Keith Souter graduated in medicine from the University of Dundee and has worked as a family doctor in Wakefield for many years. He writes crime novels and westerns in his spare time.

After winning the Fish 2006 Historical One-Page Prize with one of his short stories, he started to write a series of historical crime novels.

Visit the author's website at:
www.keithsouter.co.uk

THE FOOL'S FOLLY

It's 1485. King Richard the Third has reigned for two years in a country rife with rumours about the fate of the two princes in the Tower. There is a continual threat of rebellion by Henry Tudor. King Richard's heir, John de la Pole, is presiding over a meeting of the Council of the North, at Sandal Castle, when an unexpected death occurs in his household. Sir Giles Beeston, judge to the Manor Court, and his assistant Will Holland investigate. Soon other deaths follow and a sinister network is revealed. But whose hand is behind it, and with what purpose?

Books by Keith Souter
Published by The House of Ulverscroft:

THE PARDONER'S CRIME

KEITH SOUTER

◆

THE FOOL'S FOLLY

Complete and Unabridged

ULVERSCROFT *Leicester*

First published in Great Britain in 2009 by
Robert Hale Limited
London

First Large Print Edition
published 2010
by arrangement with
Robert Hale Limited
London

British Library CIP Data

Souter, Keith M.
  The fool's folly.
  1. Great Britain- -History- -Richard III, *1483 – 1485*- -
  Fiction. 2. Detective and mystery stories.
  3. Large type books.
  I. Title
  823.9′2–dc22

  ISBN 978–1–44480–101–9

Published by
F. A. Thorpe (Publishing)
Anstey, Leicestershire

Set by Words & Graphics Ltd.
Anstey, Leicestershire
Printed and bound in Great Britain by
T. J. International Ltd., Padstow, Cornwall

This book is printed on acid-free paper

For Ruth, with fond memories of strawberries, champagne and garden walks.
I hope you enjoy this tale of old Sandal Castle

Praise a fool and you water his folly.

Medieval English proverb

This fellow is wise enough to play the fool;
And to do that well craves a kind of wit.

Twelfth Night, Act III, Sc I
William Shakespeare

Prologue

The Church of St Mary, Cambridgeshire, June 1485

He had never been so grateful for the sudden appearance of mist. Within minutes it had advanced from the coast to cover the landscape and conceal the waning moon. Most importantly, it had given him the opportunity to make a break for it and escape from them, the trio of cutthroats who had been sent to assassinate him in his own church.

Only he would not be so easy to kill, as one of the dogs had found out a second or two before he sent him to eternal damnation.

He felt his heart skip a beat as he heard the noise of a stone or pebble skitter across the ground, undoubtedly inadvertently kicked by one of his pursuers. His hand gripped the handle of the dagger which had become sticky as the blood from the upturned blade trickled down over his fist. He willed himself to stop breathing for a moment so that he could listen all the better. He had a vague idea where one of them was, yet he could not afford to allow the third man, wherever he was, to gain an advantage over him. Professional killers, they would have been paid handsomely, so failure would be no option for them. He knew the sort of people who had sent them and they would have a basket with them in which to bring back his severed head as proof of his death.

Sacred ground! What did such as they care for that? He was a fool to believe that his own priestly calling could protect him.

And yet why should it, for they would have been told exactly who he was and of what crimes he had been capable of in his life. Crimes that he had committed in what he believed to be a good cause.

He adjusted his grip on his dagger and allowed himself a momentary vision of revenge. How he would revel in taking the lives of those bastards who had set these underlings on him; especially that fat holy toad who thought naught of betrayal, who would betray them all if he thought it would serve his own ends.

His ears suddenly pricked as he fancied he heard a sharp intake of breath nearby. He cursed inwardly, for it was hard to gauge where the sound came from. Harder than it had been inside the church, when he had sensed the approach of one of the killers as he knelt in prayer by the light of a single guttering candle in the Lady Chapel. His old training had alerted him to the first of the killers and he had swiftly draped his cloak over a kneeling stool and propped it atop a pew before merging into the shadows of the great columns. He had only just been in time, for the villain came silently with murderous swiftness, his blade ready to rake across the throat of what he believed to be a supplicant figure.

Yet he had moved even faster, silencing the bastard's mouth with one hand while he slid the dagger between his ribs into his heart. He had kept his hand over the mouth of the convulsing body as he let it crumple to the floor, all too aware of the danger of letting the others know that he had been ready for them.

In truth he had been expecting some sort of visitation ever since his Lord Buckingham's rebellion. It had been a matter of time, that was all. Only the silence of his grave could fully protect them.

He shivered, partly from the cold and partly from the fear that was threatening to squeeze his heart into nothingness. He had known men die from such terror. He chided himself for such thoughts and he gritted his teeth. 'The bastards will not succeed,' he thought defiantly. 'I will undo them — all of them!'

Thus steeling himself, he edged away from the gravestone that had offered him some scant protection and began silently negotiating a way through the cemetery, weaving between the headstones towards the far exit where the wall had fallen over. The hamlet stood just over a couple of hundred paces away and he knew that there would be a good chance of finding a horse in the stable.

But even if he made it, where was he to go? To Nottingham to seek an audience with the King? He almost laughed at the thought. Even if he could evade these killers there would be others abroad on the road to stop him reaching his majesty. It would be a great risk, but he had to take it. And if he could not get through, why then he would have to go further afield to seek those in the north.

He almost grinned as his mind saw humour in the thought. Then his thudding heart reminded him that he must first escape this mist-shrouded graveyard and the villains who so desired to hack off his head from his shoulders.

He took a deep breath and with renewed resolve reached down and felt the ground with the flat of his free hand until he found a suitable stone. He straightened, got his bearings as best he could and prepared to take his chance. He hefted the stone then tossed it away, far to his left. It crashed against a gravestone, then ricocheted across the ground and landed in shrubbery.

Instantly, they began moving, charging swiftly in that direction.

And he made for the breach in the wall and the hamlet beyond.

'I will go north,' he silently swore. 'Catch me if you can, you dogs.' He clutched his dagger in readiness.

Now that he knew they were after him, he resolved that his head would not be so easily taken.

1

Sandal Castle

The castle household was astir by daybreak, many of the servants having actually risen some two hours before that. Despite the heat of the summer, the great fires had been kindled and lit in the kitchens, the bakehouse and the Great Hall. The battlement night watch had been relieved and all around orders were being issued and acted upon, livestock were being tended to and the air was filled with the mixed aroma of woodsmoke and baking bread.

Sandal Castle had been built upon a natural sandstone ridge that towered above the small village of Sandal Magna with its ancient church of St Helens. It was a natural stronghold with clear views over the surrounding countryside. By anyone's standards it was an impressive sight. Its ashlar stones glistened in the early morning light. A great keep with four circular towers crested an impressive motte, and a battlemented twenty-foot-high curtain wall with turrets at regular lengths along it surrounded a large bailey.

Protruding above the curtain wall could be seen the roofs of spectacular halls, a number of two- and three-storied dwellings following the line of the bailey and a great central barbican with nearby drum towers connecting to the keep.

Sir Giles Beeston had risen early, having been kept awake half the night by a throbbing headache, a regular occurrence to him ever since he had been wounded by a pikeman at the Battle of Berwick upon Tweed in 1482. Although his helm had prevented a mortal blow, yet he had lost his left eye. The Lord alone knew how he managed to stay the course of the battle. He himself remembered precious little of it, except that at the close of the day when the field was won and the town claimed for England, he was proclaimed knight bannerette by his Grace, Richard Duke of Gloucester, who was now his royal liege King Richard the Third.

Giles had risen, cleansed his mouth with the goblet of watered-down wine that his assistant left by his bed every night, made his ablutions then dressed himself in readiness to ride that morning to Wakefield to preside over the Manor Court. The role of judge was one that he had only recently taken on, having been appointed Constable of Sandal Castle, by his patron John de la Pole, the Earl of

Lincoln, and he had thus far taken it very seriously. He was all too conscious that England in King Richard's reign had need of good law, besieged as it was by the ever present threat of insurrection and rebellion. A Yorkist man through and through, Giles had fought for the late King Edward at Tewksbury in 1471, then joined the household of the de la Pole family and fought proudly under the flag of the white boar, for the Duke of Gloucester during the border campaigns. Ironically, it had been that horrific wound he sustained at Berwick which had sealed his fortunes and resulted in him giving up the trappings of war and donning the coif of a lawyer. Having studied at Oxford in his youth but having little fortune of his own, he had been grateful to the de la Poles for sending him to London to further his study of the law and become a lawyer, one of the elite group that King Richard was keen to establish to dispense justice throughout England. So it was that he was conscious of the honour that his young patron, the Earl of Lincoln, had bestowed upon him by bringing him to Sandal Castle and making him Constable of the Castle and judge to the Manor of Wakefield Court.

He wore a simple tunic with a shoulder cape, and adjusted it as he surveyed himself in the mirror above his travelling chest. He was thirty-one years of age and had been aware that he was not unattractive to women before his wound. Now he stared at the ugly white scar which marred the left side of his face from eyebrow to the corner of his mouth.

'Not a pretty sight, are you?' he murmured to himself as he reached for the large leather patch that would cover his sightless eye and the upper left quarter of his face. He tied it and winced despite himself as he felt a stab of pain shoot through the scar. Suppressing a curse, he reached for his riding cap and pulled it on.

He turned at a tap on the door.

In answer to his command to enter, the heavy metal-studded door was pushed open and a young man of two and twenty summers appeared. He was a black haired, wiry youth with laughing eyes and a captivating smile.

'Are you ready to break your fast, my lord?'

Giles smiled at Will Holland, his assistant, as he buckled his sword belt. Giles was fond of the younger man, having taken him into his employ when he was in London, after Will had warned him of an attack one dark evening as he walked along Cheapside. Together they had fended off a gang of ruffians and cutpurses before retreating to

Giles's lodgings for supper. Will introduced himself as the orphaned son of a Warwickshire gentleman who had perished at the Battle of Barnet in 1471 fighting for King Edward. Giles had remembered Edmund Holland as a bluff and hearty fellow and immediately took to his son and heir, although Will had told him that meant heir to very little except a mountain of debt, for his father had a partiality for gambling.

'I fear that I have little appetite as yet, Will. I must first pay a visit to his Grace the Earl of Lincoln's physician before I can risk food.'

'Does your wound pain you my lord?'

'It does and I have run out of my physic.'

Will's face brightened. 'Shall I go and procure some for you, my lord? I could — '

'You could get some and see Doctor Musgrave's daughter, perhaps!' Giles said pointedly. He clapped his assistant on the shoulder. 'Yet I think we should go together, Will. After all, I do not wish this to take all day.'

★　★　★

John de la Pole, first Earl of Lincoln, President of the Council of the North and recently declared heir presumptive to his uncle, King Richard the Third, looked out of his window in the north tower of the keep, as he did every morning when he was in residence and surveyed the fields and woodlands beyond.

He was a well-made young man of twenty-three with the lantern jaw of the Plantagenets, coupled with the high forehead of the Chaucers. The blood of the poet ran through his veins and he saw things in his mind's eye that might have evaded those of a less imaginative nature.

The landscape swept downwards from the sandstone ridge upon which the castle stood. About three hundred paces down the hill he could see the copse of willows with the stone cross in the middle, which his late uncle, King Edward the Fourth, had erected to mark the spot where Richard, Duke of York, the rightful king of England had been killed in the Battle of Wakefield in 1460. By all accounts he had been unhorsed yet fought on with his back to the largest tree until he was finally overcome by a dozen or so swords and pikes. Some miles distant he could see the sweep of the River Calder and the Chantry Chapel of St Mary the Virgin on the bridge, where Butcher Clifford had murdered the Duke of Rutland, York's son, John's own uncle, and brother to the late King Edward and the present King Richard. He cringed at

11

the cruelty of Queen Margaret of Anjou, the wife to the hapless King Henry, for she had ordered their heads to be cleaved from their bodies and taken to York, together with that of the worthy Earl of Salisbury, to be stuck on spikes upon Mickelgate Bar. To add a final humiliation, she had ordered that a paper crown should be placed upon the Duke of York's head 'so that York could look upon York'.

John had not been born until two years after that bloody day, yet by that time Edward Plantagenet had defeated the House of Lancaster at the great Battle of Towton, when the River Cock ran red with the blood of thousands of men. There had been several battles fought between then and the battle of Tewksbury in 1471, since which time England had enjoyed peace until Edward's untimely death but two years past.

'Peace be with you grandfather and unknown uncle of mine,' he mused, making the sign of the cross as he did so. 'You did not die in vain, for our House rules and continues to give England peace and good, just law.'

John had always liked Sandal Castle, despite its ghastly history. His uncle, King Richard, had appointed him President of the Council of the North and based it at the two castles of Sandal and Sheriff Hutton. Of the two John preferred Sandal for it made him feel closer to his family roots and yet it was closer to his uncle should he have need of him. And indeed, he did worry considerably about King Richard, who had given so much for his realm, yet who had been so maligned by the Beaufort and Woodville families. Not the least of their claims was that some evil had befallen the King's two nephews, who had been proclaimed illegitimate by the Titulus Regius, the Act of Parliament that acknowledged Richard as the rightful King of England. There were claims that they had not been seen in public for two years and that they had somehow perished in the Tower of London. John had little doubt that somehow the Lady Margaret Beaufort, the mother of the upstart Henry Tudor had also had something to do with the rebellion of her cousin's husband, Henry Stafford, the Duke of Buckingham, two years before.

And now John's own good fortune, being appointed heir to the King by Richard himself, had come about through the ill fortune that seemed to dog Richard. Within a year the King had lost his son Edward, the Prince of Wales, after some mysterious illness at Middleham Castle, and then his wife, Queen Anne, just a few months later. She had died of a broken heart, everyone said.

Everyone except the Beauforts and Wood-villes, whose agents suggested that she had been poisoned by Richard.

John sighed. How he wished he could take some of the worries from his uncle's shoulders, especially since he knew that he was ever watchful in case the dreaded Tudor invasion should come from France. Of course, if it did, then he would deploy straight away, together with the armies of all of the members of the Council of the North.

The Council of the North! Ah, there was yet another sitting later that day and he had to prepare. He turned from his reverie by the window, crossed the floor of his chamber and took a seat at his desk, which was covered in documents, writing parchment, quills and a silver inkpot. For a moment he tapped his fingers on the nearest document before pushing it aside and reaching for the quill.

He smiled as images of his wife, Lady Margaret FitzAlan, at home in his Lincoln castle, flashed through his mind. A child, she needed a child and he needed a son. How he would enjoy sharing a bed with her again, when he returned home. He thought of how he would woo her before tumbling under the sheets. Images and words cascaded into his mind and he began jotting down the lines of a poem to honour her. After a few moments he finished. He leaned back in his chair and scanned his efforts, chewing the feather of his quill pen as he did so. With a smile he set it down and replaced the quill. It was a goodly piece, he thought, quite befitting for one whose grandmother, Alice Chaucer, had been the granddaughter of the great poet Geoffrey Chaucer.

'And one day there may be the blood of poets sitting upon the throne of England,' he said to the empty air of his chamber. He clapped his hands together to break his own line of thought. 'And until then, I will be a faithful royal nephew. Now to work. England awaits us.'

★   ★   ★

Doctor Anthony Musgrave, scholarly graduate of Padua, physician, alchemist and philosopher, had been up since soon after midnight, which was not unusual for him, for by nature he was virtually nocturnal. As personal physician to the Earl of Lincoln he had been given chambers and workrooms on the upper floor of the south tower of the keep.

The early hours of the night were ideal for him to climb on to the tower top itself and lean upon one or other of the embrasures in the crenellation to study the stars. Often he would be aware of the mocking mutters of the guards of the watch as they looked up at him as he darted about or stood tugging thoughtfully at his unruly grey beard while he made charts of the heavens by the light of the moon. He had reached an age when he seemed to need little sleep and, since he had been a widower for twelve long years, he had no one to complain about the hours he spent out of bed. No one, that is, except his daughter Alice who would good-humouredly cajole him when she saw that his eyes became red-rimmed and he yawned overmuch.

Usually, after an hour or so he would go to his workrooms which were always as hot as the kitchens, for in one he maintained his ovens and kilns in constant heat so that he could do his experiments on metals. Thanks to his patron, the Earl of Lincoln, he had been granted one of the few licences to legitimately practice the art of alchemy. All in all, he considered his a happy existence, free to pursue his studies, ably assisted by his daughter, whom he had taught much of the art of physic and of the peripheral arts of astronomy and alchemy. She was able to identify herbs, compound remedies or work his kilns. Not only that, but she could produce exquisite works of jewellery, silver- and gold-craft as would be satisfactory to any noble.

Alice had also risen early this day, working in her side chamber with fine files and rasps on some metalwork, for he could discern by the sounds of her endeavour that she was finishing off some piece of work. He did not see fit to interfere, since they had a tacit understanding that she would assist him when he had need of her, but otherwise she was free to amuse herself as she would.

He was busy compounding herbs with a pestle and mortar when there was a hard rap at the door and Sir Giles Beeston entered. A pace behind him was his young assistant, Will Holland.

'Sir Giles, good morning. Please, enter my parlour.'

Giles surveyed the room, which was anything but a parlour. Shelves lined the walls, bedecked with jugs, jars and bottles of potions. Bundles of flowers and plants hung from the ceiling, drying in the stifling heat of the room. A long worktable was covered in the paraphernalia of the physician, together with the crucibles, flasks and trays of the apothecary, the maker of medicines. Ledgers and leather-bound volumes covered a tall standing desk, with one large tome, a diary of some kind, open with a fresh quill laid by its side, testimony to recent note-making.

'I perceive by the pained look on your face that you are still much troubled,' Doctor Musgrave stated. A hand strayed to stroke his prodigious beard and he came closer to peer at Giles's face.

Behind him the half-open door into the side room opened and Alice appeared, a glorious smile on her beautiful face directed straight at Will.

Indeed, she was a beauty. Wearing a long green gown with a high waist, she brushed some sort of powders from her sides before she curtsied and bobbed her head to them. As she did so one could not help but notice her luxurious copper hair gathered into two great coils on either side of her head, enclosed in a net and with a garland of summer flowers threaded through.

Giles and Will bowed in turn and, at the subtlest of gestures from her finger, Will excused himself and followed her back through into her side room.

'She has something she wishes to show him, I imagine,' Doctor Musgrave said unconcernedly.

'They seem good friends,' Giles agreed with a smile. Then he winced as he felt a spasm of pain in his temple. 'That last lot of physic that you gave me is wonderful, the only problem being that I have run out of it.'

The physician beamed. 'Ah, I am glad to hear it has helped. These wounds can cause much pain for many years. It is not natural to lose an eye the way you did.'

'I would not recommend it, doctor,' Giles responded glibly, gingerly touching his eye patch almost unconsciously. 'What is in this medicine, by the way?'

'A little poison!'

Giles stiffened slightly. 'A poison?'

Doctor Musgrave had begun inspecting jars. He took three down from a shelf and began mixing their contents into a larger jug. He gave a short laugh. 'It is partly poison. There is a poisonous herbal decoction included in the whole preparation.'

He had begun to pour a thick liquid into a small flask. His eyes twinkled and he winked at Giles. 'Oh fear not, Sir Giles. In small doses most poisons have a curative ability. I use preparations from all of nature. Metals like gold, copper and quicksilver. The poisons of snakes and lizards. The flowers and fruits of the myriads of plants that God has surrounded us with in the fields, woodlands and heaths. Belladonna, aconite, and so many of the toadstools and mushrooms that we can gather in the autumn. This castle is surrounded by poisons which appear season by season, all of which I have accumulated

19

here, and which I make medicines from.'

There was a giggling noise from the side room, which both Giles and Doctor Musgrave chose to ignore.

'Divine providence has given simple physicians such as myself clues as to which plants and animals hold keys to health. We call this the Doctrine of Signatures, in that each potential remedy has a signature that will tell us about its medicinal value. Take your own case, Sir Giles, I use this herb to ease your pain.' He reached for a bunch of drying blue flowers and snapped one off. He held it up for Giles to inspect. 'What does the shape of this flower suggest to you?'

Giles eyed him askance. 'Why, it looks like a tiny helmet.'

'Indeed and so here is the signature that leads me to its secret. It is good for headaches and wounds to the head. The essential juices of this plant are in this flask. Swallow half the flask and you would feel very ill. Swallow it all and you might be dead.'

Giles sucked air between his teeth. 'You told me before, doctor. I confess that I thought that you simply didn't want me to waste precious medicine, I didn't realize that you were serious.'

'Deadly serious,' the physician returned, stoppering the flask and handing it over.

'Take but five drops in a goblet of watered wine, just like before. You may take four such doses a day, but no more without consulting me.'

The door opened and Will came out first, with Alice Musgrave close behind. From the way that Will had his hand behind his back Giles guessed that the couple were holding hands.

'Are we finished, my Lord?' Will asked.

'We are, Will. Once you release the fair Alice.'

They took their leave and descended the stairs of the keep to pass through one of the drum towers with a portcullis, before crossing an internal drawbridge to enter the great semicircular barbican. Through that they had to pass through yet another portcullis and drawbridge over the castle's internal moat to reach the castle bailey.

'I like the ring,' Giles commented, pointing to the gleaming gold ring on the little finger of Will's left hand.

Will coloured immediately, then grinned sheepishly. 'A gift, my Lord.'

'A betrothal gift?' Giles queried. 'I saw the twin of it on fair Alice's hand.'

'They are friendship rings, my Lord. She has inscribed them both with words that we chose. Hers says, 'Toute la votre — all yours', and mine has a secret inscription on the inside of the ring, against my finger. It says, 'Pour bon amour — for good love'.' He pulled it off his finger and held it out for Giles to see.

'It sounds more than friendship, Will,' Giles said after admiring its craftsmanship. He handed it back and watched Will slip it on again.

'I think it is, my Lord. You have a . . . er . . . sharp eye.'

Giles laughed. 'When you have but one, you make sure you use it. Now let us breakfast and let me sup some of this good physic, before my eye closes for good.'

★　★　★

Father Edmund Burke, the recently appointed Sandal Castle chaplain had been praying in the chapel at the top of the west tower of the keep. It had been called the Earl's Chapel ever since the days when the castle had belonged to the de Warenne family in the thirteenth century. The altar was carved from oak and covered with a fine linen cloth. On top of it was a large plain wooden cross with a plain white candle on each side. Behind the altar was an arched window with stained glass, and upon the smoothly plastered walls were painted scenes of the flagellation, the crucifixion and the resurrection of Christ. The ceiling was actually domed, where a bell had once hung during the days of the Earl of Surrey a century before.[1] On top of all of the walls clouds had been painted, with depictions of the feet of the Lord disappearing into them as he ascended to heaven.

To most of the castle residents Edmund seemed unworldly. Indeed, although he had been in position for three months now, yet he still could not get used to the strange life of the castle. It was so different from the monastic life that he had led at Monk Bretton Priory since he had entered as a lay brother at the age of twelve. Having been used to spending so many hours of the day attending masses and contemplating in private, in amongst his other work as an illuminator of manuscripts in his station in the Priory cloister, he found the lack of order in the castle hard to deal with. Yet it had been the Prior who had put his name forward for this position, and who was he to challenge such an honour, lacking though he felt in the social skills needed to minister to the needs of the great and good of a castle such as this.

---

[1] See *The Pardoner's Crime*

'Gracious Father, so I ask you to send me — ' he intoned.

Suddenly, he felt something warm, wet and sloppy land upon his tonsured head. It was followed by a peel of near hysterical cackling.

'A miracle!' cried a voice behind him.

Edmund spun round in alarm, his face aghast as he dropped his hand from his head as he had instinctively felt to find out what had smitten his head. His hand, as was his head, was smeared with fresh horse dung.

'A miracle, I say,' screeched a little man, no more than four feet in height, dressed in a strange suit of brightly coloured, motley-patterned squares. Upon his head was a strange floppy hat with three dangling liripipes. He danced back and forth in great mirth, his wizened face crinkling like an aged nut. 'I heard you asking for the Lord to send you something.' He slapped his knees. 'And he did, he sent you this gift of nature.'

Edmund's horror turned to ire. He stood up and shook his head in a mixture of disbelief and mortification at the audacity of the Earl of Lincoln's personal jester, his Fool. 'Bunce, you . . . you — !' He struggled for words.

Ned Bunce mockingly put a hand to his ear, as if to form a trumpet to hear the better. 'Aye Father, go on. You . . . you . . . what?

Should we ask for another miracle? Something like, 'give me the wit to form words'!'

Edmund advanced towards him and the little man nimbly skipped back and out of the door. 'You profaner! This is the Lord's chapel, not some . . . some — !'

'Some . . . some . . . somebody's bum! Best go clean your head, Father, before the flies start buzzing.'

Edmund stood staring at the door as he heard the patter of footsteps charging down the tower steps and the peel of Ned Bunce's laughter.

'I fear you will have to take care, Ned Bunce,' Edmund said softly, as he wiped the dung from his head. 'You should pray that the Lord is in a more forgiving mood than me.'

* * *

After breakfasting in the castle refectory, for he wished to get away promptly without having to make conversation with those members of the Council of the North who had risen early, and having taken five drops of Doctor Musgrave's potion in a goblet of weak wine, Giles began to feel the pain in his head and face subside. As it did so, his sense of well-being and humour began to return. In part this was due to the antics of Ned Bunce who had entered, curled up like a ball, and rolled himself along to be stopped by Will Holland's boot.

'What mischief have you been up to now, Ned Bunce?' Giles had asked.

The Fool had risen with an innocent expression on his face. 'Why none, sir. Except for paying a call on Father Burke and witnessing a miracle.'

As he told them, illustrating his tale with an impromptu exhibition of Father Burke's reaction, both Giles and Will found themselves laughing heartily.

'Oh, and then I fear that his Lordship, my master the Earl of Lincoln, might wonder where he is when he leaves his chamber this morning.'

'What have you done, Bunce?' Giles asked suspiciously.

'Me, sir? Nothing sir. But as I passed his chamber door I noticed that some villain had hung one of the tapestries over his door. He is sure to walk straight into it when he opens the door.'

Will almost snorted with amusement, but Giles gave him a censorious glance.

'You need to take care, Bunce. Playing tricks on the heir to the throne is not the cleverest of things that you have done.'

Ned Bunce put a finger to his mouth and

pursed his lips as if in fear. 'Why, that must be why they call me 'the Fool'! But why do you think that it was me, Sir Giles. I am not tall enough to hang tapestries above doors.'

'You seem to regularly get where people would not expect you,' Giles countered.

'And I thought that I was doing the right thing by letting my Lord sleep and coming to tell the important people that such a knavish trick had been played upon my Lord.'

Giles shook his head good-humouredly. 'You are a nuisance, Ned Bunce.' He nodded to Will. 'Perhaps you could get some of the servants to undo Bunce's little jest before the Earl finds out and is upset.'

'I doubt if the Earl would be upset, Sir Giles,' Will returned. 'I know of few men with such a goodly disposition as the Earl of Lincoln. Yet still, I shall see that it is done.'

When he had gone Ned Bunce leaped up into his vacated seat, regardless of Giles's look of remonstrance.

'Wine! Wine I say!' Bunce called, thumping his fist on the table.

One of the refectory servants appeared instantly. 'I'll give you wine, Ned Bunce. This is no tavern.' Then deferentially to Giles: 'Shall I have the Fool removed, Sir Giles?'

Giles shook his head. 'But I agree, no wine for him. It may make him more troublesome.'

27

Bunce frowned like a frustrated child and emphatically placed his elbows on the table, then sank his chin into his cupped hands. 'Why does everyone hate poor Ned Bunce? Dickon of Methley, the falconer, was just as ungentle with me this morning. And all because I think he is unkind to use those straps to tie his falcons and hawks to their perches.'

'What did you do, Bunce?' Giles asked, with a shake of his head.

'I untied them all and shooed the birds away.'

Giles grinned. 'And did they go?'

The jester shook his head sadly. 'Foolish birds, they wouldn't budge. They do nothing except for the fat falconer.' He held out his right hand, which still held the odour of horse dung. The tip of his thumb was bloody and swollen. 'One of the bad tempered birds thought my thumb was a mouse and almost took the top off it. If I hadn't been so fast then — '

'You mean if I hadn't been so fast, you damned little Fool!'

They both turned at the entry of a stocky man dressed in hunting clothes, with a leather jerkin that had numerous pockets about it, and with a belt from which hung several straps, bags, a catapult and a couple of knives. He had a full-brown beard, a curved, hawk-like nose and strangely sharp piercing hazel eyes.

'Why it is old hawkface himself,' Bunce said quickly. 'Have you tied all those poor birds up again?'

'I will tie you up if I find you messing with my birds again,' Dickon snapped back. He bowed to Giles. 'I am glad that I caught you, sir. I meant to ask you, about tomorrow, will you be hawking with the rest of the Council party?'

Giles pursed his lips. 'I had not thought to do so, Dickon. Yet it would be a good opportunity for me to have some conversation with some of my Lord's fellow councillors. Yes, I shall come.'

Dickon coughed diffidently. 'You will forgive me asking, Sir Giles . . . but have you done much hawking?'

'As much as most folk, why do you ask?'

'It is just that I would not want any accidents, Sir Giles. I will need to match you up with the right sort of bird. You having only one eye, if you don't mind me saying.'

Ned Bunce howled with laughter and rolled off the seat on to the straw-covered floor. 'Oh subtle, hawky Dickon! Don't risk offending your betters.'

Dickon flushed and stuttered with embarrassment.

'Have no fear of embarrassing me, Dickon,' Giles replied. 'I can handle a falcon well enough. And fear not about my eye. It does not miss much . . . if anything.'

Bunce picked himself up and snorted with glee. 'That's good, Sir Giles. Don't miss anything here. Not in this den of thieves and rogues.'

'Watch that tongue of yours, Ned Bunce,' Giles warned, good naturedly.

The jester immediately thrust his tongue as far out as he could and crossed his eyes as if attempting to see it the better. 'I will watch it, Sir Giles. How long for?'

Dickon the falconer cuffed him gently across the head. 'What Sir Giles meant is that you need to keep a civil tongue in your head, as you well know, Ned Bunce. Now be off with you or I will set that gerfalcon on you again. He has already tasted your thumb and I think it might have whetted his appetite for a little jester's tongue.'

Ned Bunce gave a mock shriek and dashed from the refectory.

'If you have a moment, Sir Giles, I think I have the very bird for you. It would be good to let it have sight of you.'

Giles liked the falconer's no-nonsense

approach and his obvious fascination and concern for his birds. He followed him out across the bailey, which by now was thrumming with activity. Servants moved quickly hither and thither with baskets and pails, a couple of wheelwrights worked on a cart and the various swineherds and ostlers were at work. The castle falconry was in the mews. Outside it, on a series of blocks, a number of birds were perched, tethered by long straps. Various types of long-winged falcons sat alongside short-winged hawks. Beyond them was an open door leading into a dark cavern-like room with a straw-covered floor, which smelled strongly of droppings. As they approached, the birds all turned their attention upon them, their heads seeming to swivel as they kept them in sharp focus.

'A moment, Sir Giles,' said Dickon, dashing into the dark recess, returning after a moment with a bird on a gauntleted fist. 'I call this one Lightning. He is a 2-year-old tercel, a male peregrine falcon.' He handed Giles a spare gauntlet. 'Would you care to put on a glove and let him get used to you?'

The castle constable did as was suggested and after a few moments, he ventured to stroke the bird's plumage.

Will appeared. 'I had the tapestry removed, my lord. Fortunately, the Earl is still not about.' He looked admiringly at the bird on Gile's gauntleted fist. 'A fine bird. He seems to have taken to you, my lord.'

Dickon gave a short laugh. 'Aye, I thought he would.'

'What made you say that, master falconer?' Giles asked.

'It was what you just said about your eye not missing much. Well, nor do Lightning's.'

2

Messages

The road from Sandal Castle to Wakefield took a meandering course down the hill past the village of Sandal Magna with its hostelry, ancient church and surrounding hotchpotch of timber-frame houses and wattle and daub dwellings. Some had animals in small enclosures and others devoted their attention to vegetable patches and flower gardens. At the edge of the village they passed a well-stocked fishpond where a couple of urchins were throwing stones in a vain attempt to stun the fish.

'Hey!' bellowed Will, as he and Sir Giles approached. 'Be off with you or find yourself in the Manor Court.'

The urchins needed no second word. They had looked up at once, their eyes seeming to open wide in fear, then swiftly raising their hands to tug at forelocks, they rapidly pulled hoods up and scurried away, running along the unploughed balks that divided the surrounding fields.

Will laughed. 'There is a fine thing, my

33

lord. A firm voice and a sight of the King's authority and they are off. I wish that we could dissuade more people from breaking laws as easily as that.'

Giles indulged him with a smile. 'They are but lads doing what lads of all rank do. I suspect that you also tried to stun a fish when you were a boy.'

Will grinned. 'Aye my lord, and like them I missed. They say the trick is to aim a couple of feet nearer you than the fish.'

'There you are right, Will. The water distorts the picture of what you see. Much as happens in life, when many things are not as they seem.'

'How is that, my lord? I am not sure that I understand you.'

'Well, take those lads. They seemed to run off at the sound of your voice and at the sight of us on horses.'

'They showed due respect, my lord.'

Giles shook his head. 'You know well enough that they were just young boys, of an age when they have reason to be wary of bigger boys and of grown men. Yet you saw the fear on their faces. They were more fearful of my eye patch, for they would be told that masks and such things are used by robbers, monsters or executioners. You are used to my eye patch, but they possibly thought that they had seen one to be fearful of.'

'You mean they may have thought that they had seen a premonition? That you were an executioner? Why my lord, that is possible, is it not? I mean, such as they may well end up on a gallows one day.'

They rode on past fields of swaying cereals and root crops, and with here and there fields of rhubarb and liquorice, both specialities for which the manor was famous. As they went they passed groups of merchants, itinerants, and shepherds with their flocks and the odd farm labourer driving a few cattle before him. To the east was a great expanse of heathland, while to the west the area was heavily wooded.

After a few minutes of silence Giles sighed. 'I hope that you are not right about those lads we just saw, Will. True, this very morning may well result in me trying several miscreants who deserve the final penalty, yet there will be others who have felt forced to turn to crime in order to feed their families. It is my task to make sure that they are all heard and that the law is served fairly and that justice is served out when it is appropriate.'

Will stroked his shaven chin. 'You do not talk the same as my last teacher of law, if you will forgive my impertinence, Sir Giles. He taught me that the law and justice are the same thing. That we have the rule of the law, and that justice is served when people are dealt with for breaking those laws.'

Giles gave a short laugh. 'That is an interpretation, yet I believe that the function of a judge is to exert fair judgement. He must listen and consider everything about a case. Otherwise our gallows will never be empty and we will only ever have a population that lives in fear. That is wrong, Will. People should be respectful of the law, yet not be fearful. It is there for protection of all the people.'

Will chewed his lip and was thoughtful for a few moments as the road followed the gently undulating terrain. They overtook an ox-cart which was heavily laden with grain on its way to one of the Wakefield soke mills.

'Does that go for all ranks of people, Sir Giles?'

'Of course! From noble to peasant. That is the sort of law that King Richard wants for his people. And that is precisely the sort of law I practice. Fair and just.'

The road descended to the River Calder and they crossed the stone bridge that spanned it and upon which stood the Chantry Chapel of St Mary the Virgin. It was one of the four Chantry Chapels of Wakefield, which had been erected on the four main roads leading into Wakefield. Of the four it was particularly renowned for the richness of its sculptured parapet and pinnacled canopies, so typical of the architecture of the preceding century.

'I always feel uneasy when we cross the Calder, my lord. The bloody deed that was done here makes a mockery of justice.'

The door of the chapel was open and already several people had entered to get the resident priest to say a prayer with them before they began their undertaking of the day.

'You mean the slaying of the Earl of Rutland by Lord John Clifford?'

'It was cold-blooded murder, my lord. The Earl of Rutland was a mere lad, unarmed and bound. The unknightly Clifford butchered him. Where is the protection of the law there, Sir Giles? One noble killed another at this very spot in front of a house of God.'

'It was war, Will. Just after the heat of the battle. Evil things happen in such circumstances. Lord Clifford is said to have claimed Rutland's life, because the Duke of York, Rutland's father, had slain Clifford's own father, Lord Thomas Clifford, at the battle of St Albans in 1455. It was a killing done in revenge. He thought he was just in taking Rutland's life.'

'So was it just?'

Giles shook his head and urged his horse on over the bridge towards the hill that led up the Kirkgate towards Wakefield.

'Of course it was not just, Will. It can be understood, but not condoned. There was no justice in that act of malice. Yet Lord Clifford did not enjoy his revenge for long, since he died with an arrow through his throat at Ferrybridge, before the great battle of Towton in 1461, when Edward Plantagenet fully won the crown for his House.'

Will grimaced. 'That must have been a painful death, my lord.'

'It would have been. By all accounts he had removed his bevor for some reason, thereby exposing his throat. A bowman took the opportunity and despatched him.'

'Then it was a lawful death?'

Giles raised his right eyebrow and gave a short laugh. 'You ask some difficult questions, Will. It is a fact that the law is automatically on the side of the king. Towton was a battle for the crown of England, fought by the armies of two 'legally' crowned kings. At the time it happened it was both lawful and yet unlawful. Yet since the House of York won the battle, it became lawful.'

Will frowned. 'The law is hard to comprehend at times, my lord. In the case of this Lord Clifford, he was a child-murderer. I think his death is a good example of divine justice.'

Giles clicked his tongue. He liked the way that his young assistant's mind worked. He questioned everything and he hoped that in time he would become a seasoned lawyer like himself.

'Well, let us go and see what legal dilemmas the Manor Court holds for us today. Watch and listen and then we will see whether you think the judgements that I hand out today suit your idea of justice or not.'

★   ★   ★

As John de la Pole, the Earl of Lincoln, walked briskly across the bailey courtyard the servants, workmen and guards deferentially made way for him to pass through. Two guards stood at attention as he approached the stone staircase that led to an upper porch supported on an ornate octagonal column. Above the door was a large, rather splendid sundial that indicated that the tenth hour approached.

'Are the Council of the North members already here?' he asked the nearest guard.

'I believe that twelve of the Council lords are present, sir.'

39

Lincoln allowed himself a smile. That made them one short. He had a good idea of who would not yet have arrived. He nodded and skipped up the stairs just as the heavy wooden door was pulled open. He entered, aware that his approach had been expected and observed through the small grille in the door. One of the clerks was waiting in the semicircular oriel gallery. He bowed and stepped backwards to allow Lincoln to sweep past him through the Presence Chamber with its walls bedecked with pikestaffs, swords and banners, one with the coat of arms of the Duke of York, in remembrance of his grandfather, and one bearing his personal coat of arms with the rampant lions.

Although the spontaneous opening of doors and curtains was perfectly normal for one of his exalted station, yet the poetic part of him yearned for some normality. He often wondered if he could get away with disguising himself and acting the part of a commoner, of a servant. There was something appealing in the thought of opening doors for someone else, of standing and listening without having always to perform. He sighed at the thought, for expectation was one of the key features of his life. He was expected to perform, to lead, govern and always be wise. Yet he was not yet twenty-three years of age and already he had to govern and keep the unruly under control. He smiled ruefully at the thought, for it was as nothing compared to the task his uncle the King had in trying to control the disparate regions of England.

'Shall I announce you, my lord?' the clerk asked, quickly scuttling ahead to reach the door into the Great Hall first.

'Are all of the Council members present?' Lincoln asked rhetorically.

The clerk, a young man by the name of Brakespeare, shook his head slightly. The corner of his mouth twitched nervously, for he was unsure how the Earl would react. 'I am afraid to say that the Earl of Northumberland has not yet arrived at the castle, your Grace.'

'Thank you. I need no announcing,' Lincoln replied with a thin smile.

He pushed open the heavy wooden door and entered. He stood at the entrance for a moment and surveyed the room.

Sunlight shone in through green glazed glass in three large mullioned windows, inlaid in the middle of each with stained-glass falcons. Large tapestries hung from the walls and a fire blazed in the great hearth beneath the arms of the de Warenne family, the original owners of the castle before it became a royal base. At the far end of the hall, on top of the dais, was a high table, around which a dozen nobles, knights and a few clerics had been sitting and talking animatedly. At the Earl of Lincoln's entrance they had all stopped talking, scraped back chairs and stood awaiting his pleasure.

Lincoln clapped his hands together and sprang down the steps into the main hall. As he did so he placed a hand on the grip and pommel of his sword and walked up between the two rows of trestle tables that had been put out in readiness for a banquet that evening.

'My lords, welcome one, welcome all,' he cried as he mounted the dais and took his seat at the head of the table.

Immediately, Christopher Brakespeare, the clerk, lay the pile of documents that he had been carrying before Lincoln, then backed off the dais to take a position at a small table below, where he had already placed ink, quills and parchment ready.

The lords bowed, and then at a sign from the Earl they took their seats. As they did so he ran an eye over them. For the most, they were good and true men, yet there were several that he always felt merited both a degree of caution and on occasion a firm reminder of their place in the hierarchy of the land. He spied the small and portly Sir Roger

Harrington of Durham with his russet-coloured long gown and red hair poking out from beneath the capuchon that he usually wore. Next to him was the melancholic looking Lord Thomas Scrope of Masham, whom Lincoln had formed an acquaintance with at the coronation of King Richard. And then he heard the perpetual cough and rasping breathing of the Abbot Mallory of Monk Bretton, who seemed to have been suffering from the consumption for as long as anyone could recall. And yet for all of his wheezing and complaints about his health he was remarkably well fleshed, which even the gown of his order of black monks could do little to conceal.

'Is everyone here?' the Earl asked the assembly.

Sir Roger snorted with derision. 'All but one, my lord. Henry Percy, the Earl of Northumberland, has seen fit not to grace us with his wisdom and presence.'

There were general mutters around the table, for everyone knew well that the Earl of Northumberland, descended from the one they called Harry Hotspur, had been peeved when King Richard had first formed the Council of the North the previous summer. The King's aim was to bring government to the northern shires, essentially mirroring the

43

Council in London, yet having it run by nobles and clerics who could identify with and had an interest in representing the folk of the north. Henry Percy, being the head of the most powerful family in the north and a firm friend of the late King Edward, had resented the very existence of a Council of the North and had grudgingly accepted a place on the Council, although he had fully expected to be made head of it. However, when King Richard's heir presumptive, John de la Pole, was appointed instead he had proven to be a less than enthusiastic member.

'He should be brought to task, my lord,' said Abbot Mallory.

'I agree,' chirped in a lean, middle-aged black-haired man with a pointed beard which seemed to bristle out from an aggressive chin. He was wearing one of the modern chimney hats. 'It is an insult to the Council, to your presidency and to his majesty.'

Lincoln sat back and stroked his upper lip. 'You think so, Sir William? How exactly is it an insult to the King?'

Sir William Stanley of Holt, formerly Lord of the Honour of Skipton and brother of Lord Thomas Stanley, the Earl of Derby, leaned forward and tapped his forefinger emphatically on the table. 'This Council carries out his majesty's work. You are his majesty's chosen heir and president of the Council. To miss a prearranged meeting of the Council is insulting to all.'

'And how should I respond to this insult?' Lincoln asked the assembly.

'Fine him!'

Lincoln smiled. 'I fear that only his majesty can fine him, Sir Peregrine,' he said, addressing a blond hatless knight with a heavily pock-marked face.

Sir William took a sharp intake of breath, then:

'Take some of his precious land from him.'

'Nor is that so easily done, Sir William. Only King Richard could do such a thing. And that is hardly the sort of thing that he should be burdened with when he has so many burdens already.'

Lincoln was well aware that both Sir William and his brother Lord Stanley were greedy for land. Sir William had been made Lord of the Honour of Skipton in 1462 after the Butcher, Lord Clifford, had been attainted and had all his lands stripped from him. Sir William had enjoyed his estates at Skipton until 1465 when these were exchanged for the castle, lordship and manor of Chirk in the Marches of Wales, so that Richard, King Edward's favoured brother, could effectively be master of the north.

Although neither Stanley nor Northumberland held those lands, it was well known that the two were not friends and both coveted the holdings and titles.

'I think that mayhap the Council members are too eager to judge without knowing all the facts,' Lincoln said.

Sir Roger Harrington raised his hands questioningly. 'Surely the fact that he is absent is all that we need to know, your Grace.'

'Perhaps you have not been using your ears, my lords,' said Lincoln indulgently. 'If you had you would have heard the sound of a horse crossing the drawbridge. And if you had been observant you might have seen who was riding that horse.'

'Why, is he here?' Abbot Mallory asked.

There was a rap on the door and in answer to Lincoln's gesture, Christopher Brakespeare swiftly went to answer the door and ushered in a messenger in the livery of the Earl of Northumberland.

Moments later Lincoln was reading a letter written in what seemed to be a shaking hand. The Council members watched in interest as his lips curled into a slight smile and he slowly folded the letter.

'It seems that his Grace the Earl of Northumberland is abed with the sweating sickness. He had tried to rise this morning, but had to return and is now being bled by his physicians.'

After despatching the messenger to the kitchens for refreshments before returning with a message of good wishes for a speedy recovery, the Earl of Lincoln reached for the pile of documents.

'You see, my lords, it is a good policy, I believe, not to make hasty assumptions. In such ways do men wage unnecessary war and risk the loss of their heads. Now, shall we to the business of government?'

'If I may say so, my lord, you have a wise head upon young shoulders,' Abbot Mallory ventured. It was followed by murmurs of assent from around the table.

Lincoln acknowledged the complement with a smile. But before he began introducing the first item he had already made a mental note to find out if the Earl of Northumberland truly had been afflicted by the sweating sickness. It was not in his nature to be suspicious; he simply considered it wise to be cautious.

★   ★   ★

Dickon of Methley had set out from Sandal Castle in his old, specially modified cart pulled by his favourite old piebald pony. The cart was covered in a wooden canopy inside which were a series of spars upon which six birds could perch, each hooded and tethered a safe distance from the others. It was his usual practice to fly the birds before a proper hunt, as had been arranged for the morrow. In the cart he had two gerfalcons, a peregrine falcon, a tercel, a goshawk and a merlin, All of them bred to kill and each suited for different types of terrain and different types of prey. The falcons were ideal for the open country, while the shorter-winged goshawk and merlin would be good if the hunt went into the woods.

Dickon knew that he was about thirty and five years of age. He had been a falconer at the castle all of his life and had only left the Manor of Wakefield once in his life, and that had been to do battle on behalf of his lord and master. He had been a youngster when he had gone to Towton and fought for Edward, Earl of March, who although he had already been crowned king, upon that bloody day became unquestioned king of England. Dickon could still bring back the emotions of that day; the fear, the revulsion at so much loss of life, and yet the exhilaration of seeing the mighty, handsome giant that was King Edward. Most of all, though, he could sense the feeling of revenge, of justice after the murder of his master, Richard, the Duke of York. The horrors of Towton occasionally came back to him in his dreams, but not so terrifyingly as the sight, albeit from the battlements of Sandal Castle, of his master being dragged from his horse, putting up a fight, but then being hacked to death. He had been fortunate to escape from the castle with his grandfather before the Lancastrian horde was unleashed upon it.

But these were happier times. His old master's son, Richard, was on the throne, after the death, God rest his soul, of King Edward. And his grandson, the Earl of Lincoln, was the President of the Council and the owner of the castle. Strangely, Dickon felt a sense of pride in serving him, for he seemed as clever a man as any he had ever met, despite his youth.

'Pah, what are you thinking about, Dickon?' he chided himself. 'He is twenty-three! That is some four years older than King Edward was when he won the field at Towton. Come on now, let's be having these birds in flight and make sure that they are fit and ready tomorrow, and hungry enough to kill.'

Dickon had learned his craft from his grandfather, his own father having succumbed to the plague when he was four. The old man had taught him well. He had taken him out as a youngster and shown him how to climb trees to snatch new birds as 'eyases', or nestlings straight from the nest, or net 'branchers' that had just left the nest for the first time. Then he had shown him the secrets of the long process of training a bird. First by trimming its talons, 'seeling' its eyes by temporarily stitching the eyelids together, and attaching the two jesses, strips of leather with rings at the end to their legs. He taught him how to attach the two bells, each with a different pitch so that by hearing them when the bird was in flight, even in thick mist, he could pinpoint its height and its direction.

How Dickon had taken to it all. He loved everything about the art; the training of a bird so that it would recognize him as its master, and the sound of his whistle as a signal for it to come to his hand; teaching it to feed, to drink and finally to hunt and kill. More than that, though, his grandfather had taught him to recognize when the birds were not well and he had schooled him in the making up of remedies to give. He could compound mixtures of spices, snake meat, vinegar and various powders, all of which seemed to work at least as well as did the human medicines given by the local apothecary or wise woman. He could honestly say that he had affection for them all, just as he knew that they all had a feeling of some sort for him.

He spent about a couple of hours flying each one in turn, gauging by their weights on his gauntleted fist when they had flown enough to be ready to rest until the morrow.

'Come now, Lightning,' he said, putting back the merlin and taking out the tercel. 'You have got to show Sir Giles that I know my craft. I have promised him that you are a bird that can spot things when they need to be spotted.'

He gently unhooded the bird and stroked its plumage. Then searching the skies he shook his head. 'It looks as if the others have scared off all of your feathered friends. We shall just have to let you have a fly round and then you can have this dead mouse that is left in my pocket. I will cast it into the sky with my catapult and we shall see if you can catch it before it hits the ground.'

A movement of the bird on his gauntlet alerted him and he followed its gaze, spotting the distant point that was moving slowly towards them from across the tops of the woodland that bordered the heath.

'Clever boy, Lightning,' he said, making a throwing action with his hand and launching the bird into the air.

The tercel soared higher and higher

circling above the advancing pigeon, which sped on, graceful in its own right. Then it dived, suddenly swooping from a great height, taking the pigeon in a mass of feathers, breaking its neck in the grasp of its powerful talons and killing it instantly.

'Good bird!' Dickon enthused delightedly a few moments later as the carcass of the pigeon was deposited at his feet and Lightning landed on his outstretched gauntlet. 'Looks like you have provided me with pigeon pie for supper tonight.'

He reached inside a pocket and drew out the promised dead mouse, which was eagerly snatched in the deadly beak. He sang to it, as he did to all his birds, then hooded it and replaced it in the darkness of the cart.

It was when he reached down to pick up the pigeon that his eyes widened in surprise.

'Well, well, you clever bird, Lightning. Now here is a surprise. Whatever it means.'

★   ★   ★

Will had been pleased that Sir Giles had sent him out to purchase food and ale before he called for the last case of the session to be presented. It had been a relatively uninteresting morning as far as Will had been concerned, as most of the cases had been uninspiring. There had been the usual series of disputes, minor misdemeanours and breaches of the town's peace or of the curfew. His interest had been whetted just once in the case of a woman who it was said had brought about her mother-in-law's death through witchcraft. Sir Giles had skilfully cross-examined all the supposed witnesses and exposed the evidence as being meaningless and the whole case being based upon spite and jealousy. He quashed the case but sentenced the two discredited witnesses to three days each in the stocks, the sentences to begin forthwith.

As he left the Manor Court, Will had taken the opportunity to wander around the town streets, soaking up the atmosphere of the busy market day.

Wakefield was not a pretty town, Will thought, when he compared it to the great cities of London or York, yet it was clearly quite prosperous and not without its own charm. It had four main roads leading into it, each of which had a chantry chapel and a tollgate which closed at the eight o'clock curfew. Three of the roads met at the market place, which was called the Birch Hill. Within this area there was a pond, a market cross and a large circular area called the Bull Ring. This was so named because bull and bear bating regularly took place there when fairs were held. On market days such as this day, it was strewn with market stalls and temporary animal pens, and was thronged with people. Not far from the Bull Ring was the Tolbooth or town prison, and close to it was the Wodehalle, the Moot Hall where the Manor Court was held. Further down the hill was the Church of All Saints with its mighty spire.

Will threaded his way down the Northgate, a basket of bread, cheese and apples in one hand and a flagon of ale in the other. On either side of the wide ox-cart and pack-horse rutted road were gabled wooden houses, most with undercrofts for animals or for storing supplies, and with rooves of thatch or reeds. Side streets and narrow alleys ran off it and from them came odours of wood smoke, baking bread and cooking. Dung heaps, puddles and refuse of all sorts had to be negotiated by the crowds of people and animals that ambled along in a zigzag manner in the heat of the sun.

He crossed the Bull Ring and entered a small square in front of the Tollbooth. To his surprise the two ex-witnesses in the case of the woman accused of witchcraft were already locked in the stocks and were being berated with abuse, rotten vegetables and pig dung. Urchins ran hither and thither goading them and amusing the crowd that had formed to take pleasure in the misfortune of others.

Will stopped for a moment to watch a woman, whom he recognized as the wench who had so recently stood in the accused's person's pen charged with witchcraft, approach them with a bucket of some sort of excrement. The crowd roared with laughter as she applied it pitilessly with a wooden spoon. It was not a pretty sight, but he supposed that Sir Giles would say that it was both lawful and just.

He walked on towards the Wodehalle where he hoped Sir Giles would be just about finished. It was a large timber-framed building capable of holding up to 200 people. Above its door was the emblem of the de Warcnne family, the original lords of the Manor of Wakefield, and above that was a small sundial. He was just about to reach for the door when he heard the rumble of cartwheels behind him, then someone called out his name.

'Master Holland! A word.'

He turned and saw Dickon of Methley, the castle falconer drawing his covered cart to a halt. Almost immediately several street boys had gathered round and started tugging at his sleeves, and leaned over to get a glimpse inside the cart.

'What have you in there, Master?' cried one.

'Falcons,' replied Dickon. 'And every one of them could see off any one of you. Now get back and keep away from them.'

Will smiled, for although Dickon spoke warningly to them he did so in a tone that was not harsh, as such as they were used to hearing.

'What can I do for you, Dickon?'

'Is Sir Giles still in the court?'

'He is. I have just bought food and ale for his lunch.' Will looked curiously at the falconer. 'This is an unexpected meeting, Dickon. What brings you to the Manor Court?'

'I thought that since Sir Giles is the Constable of Sandal Castle I should show him this. My tercel, the one that I had chosen for Sir Giles to fly tomorrow at the hunt took a pigeon.'

'And you want to give Sir Giles it as a gift?' Will asked doubtfully.

'In a manner of speaking, Master Will,' he replied, reaching into one of his voluminous pouches and drawing out the body of the pigeon. 'But I thought he might be interested to see what it was carrying.'

Will's eyes opened with interest when he noted the small leather pouch attached to one of its legs.

'Is it a message?'

Then as Dickon nodded:

'What does it say?'

The falconer shrugged his shoulders. 'I cannot read, Master Holland. That's why I came straight here. I thought it might be important.'

Will grinned at him. 'Then let us deliver the message to him.'

And pushing the great door open he led the way inside. The day just seemed to be getting interesting.

3

The Fool's Folly

Sir Giles had just dismissed the court. Will and Dickon waited for the crowd to teem past them and then Will led the way to the Rolls Office.

The inside of the Wodehalle, as the Moot Hall was known locally, was as large as a barn. It had been built at the end of the thirteenth century in order to hold the Manor Court on behalf of the lord of the manor. In those days the people of Wakefield, including the burghers, guildsmen, yeomen and bondsmen, and the serfs, villeins and tenants of the Manor of Wakefield, which stretched from Normanton in the east to distant Halifax in the west could all be called upon to attend. Indeed, in the past, there had been occasions when the Moot Hall was packed to the point that the great doors had to be thrown open so that the court audience could spill out around the square of the Tolbooth and the stocks.

There was a dais in the main hall, upon which was a large oak table with several chairs for the judge of the court and occasionally for visiting dignitaries, such as the Earl of Lincoln. These and the twelve stools to the left of the dais for the members of the jury were all now vacant, as was the three-sided wooden pen which faced the table for whoever was addressing the court or being addressed by it.

Two of the town constables were standing around waiting for a third man to dismiss them. This third person was the court bailiff, a sour-faced fellow in a long gown who was tidying documents and ledgers. He looked up as they approached the dais.

'Ah, Master Holland,' he said, unenthusiastically. 'The judge is in the office. He is expecting you.'

'He will be wanting his lunch, I expect, Master Crowther,' Will said cheerily.

'Then he is lucky,' one of the two constables remarked pointedly. 'The court is empty and so is my stomach.'

'You hold your tongue, Tom Toliver,' the bailiff snapped. 'The court business is not over until the Court Rolls are safely inside the Rolls Office. Your duty is to see that they, and I, are safe.'

'As you will, sir,' replied Tom Toliver stiffly. He was a short, stocky man who looked as if he liked to eat regularly, unlike his fellow constable, Bartholomew Crofton, who was tall, lanky and had the red-nosed look of the bucolic. A blue band on Tom Toliver's livery indicated that he was the senior of the two.

Constable Crofton winked at Will and Dickon. 'Take your time, Master Crowther. The Court Rolls are our greatest joy and pride. We can eat and sup to our hearts content once you are safely in the Rolls Office. Is that not so, Tom?'

Will grinned and gestured for Dickon to follow him behind the large screen at the back of the table. He tapped on the door and was bidden to enter.

Giles was sitting at a table studying a vellum scroll. He still had his iron-grey coif on, the close cap that was his badge of office as a judge. Together with his eye patch it made him a striking, if forbidding figure.

'Ah, food and ale!' he exclaimed cheerfully as he looked up and saw Will. Then he raised a quizzical eyebrow as he spotted Dickon enter behind him.

'My lord, good Dickon the falconer has a strange thing to show you.'

'Then he can show me as we eat. Is there enough for three, Will?'

Dickon looked aghast and began to protest, but was silenced when Giles raised a dismissing finger.

'Lay the food out on that spare table, Will,' Giles went on, looking beyond him at the entry of Master Crowther, his arms laden with the ledgers, documents and vellum scroll upon which he had written all of the proceedings of the morning session, under Giles's direction. 'I will cast my eye over the morning's proceedings with Adam Crowther here, then he can lock up the Rolls and be off.'

The bailiff looked slightly taken aback at the use of his Christian name by the judge, then his lips seemed to soften into the semblance of a half smile of pleasure. He laid the scroll down on the desk and Giles sat down and read swiftly.

'You are a good and learned clerk, Adam Crowther,' Giles said at last. 'You transcribe well and keep excellent records. This is the basis of good legal practice.'

A tinge of pink formed on the bailiff's cheeks. 'We are proud of the Wakefield Court Rolls, Sir Giles,' he said, standing deferentially a pace away. 'It is an honour to look after them.' He turned and unlocked a large chest that took up a whole corner of the room. He lifted the lid and dropped the front to reveal numerous pigeonholes containing countless fine vellum scrolls, all neatly labelled and methodically arranged. Dating back to 1274 and written in a mix of English and Latin, they represented a continuous record of all of the dealings of the Manor Court since then.

'May I lock them away, Sir Giles?'

'Please do and then you may go yourself.'

The bailiff carefully stowed the latest Court Roll into a pigeonhole and locked the chest. Then he opened a cupboard and stowed the ledgers and other documents away, before locking that too.

'I shall let the two constables go now, Sir Giles, but I shall wait in the court until you have finished and then I shall lock the Moot Hall myself.'

Giles pointed to the table where Will had laid out what seemed to be a mini-feast. 'Would you care to eat with us?' Giles asked.

Adam Crowther shook his head emphatically. 'It is not my time to eat, Sir Giles. If you need me, just call.'

Will grinned when he had gone. 'He is a stickler for order and status.'

'He is a useful and clever clerk,' Giles replied, sitting down and removing his coif, which he placed in a small box by his side. 'Now, what is it that you have to show me?'

With some prompting Dickon repeated his tale, finishing by bringing out the pigeon and laying it on the table in front of Giles.

'Have you looked inside this little leather bag?'

Dickon nodded uncertainly. 'I did, sir. But just to check. I saw writing on it, and as I said to Master Holland, I am not an educated man and I cannot read. That is why — '

'Quite so,' Giles interrupted as he undid the bag and withdrew a small piece of parchment. 'You have done well, Dickon.' He looked up at the falconer and smiled. 'As did your falcon, Lightning.'

Then turning his attention to the parchment, he unrolled it and flattened it on the desk. There were two lines written in bold sloping handwriting. He read it aloud:

'*The nightingale flies north to sing.*

Do not fail the love that is thine.'

Will and Dickon looked blankly at each other.

'A strange wording, my lord,' remarked Will.

'Strange indeed,' Giles agreed. 'As to whether it is of any significance, who can say. We could do with knowing who sent it and to whom. Have you any ideas, Dickon? You are our falconer. Are there any people in the area who would have trained messenger birds?'

Dickon pursed his lips in thought. 'I cannot rightly say, Sir Giles. I have heard of pigeons being used thus, but I have never seen it myself. Yet it should not be difficult. They would just have to know how to handle the birds, then arrange for them to be taken to the other person, the person who had need of sending a message. The two people would probably exchange pigeons, then when they needed to send a message they release one and it would find its way home.'

Will broke off some bread and cut a wedge of cheese to lay upon it. 'So someone is waiting for this message that Dickon's falcon intercepted? But what does it mean. It sounds to me like a message between lovers.'

'Indeed a possibility. Especially if they are illicit lovers,' Giles replied.

Then, thinking he heard a movement from without he pointed at the door and nodded to Will, who understood his glance. Will rose and crossed to the door, then suddenly yanked it open. He stepped out and they heard his steps walk down the corridor, then come back as he went to check in the court hall.

'Nothing, my lord. I think that the bailiff must have stepped outside.'

'I wonder?' Giles mused as he untied the little leather bag then inserted the rolled-up piece of parchment. Putting it in his pouch, he pointed at the pigeon.

'The bird is yours, Dickon. Do with it as you will.'

The falconer thanked him and replaced it in his own pouch. 'It will make a good meal this evening, Sir Giles. It will be a good omen for the hunting tomorrow.'

Giles accepted the mug of ale that Will handed him. It could well be a portent of some sort, he thought. But whether it was of good or of evil was a matter that he would need to think about.

* * *

It was late in the afternoon when Edric, the second cook's assistant went down to the cellars beneath the Grand Hall undercroft to bring up a cask of Bordeaux wine in readiness for the feast planned for the Council of the North that evening. Always a nervous youth, he was forever being teased about his jumpiness. Scared of his own shadow, the kitchen staff proclaimed, which had the effect of making virtually every one of the castle servants delight in making him jump whenever the opportunity arose.

With a spluttering torch held above his head he advanced down the steps into the cool cellars and almost fainted when he turned the first corner and tripped over a body lying on the floor.

He gasped and jumped backwards, almost falling backwards as he slipped in a puddle of sticky liquid. In the circle of light cast by the torch he saw to his horror that it was red. Tremulously, he held the torch out to see by its light whose body it was.

The castle jester was lying on his back with his eyes staring upwards and his mouth hanging open.

'N-Ned Bunce,' he whispered, extending a foot and prodding him with his toe. 'Are you dead?'

'No!' the jester cried, suddenly sitting up and raising a flagon of wine which Edric recognized to be the source of the sticky red puddle. 'Why do you ask?' he slurred. 'You look as if you've just seen a ghost!'

As Edric let out the scream that had for some moments been threatening to erupt from his lips, Bunce began to cackle, a loathsome noise that only ceased when he put the flagon to his lips and slurped its contents noisily.

Noisy footsteps clattered down the steps.

'What the hell is going on down here?' demanded the angry voice of Peter Griddle, the second cook as he charged down the steps and turned the corner.

'Edric, you damned milk-sop! Stop that

caterwauling!' Then spying the jester and the flagon of purloined wine:

'Bunce! You drunken sot!' He held out a hand. 'Give me that flagon of wine or so help me I will — '

'Or you will pine, pine, pine!' cried Bunce, leaping to his feet and then ducking, he charged past. 'And I am not drunk,' he called over his shoulder. 'I am fine, fine, fine!'

Peter Griddle's face went red, then he cuffed the whimpering Edric on the side of the head. 'Shut up, you numbskull, or someone will take care of you.' He turned his head and spat into the puddle of wine. 'Like they might take care of that little runt, Ned Bunce!'

* * *

Alice Musgrave had been six years old when her mother had died, which meant that she had received a less than conventional upbringing from her father. Doctor Anthony Musgrave had treated her progress from childhood to adulthood as an experiment. This was not to say that he had been neglectful in any way. Indeed, he had taught her things far beyond the normal range of subjects usually studied by a young lady of her class. While he had been careful to accept the help of his sister in teaching Alice about music, literature, painting and drawing, he had ensured that she knew how to read the classical languages of Greek and Latin and to converse in French and Italian. More than that, he had taught her mathematics, as well as trained her in the practical use of metals, the fashioning of jewellery and the preparation of medicines. And building on those skills he had allowed her to assist in his experiments in alchemy and in his observations of the planets, thereby giving her a rudimentary knowledge of astrology.

For several of her teenage years she had travelled with him around the great courts of Europe until he had settled in England and obtained the welcome patronage of the Earl of Lincoln. For two years, the two happiest years of her life, they had lived at Sandal Castle where she had effectively looked after her father's needs and been his assistant in his great works.

And then Sir Giles Beeston had been appointed as Constable of the Castle and judge of the Manor Court, under the Earl's patronage, and she had met his assistant Will Holland. The attraction between them had been mutual as well as obvious for all to see. Their meetings were, of course, always carried out with decorum, living as they did under the auspices of the Earl, and yet without interference from Doctor Musgrave, for he took a great interest in studying the phenomenon of love.

Their chambers on the top floor of the south tower were private and virtually self-contained. Her father kept his alchemy oven and kilns perpetually fired in one room and used another for consulting with patients and preparing remedies. Next door to this there was a small kitchen where she brought the same principles of experimentation to the preparation of food that he had shown her from alchemy. This meant that some of the meals she produced were inspired and others were inedible. The meal that she had prepared for her father and Will Holland that evening was, she believed, in the inspired class.

'It smells delicious, Alice,' Will said as she opened the door in answer to his knock. 'Roast rabbit unless I am mistaken?'

'Roast rabbit in a sauce of shallots, with rosemary and a few other things of my devising,' she said, wrinkling her nose in that way that sent shivers up Will Holland's spine. Her eyes opened in delight as he brought his hand from behind his back and produced a posy of flowers.

Will cast a quick look over her shoulder

and smiled when he saw that they were yet alone. He dipped close and brushed her lips with his. Alice responded, her cheeks colouring instantly. Then she took his hand and led him into the room, where a table had been laid for three people.

'My father should be with us in a moment,' she said, steering him to one of the chairs. 'I hope you are hungry because I have made enough — '

'Goodness, Alice, that smells good,' came Dr Musgrave's voice from the far doorway. 'It is a pity that I cannot enjoy it with you.'

Alice stared at him uncomprehendingly. 'You cannot enjoy it, father? Why not?' She scowled and her lower lip seemed to quiver petulantly. 'You know that I have been preparing it for the past two hours. And I had asked Will to be our guest.'

The physician turned and blinked at Will, as if seeing him for the first time. Then he smiled, stepped forward and patted him on the shoulder. 'Then he will enjoy your company without me, my sweet child. Regrettably, my presence is needed by my lord, the Earl of Lincoln, at the feast this evening.'

'Ah yes, sir,' said Will. 'Sir Giles is attending also. I think he has a message he wished to discuss with the Earl and his guests. I am sure he would value your opinion.'

Doctor Musgrave held out his hands beseechingly. 'You see, daughter, I have no choice. I must away, and you two must enjoy your own little feast.'

'But father, we — '

'Farewell. Good appetites.' With which he let himself out.

As soon as the door closed the two young people stared at each other before falling laughing into each others' arms. Then they fell into kissing.

'But what do you think of the messages on our rings?' Alice asked at last, reaching for his hand.

'I think the messages we chose are ideal, my love. I am all yours, and you — '

' — have all my good love,' she whispered, kissing his hand.

'You are so clever not only to make these rings, but to engrave them so beautifully. And I love the embellishments you added. Rosemary leaves on yours, and three saints on mine.'

'They will protect you, my darling. From all evil.' She squeezed his hand. 'Now tell me of this message that Sir Giles has to impart.'

Will told her of the message found on the pigeon. 'I must admit that it unsettles me. Sir

Giles clearly thinks that it is not an innocent message.'

Alice frowned so that three little lines creased her brow. Despite himself Will laughed. 'But we should not let it worry us now. Shall we sup?'

'We could,' Alice said softly. 'Or we could talk about our betrothal, now that we are alone.'

Will noted the flush of her cheeks and the quickening of her breathing, and as he did so he also felt his own cheeks begin to burn. He quickly averted his eyes towards his toes. Yet it was no use, for his eyes found themselves returning to gaze on the beautiful face that was upturned to him.

'Alice, I love you,' he said huskily.

'And I love you,' she replied demurely. Then she whispered. 'Shall we lie together now?'

* * *

The music of viol, flute, harp and clavichord floated down from the quartet of musicians in the minstrel's gallery of the Great Hall as the Earl of Lincoln entertained his Council of the North. Whereas normally he and his favoured guests would have eaten at the top table on the dais at the end of the hall, on this occasion he had eschewed the dais so that all would eat on the same level. Lincoln had learned from his uncle, King Richard, that there were times to assert one's dominance and times when it was best to play politics.

One part of his mind was in fact silently composing a comic poem about the sensitive and prickly nature of pride among the nobility and senior clergy of the realm. He smiled to himself as he thought of a rhyming couplet which perfectly parodied the preening, peacock-like vanity of those who sought advancement through being obsequious, as several present most assuredly did.

He was sipping wine from his goblet when the rasping, wheezing voice of the Abbot Mallory of Monk Bretton intruded on his silent reverie.

'My lord, he really is most irritating. If I were you I would have him — '

Lincoln glanced at the abbot and frowned. 'Who did you say was irritating, my Lord Abbot?'

'Your Fool! He seems to have no sense of respect for the privacy of his betters. I went for my nap this afternoon after our meeting, and when I drew back the blankets on my bed I found it covered in worms.'

Lincoln fought back a smile. 'Worms, eh? And you are sure that they were set there by my jester, Ned Bunce?'

The abbot had been gnawing on a chicken leg. He smacked his lips and tossed the bones down on his platter then dipped his fingers in a fingerbowl by his side.

'I suspect him, my lord.'

'But you do not know that it was he?'

The abbot bit his lip then reluctantly shook his head.

'Ha! Innocent Bunce, innocent Bunce!' called out the familiar voice of the jester. Then he suddenly popped his head up from under the table, opposite the abbot. In a trice he jumped out and executed an ostentatious bow to Lincoln, then followed with a surly imitation to the abbot.

'Ugh! What a horrid thing for anyone to do! Bunce hates worms,' he said, screwing his eyes up distastefully.

He mockingly shielded his mouth from the abbot and whispered theatrically, so that all in the Hall could hear him:

'Nasty, dirty worms!
Bunce thinks it glum
Maybe those dirty worms
All slipped from the Abbot's — '

But instead of vocalising the last word he turned round and bent over to point his behind at the guests. He waggled it and slapped it noisily.

74

At this, Lincoln and half of the guests burst out with laughter, much to the obvious displeasure of Abbot Mallory, who thumped his fist on the table.

'You see what I mean, your Grace? Such impertinence.'

Lincoln pointed a warning finger at the jester. 'Ned Bunce, I fear you will go too far one day.'

Bunce immediately turned a cartwheel then stood pointing at his short, stumpy legs. He put on an exaggerated crestfallen expression and raised his hands helplessly.

'Far, your Grace? On these legs?'

Lincoln chuckled despite himself. Then he turned to Giles. 'And what say you, Sir Giles? What is the legal opinion on the jester's crime?'

Giles had been nursing a headache, but smiled indulgently and leaned forward to nod at the abbot. 'I sympathize with Abbot Mallory's shock upon finding worms in his bed, your Grace. Yet I am not sure that one could justly call this a crime. At worst it is an invasion of the good abbot's privacy, but no harm has been done to him, except perhaps to his pride.'

The Earl of Lincoln smiled at Giles's choice of words and wondered if the Castle Constable had somehow divined the fact that he had been composing a poem on that very subject.

'It is surely a joke,' Giles went on. 'A jest such as one might expect from a jester. That implies that it was Bunce who did it, yet unless he admits that he did put the worms there, then there is little more to be said.'

Sir Roger Harrington of Durham slapped the table. 'I know how we might get the truth from him, my lord.' He waited until Lincoln nodded his head for him to continue.

'Put him on the rack, your Grace. He looks as if he could do with a little stretching.'

The remark, delivered without any obvious humour occasioned general hilarity throughout the hall.

'Or we could feed him one of those worms,' suggested Sir William Stanley of Holt. 'It might cure him of these pranks.'

Ned Bunce's face registered horror, then fear and he stood there with his knees knocking in exaggerated fashion.

'Poor innocent Bunce,' he cried. 'He needs a drink to calm his nerves.' And without asking permission he grabbed the abbot's goblet and downed it in one draught.

The abbot glared at him and he stared back, his eyes crossing over comedically.

'Now Bunce feels . . . sleepy!' he said, as he slid to the floor and immediately curled up.

He began to make loud snoring noises.

The Earl of Lincoln laughed. 'Well, it looks as if the trial of Bunce is over for the time being. You may stay there, Bunce, and sleep, as long as you do not snore.' He looked down the table and nodded at his personal physician, Dr Musgrave. 'And if you keep snoring, then the good Dr Musgrave here has my permission to either bleed you or give you one of his enemas.'

The jester immediately went quiet and rolled over, much to everyone's amusement.

Lincoln clapped his hands and a servant appeared.

'A fresh goblet for the abbot and more wine for everyone.'

When goblets had been recharged, Lincoln stood and raised his in a toast. 'Let us drink to the King's health, and to absent friends!'

The assembly rose with much scraping of chairs on the stone slab floor, and drank the toast.

'I hear that the Earl of Northumberland is not able to come this day,' Giles remarked, casually.

'He sent a message,' Lincoln returned. 'We wish him a speedy recovery, of course.'

Giles noted the muted silence that had fallen on the gathering. He took the opportunity to tell them about the falconer,

Dickon of Methley's discovery of the message attached to the leg of the pigeon that his falcon had taken. As he did so he drew out the small leather pouch and produced the parchment message. He read it out.

'A strange message,' Lincoln said, stroking his chin. 'Does it mean anything important, do you think?'

Giles had been watching the gathering as he spoke. No one seemed to register any particular surprise at it.

'Oh, it means something to someone, I am sure,' Giles replied. 'But it may be of no import at all. Perhaps a message between lovers?'

'Do you know what direction the pigeon was travelling?' Dr Musgrave asked.

'Towards Wakefield, or beyond, from the south.'

'A mystery for the present, then,' Lincoln pronounced.

'One that I am pondering over, my lord,' returned Giles.

Ned Bunce gave a single loud snore then turned over again.

★ ★ ★

It was dark by the time the outline of Sandal Castle loomed up ahead. He was weary from much riding and had only dared to stop at secluded spots to rest his horse.

'It is too dangerous to lurk near the castle tonight,' he mused to himself. 'There might be more of them after me and they might be closing in soon, so I must get to Wakefield and seek a safe place to lie up and think. And sleep!'

He drew his cloak about him, feeling the comforting touch of the sword hilt beneath it, a trophy he had taken from the first noisy assassin that he had ambushed and dispatched near Tamworth.

He fancied he could hear revelry from the direction of the castle. Sounds travelled at night and his mind conjured up a picture of a welcoming fire, a mug of ale or wine and a plate of piping hot food.

He almost jumped when he heard a rustle in the nearby undergrowth. He stopped, pricking up his ears and listened for a few moments, until he assured himself that it was no more than the movement of some small animal foraging for food.

He coaxed his mount onwards, making his way quietly to Wakefield, where he imagined he would somehow have to enter the town after curfew time. It would probably mean having to tether his horse some distance outside the town and take to his feet.

'The bastards,' he whispered to himself. 'They will not take me before I do what I have to do.'

★ ★ ★

The moon had come out from a bank of scudding clouds, much to the relief of the two men of the watch, for patrolling the battlement walk was a thankless task at the best of times, but an especially difficult one in darkness. There were usually six of them at any time, each given a segment of wall to watch over, to ensure that no one crept up on the castle during the night. The two had met up at the last turret on the curtain wall before the wall swept up to meet the keep.

Not that it would give any attackers much joy if they did sneak up and avoid the watch, for Sandal was regarded as pretty near impregnable. The danger would lie in a siege, such as had happened all those years ago when Richard, Duke of York, had been goaded out of the safety of the Castle to his death.

'Look, he's at it again,' said Guardsman Mason, the younger of the two guards, pointing to the figure outlined between the crenellations atop the south tower. 'Bloody

80

old witch, that's what I say.'

'Watch your tongue,' hissed Jarman, the older guard. 'What you think doesn't matter a cat's paw. These are powerful folk. They could have the lives of common folk like us snuffed out like that!' He snapped his fingers with his free hand, then tapped the long pole of his pikestaff on the battlement floor. 'All of them are friends of the king. You know and I know what they say about his majesty and how he deals with them that gets in his way. If it is true, then our lives don't mean a tallow candle.'

Suddenly, the air was pierced by a shout and they both looked up at the south tower.

Dr Musgave was waving frantically and shouting at them. Then, when it was clear that he had their attention, he pointed down at the internal moat that surrounded the barbican, separating it from the bailey and the keep on the motte.

They both peered down and saw in the moonlit waters of the moat that something was floating. At first it looked like the body of a small animal lying face down in the water. Then they saw the three long liripipes of a jester's hat splayed out on the surface of the water.

'My God!' gasped Mason. 'It is the Fool.'

'It is,' agreed Guardsman Jarman, turning his head and spitting dispassionately. 'Looks like somebody might have finally got rid of the little bastard.'

4

Down in the Dungeon

The corpse of Ned Bunce was pathetic to see, having been unceremoniously dumped on his palette bed in one of the old horse stalls in the stables, which had been his home for the past two years. A crude door was all that had screened him and his meagre possessions from the noise and the smell of the horses, and the continual harassment of the ostlers and stable boys.

Although Dr Musgrave had persuaded the guards to fish his body out of the moat during the night, it was not until after cockcrow that Sir Giles had been informed of the jester's death. He had been less than pleased that they had not seen fit to disturb his sleep with the news. Giles had no doubt that the reprimand that he had given to the sergeant of the watch would be passed on, indeed probably multiplied, to the men of the watch. If it was, then he had no sympathy, for he was furious that the jester's death had been treated as a matter of little concern.

He knelt down over the body and looked at

the face, which was as pale as alabaster and yet mottled with a red rash like the underbelly of a fish. His eyes looked huge and were staring sightlessly up at the timbers above, while his purple tongue stuck out between almost black lips, which were curved into a fixed, macabre grin. It looked as if he had died in the very act of blowing one of his irreverent raspberries.

Will was looking over Giles's shoulder. He looked distinctly queasy at the sight of the little man's face. He commented upon the curious expression.

'It is the sardonic mask of death,' Dr Musgrave volunteered. 'It is common after death. The muscles around the mouth contract, pulling it into this bizarre semblance of a smile.'

'Did he drown, do you think?' Giles asked, standing up again.

'Almost assuredly.'

'Could he have been drunk?' Giles persisted. 'He had certainly taken wine at the feast, and I hear that he had been chased out of the cellars earlier on.'

'That is possible, Sir Giles.'

'But is there a way that we can find out?'

The physician had been tugging pensively at his beard, but now fixed Sir Giles with a shrewd regard. 'It is possible, but it would necessitate opening his stomach. And we will only know if he had drunk a great deal and died before it disappeared from his stomach. It is only a small chance that we could say conclusively.'

Will stared at him with open-eyed disbelief. 'But surely we cannot desecrate his body? My lord, you cannot permit this.'

But Giles stayed him with a raised hand. 'Not so hasty, Will. If Dr Musgrave is able to help us detect the cause of Ned Bunce's death, then the law will rule that there is no transgression.'

Will looked doubtful, yet bowed in submission. 'I am not sure that I agree, Sir Giles, but as always I hope to learn from your instruction.'

'I hope that will be the case, Will,' Giles replied, clapping the younger man on the shoulder. 'Yet before we do anything I would like his Grace, the Earl of Lincoln, to be informed of the death of his Fool.'

There was the crackle of a foot on straw and they turned upon hearing Lincoln's distinctive voice.

'I am already informed, Sir Giles. I see that my poor Fool will make me laugh no more. What folly was this? Did he drink too much of my wine and fall into the moat?'

'It looks like it, your Grace,' Giles replied.

Lincoln puffed his cheeks. 'A sad day then. Bunce was the best Fool that I ever had and he will be hard to replace.' He looked down at the sad figure and shook his head.

'He was never a pretty sight and seems less so now.'

He tapped his teeth for a moment, then:

'I shall have him buried on the slope leading down to the copse of willows and my grandfather's cross. I would like to be able to see his grave from my window. I think that I shall write a poem about him. I shall call it *The Fool's Folly*. That is appropriate, don't you think?'

The three others murmured assent, albeit more through politeness rather than actual agreement. None of them was sure whether the Earl was genuinely sad at the death of his Fool, or merely felt inconvenienced.

'Actually, there are certain formalities that I must attend to first, my lord,' said Giles. 'This man has died unexpectedly in the Castle grounds. I must make certain investigations before I can record the cause of his death.'

Lincoln nodded dispassionately. 'Do whatever you need to do, Sir Giles.' He gave a short hum then immediately changed the subject. 'Will you be joining us on our hunt this morning? I hear that Dickon the falconer has a bird chosen for you. That bird that you told us about last night.'

Giles shook his head apologetically. 'I fear not, your Grace. It would be best that I make my investigations first.'

Lincoln nodded. 'A matter of duty, eh, Sir Giles? I commend you for that. So we shall see you after our return.'

He clapped his hands and breathed deeply then exhaled swiftly, as if blowing away any unpleasantness. 'It looks like a good day for hunting.'

Once he had gone, Giles turned to Dr Musgrave. 'Will you be able to do this examination we were talking about this morning?'

The physician nodded. 'I suggest that the dungeon would be the most appropriate place. No one will disturb me as I carry out the operation. It will not, of course, be pleasant.'

Will still looked troubled. 'But Sir Giles, I thought you were going to tell his Grace, the Earl of Lincoln, and seek his assent?'

Giles patted his young assistant on the shoulder. 'You have much to learn about royalty, Will. His Grace is no Fool. He knows exactly what we are going to have to do and he just gave his assent.'

* * *

87

The news of the jester's death spread instantly around the castle. The initial overall reaction was one of shock, but gossip and tittle-tattle revealed a variety of opinions about the Fool. There were those who were visibly upset and saddened, others who felt a certain relief from the jester's incessant irritation, and yet others who felt justified in their prophetic abilities in having at some time or other predicted that he would come to a bad end.

Dickon was foremost among those who expressed sorrow about Bunce's death. He had heard about the incident as he finished loading his cart with his birds and dashed over to the stables where he waited deferentially for the Earl of Lincoln to come out. Then he went in and, catching Will's attention, requested that he be permitted to see the Fool one last time.

'Despite all of his faults he will be sadly missed,' he said, making the sign of the cross before him and bowing his head as he looked down at the body of the jester.

'I just hope that he enjoyed his last meal and however many flagons of ale or wine he washed it down with.'

Giles pursed his lips. 'Are you saying that he liked his cups too much, Dickon?'

The falconer grunted assent. 'Aye, and it

appears to have been the death of him. Is he to be buried in the cemetery of St Helens, my lord?'

Giles shook his head. 'The Earl of Lincoln wants him to be buried within sight of his tower window.'

'And he is going to write a poem about him,' added Will.

Dickon gave a rueful smile. 'The Fool would like that. He was a conceited little sod, but he loved the Earl.'

'We must prepare his body,' Giles said. 'Since you were his friend, would you care to move his body for us?'

Dickon nodded immediately. 'It would be my pleasure, Sir Giles. Where shall I take him?'

'We shall prepare his body in the dungeon in the barbican. Dr Musgrave will lead the way.'

And as Dickon knelt to reverently wrap the jester in an old horse blanket that lay beside him on the palette Giles nodded to Will to open the door of the stable stall.

'Come on, old friend,' Dickon said, gingerly lifting the small wrapped bundle. 'Let us prepare you for the last great journey.' He turned and nodded to Dr Musgrave. 'Lead the way, if you will, Doctor. It is a privilege to carry him before I must away with the hunt.'

The little party filed out and crossed the already busy bailey courtyard towards the drawbridge that led over the inner moat to the barbican. Servants and castle folk stood aside to let them pass, everyone bowing and signing the cross as they realized that Dickon was bearing the mortal remains of Ned Bunce the Fool.

*   *   *

The castle dungeon had not been used as a prison for many years and no one except Dr Musgrave ever visited it. Being under ground and well away from prying eyes it was the perfect place for him to go to perform his anatomical studies on the carcases of castle animals or pets which came his way after their deaths.

Dr Musgrave had barely noticed Ned Bunce during his life, merely considering him a nuisance that one had to endure when living in a castle under the patronage of a noble. In death, however, he warmed to the intellectual challenge that dissecting his corpse would give him. He viewed it as an opportunity to assist Sir Giles in ascertaining the cause of the jester's death and as a chance to legitimately examine the internal organs of the human body.

After taking the body to the dungeon and laying him on the work bench in the centre of the great square dungeon they had all retired to break their fasts. They were still at table when they heard the clatter of numerous horses, dogs and the rumble of Dickon's cart crossing the outer drawbridge on their way to the hunt in the Old Park to the east of Wakefield. The East Moor in particular would almost certainly assure them of good sport.

At first Giles had intended that Will should observe the examination and make whatever notes he felt were needed, but being aware of his reservations about the process, and the pallor of his face as they descended the steps to the dank dungeon, he relented and sent him off around the castle to reconstruct Bunce's movements that day.

For himself, although he had seen many atrocities on the battlefield, and also attended executions and several postmortem examinations in his capacity as a judge, yet he did not relish the sight that he was about to see.

The dungeon was fairly dank, with metal rings and chains hanging from the walls, an old rack shoved into a corner of the deep straw-covered floor. A spluttering torch burned on each wall, adequately illuminating the chamber and sending oily smoke upwards to form an eerie cloud above the macabre scene on the bench. By its light Giles fancied that he saw movement in the straw near the walls.

'Rats!' Dr Musgrave said with a thin smile, noticing Giles's head movement. 'But they will not disturb us while we have the light on. They fear our presence. It is only if we leave Bunce's body here after the examination that they would come out to feed.'

Despite himself, Giles shivered. He had seen the mess that rats can make of a dead body.

'Shall I get some men down to clear them out?' Dr Musgrave asked. 'They are quite easily caught. As you can see, I often use them in some of my experiments.' He nodded to a pile of empty cages in the far corner.

Giles declined to ask what sort of experiments the physician meant. He bit his lip then shook his head. 'We will not leave Bunce's body to them,' he said. 'Yet I think that they may prove useful to us before we have finished. Please carry on, Doctor.'

The doctor grunted, pulled back the blanket and began undressing the body. Then he opened the wooden chest that he had brought with him and from it started to lay out a selection of knives, scalpels and saws.

'What do you make of his general

appearance?' Giles asked. 'Does he look as if he has drowned?'

Doctor Musgrave bent closer to the face, peering into the staring eyes with their network of bloodshot vessels. Then at the fixed sardonic grin, the blackened lips and the purple bloated tongue.

'It certainly looks likely. He was found face down in the water of the moat, presumably from having just tumbled in. He is only a little fellow and it is unlikely that he could swim.'

'What do you make of that mottled appearance on his face?'

'Drowned men can look thus, Sir Giles.' His brow creased in thought. 'They say that if a body has been in the water for a while the skin will turn fish-like.'

He pushed his sleeves up beyond his elbows and then ran his hands all over the body and over the head, feeling for any breaks in bones or evidence of any bruising. He rose and shook his head firmly. 'And there is no sign of violence of any kind.'

Giles had brought a small book and writing box. He selected a quill, inked it and made some initial notes. As he did so, Dr Musgrave selected and tested a scalpel for sharpness.

'There will be little blood with this first incision,' he said, applying the blade under the base of the jester's breastbone, cutting in one long straight line all the way down the abdomen to the top of the pubis. Then separating the edges of the wound he grasped the muscle layer with a pair of fine tongs and started to open the abdomen. Immediately, coils of glistening pinkish bowels started to emerge through the incision. He reached in and started to pull them out of the abdominal cavity.

'These are the small bowels, Sir Giles. I just need to follow them up to the stomach. Then I shall open it and then perhaps we will have the answer you seek.'

Giles looked up and nodded, aware of the patina of perspiration that had formed on his brow.

★ ★ ★

Will had taken the opportunity to pay a call on Alice and found her busily preparing small bottles of valerian tincture.

'My father saw a spate of servants this morning while you and Sir Giles had gone to breakfast. They are all on edge after Ned Bunce's accident. He has left me to make up his prescriptions while he does some examination of the poor man's body.'

'They are opening his stomach to see if he

had drunk too much, although I cannot see what difference it will make,' Will volunteered. 'Fortunately, Sir Giles spared me from seeing it. I have little stomach for such a thing.'

Alice grimaced. 'I do not like to think of that.' She shivered and shook her head as if to banish the thought. Then:

'It will not seem the same without Bunce's merry little ways.'

'His irritating little ways is how many folk seem to see them.'

'I liked him, Will. He made me laugh.'

Will laughed. 'I imagine he had a soft spot for you.' And ensnaring her waist he kissed her neck. 'As have I, my love.'

Alice sighed as the feel of his lips upon her neck sent shivers of delight through her body. Then before he could find her lips she pushed him gently away. 'No! Behave yourself, Will. I have these potions to prepare and then I must deliver them. And anyway, you must have work to do yourself.'

Will reluctantly stood back and nodded. 'I have the task of seeing how Bunce spent his day, of finding out who saw him and at what times.'

'Edric, the second cook's assistant is one, at least,' Alice told him. 'He is a bundle of guilt this morning and was one of those who visited my father.'

'Guilt?' queried Will. 'Why so?'

'I do not know. All my father said was that I must give him some valerian tincture.'

'Then why don't I deliver it for you, my love? It would be a good place for me to start my investigation.'

He accepted the small bottle she handed him and stowed it in his pouch alongside the small sheaf of parchment and writing accoutrements that he had in readiness to record his investigations.

He leaned forward to bid her farewell, but this time she did not resist as he sought her lips.

★   ★   ★

John de la Pole, the Earl of Lincoln, did not enjoy falconry as much as he pretended to. Although he was fairly adept at it and could handle his bird as well as any, certainly better and more successfully than any of his party on this particular day, yet he preferred to simply ride. The problem with hunting was that it demanded one's attention in order to talk to and fly the bird. On this day he was feeling sadder than he had since the death of his cousin, young Edward, the Prince of

Wales, the year before. Although those in the Council of the North would doubtless consider him weak, yet he was deeply saddened by the death of his jester and all he wanted to do was go off and think so that he could compose the poem to honour him.

'The Fool's Folly,' he mused aloud. 'Oh Fool, how you made me laugh — '

'What was that you said, my lord?' Sir William Stanley of Holt, who was riding close by, asked curiously. 'Are you dwelling on the unfortunate death of your Fool?'

Lincoln looked round with a trace of embarrassment. He had not realized how far they had ridden from the main hunting party. 'Yes Sir William, he was on my mind. Bunce had been in my service for many years. He was a faithful servant.'

'A good quality, my lord,' said Stanley, stroking the head of the merlin that perched on his gauntlet. 'A person in your position must be sure of the faithfulness of those around him.'

'Meaning what, exactly, Sir William?'

'These are troubled times, my lord. England needs a firm ruler now more than at any other time.'

'We have a firm ruler, Sir William. My uncle, King Richard, sits on the throne and rules with a firm and fair hand.'

Stanley quickly bowed his head. 'Of course, your Grace. I meant no disrespect. I merely meant that you, as the president of the Council of the North, must be assured of the faithfulness of the members who serve on it.' He looked over his shoulder as if to ensure that they were well out of earshot of the other hunters. 'I give you my word that I for one will always serve you well. Now and in the future.'

Lincoln stared back impassively, even though he felt a flame of temper begin to flicker. The blood of the Plantagenets flowed through him and he knew that he had to keep his temper curbed. It was another thing that he had learned from his uncle, a well-known hothead before the death of his son and his beloved wife, Queen Anne, earlier in the year. And as he thought of his uncle he realized how he missed him and wished that he could be there with him now, able to enjoy a short release from the cares of his crown and the threat of another uprising.

'And do you speak of your loyalty to my uncle the king?'

'I swear that with all my heart, my lord.'

'And in that do you speak for all your family?'

Sir William's shrewd eyes fixed on him. 'My family has always served the House of

York, your Grace.'

'Really? Your brother, Thomas, Lord Stanley the Earl of Derby, was friend to the late King Edward, but less so to his brother, King Richard. And he is still confined to his home along with his wife, the Lady Margaret Beaufort, two years after the rebellion of the Duke of Buckingham.'

'They are loyal to the throne, my lord,' Stanley persisted.

Lincoln pursed his lips. 'Yet Lady Stanley's son, Henry Tudor, he who opposes King Richard, is not loyal.'

'He is a renegade, my lord.'

'Yet he is loved by his mother, I hear.'

'All mothers love their sons, my lord.'

'Ah yes, and Margaret Beaufort has loved many men, as husbands, has she not. Let me see,' said Lincoln, staring into the distant moors. 'There was her first husband, my own father, the Duke of Suffolk. The marriage was annulled when they were eleven or so, I believe. Then she married Edmund Tudor, the Earl of Richmond, who gave her a son, the Henry Tudor who now looks on my uncle's crown from France.'

Sir William's cheeks grew red above his pointed beard, but he said nothing.

'Then she was married to Sir Henry Stafford for a while until he died and she married your brother. Why, Sir William, in a way, you and I could almost be related!'

'I fear that you play with me, my lord.'

Lincoln smiled. 'Why no, Sir William, I am just grateful to know that my uncle and I have the loyalty of your family. Or all of them except Henry Tudor, your step-nephew.'

The peregrine falcon on Lincoln's wrist began to fidget and pecked at his gauntlet.

'Was there anything else, Sir William?'

'I had intended to talk about the faithfulness of those who are not here, my lord.'

'Ah, you mean Henry Percy, the Earl of Northumberland? I thank you for your concern, Sir William, but I believe that I have the matter in hand. Now, shall we let these birds have some exercise? I have lost one good servant already this morning. I have no wish of upsetting Dickon, my falconer, by not flying his pride and joy.'

★   ★   ★

The dungeon smelled like a charnel house.

Sir Giles held his hand over his nose as he watched the doctor pour the stomach contents into a brass basin.

'An unpleasant-looking mess,' the physician said, as he dangled the tongs he had used earlier in the basin to move barely digested lumps of meat around in the dirty, viscous red liquid that bathed it. He leaned closer so that his nose was almost inside the basin and sniffed repeatedly. 'It looks and smells like wine,' he reported.

'Which is what we would have expected. Yet we know that he had drunk some wine, the question is, was there enough to make him lose balance and fall into the moat?'

Dr Musgrave frowned. 'I am unable to say, Sir Giles. How much is too much, especially with a little fellow such as this?'

Giles scratched a few notes then stood stroking his chin with the feather of the quill. 'What food is in his stomach?'

The physician prodded with his tongs, moving lumps about. He selected one lump and lifted it up to inspect it closer. 'There is certainly bread here, but also meat. This, I think is fowl, Sir Giles. Pigeon, unless I am mistaken.'

'Pigeon?' Giles repeated as he jotted another line of notes.

'I am sure of it now. And it smells as if it was probably cooked in garlic. Not a herb that I enjoy myself.'

'We shall come back to the stomach contents in a moment,' said Giles. 'What I would like you to do now is to open his chest and examine his lungs.'

'His lungs, Sir Giles?'

'It is an idea I have. I have read that a drowned man will have water in his lungs.'

'Most assuredly he would.' He looked puzzled for a few moments then reached for a scalpel and extended the incision upwards over the breastbone to the base of the corpse's throat. Then with the tongs in one hand and the scalpel in the other he dissected the skin back from the muscles of the chest. Old, dark blood oozed from severed blood vessels, making it ugly work. Finally, picking out a pair of heavy pincers from his instrument chest he cut upwards through the left side of the chest wall, crunching several ribs at a time. He repeated the process on the right side before laying the pincers down, getting hold of the front of the rib cage and lifting it up to expose the heart and lungs.

'Do you wish me to remove the lungs from the body?'

Giles winced as he felt a stab of pain from his old wound. From experience he knew that he would need some more of the doctor's potion soon, else the pain would get a good hold. Steeling himself, he shook his head. 'I think not. If you just squeeze his lungs the water will come from his mouth, will it not?'

The doctor reached into the chest cavity and, getting hold of each pinkish-grey lung, squeezed firmly.

Apart from a macabre death rattle as air was forced from the lungs up the dead man's throat, there was nothing.

'There is no water in his lungs. I begin to understand what you are thinking,' Dr Musgrave declared, as he washed his hands and arms in one of the buckets while Giles made further notes.

'And now, Doctor, I think that it would be useful if you were to catch two of those rats of yours.'

★ ★ ★

Will had spent all morning talking to various people. Edric had indeed been upset when he heard that the jester's body had been found in the inner moat. The guilt he had expressed to Dr Musgrave had been due to the fact that he had discovered Bunce stealing wine in the cellars and he somehow feared that it had been because he had not stopped him from drinking that he had come to his fate. Will gave him the potion from Alice and was amazed to see how quickly it calmed him down.

Gradually, he had built up a picture of

Bunce's contacts throughout the day. There did seem to be a few gaps, but he hoped that it would be enough for Sir Giles to work on.

Feeling bold, he plucked up courage, made his way to the barbican and descended the stairs to the dungeon. He banged on the great door and after identifying himself was bidden entry by Sir Giles.

The sight that greeted him was not as bad as he had imagined. The corpse of Ned Bunce had been wrapped up in the blanket that he had been carried down in by Dickon and lay on the bench in the middle of the chamber. The bench itself had clearly been swabbed by Dr Musgrave, who stood on the other side of the bench from Sir Giles.

'H-have you finished to your satisfaction, my lord?' Will ventured, coming in and seeing that they were both looking down at two cages that had been placed beside the body.

'We have finished, but I am far from satisfied,' Giles returned, looking over his shoulder at his assistant. 'Come in and close the door, Will.'

Will did as he was told and joined them at the bench. 'Two dead rats,' he commented. 'Had they starved to death down here?' he asked with a half smile.

'They were not dead until a moment ago,' Giles replied. 'We watched them die a horrible but swift death.'

'How so, my lord?'

'Poison!' Dr Musgrave exclaimed. 'We fed them some of the food that was in Bunce's stomach. It was poisoned. I think that Sir Giles expected it to be.'

Giles raised a hand to massage his throbbing temple. 'I had suspected so, yes. I did not really think that drinking himself senseless would have resulted in him drowning. No, Ned Bunce was already dead before his body was pushed or slid into the moat. This was no accident, but cold-blooded murder.'

'But by whom, my lord? And why?' Will asked in horror.

'Those are the questions that we are going to find out Will.' He gritted his teeth. 'I have a feeling that we must find out swiftly or Ned Bunce will have died in vain.'

5

Summons

Sir Giles found to his dismay that he had waited too long before taking more of Dr Musgrave's special skullcap potion. Will went to the kitchens and returned with a goblet of weak wine for him to add the potion to. But as often happened, the headache escalated and reached disabling proportions, so that he was forced to go and lie in his darkened bedchamber with a vomit bowl by his side for most of the afternoon. It was only the blessing of sleep which finally gave him ease, and he awoke with a start upon hearing a pounding on his door.

It was the good Will, come to check that he would be able to go down to dine with the Earl of Lincoln and the rest of the hunting party.

'Have I been asleep all of the afternoon?' he asked, sitting on the side of his bed and massaging his temples.

'You have, my lord. I have checked on you twice, once while you were incapacitated with sickness and the other while sleeping like a babe. I did not like to disturb you.'

Giles stifled a yawn. 'I am grateful, Will. Yet it means that I have not properly started my investigations. I need to arrange for the Manor Court to sit in Wakefield tomorrow, and I — '

'I have taken the liberty, my lord,' Will interrupted. 'I sent a message to Master Crowther, the court bailiff, saying that it was likely that you would wish to hold a hearing into an unexpected death.'

'Did you say more?'

Will shook his head. 'I said that it was the death of the castle jester, which I thought would be enough to satisfy him. To say more I deemed would be beyond my authority.'

'Well done, Will. That is exactly as much information as I would have wished to be imparted.' He sighed. 'It will not be an easy sitting, I fear. Especially when I talk to the Earl and tell him what I propose.'

★ ★ ★

Dickon had been in a gloomy mood all day and could not shake off a feeling of dread. The hunt had gone exceedingly well and all of the birds had performed well, as had the hounds in getting birds airborne or conies and hares on the run. They had returned with a cartload of assorted prey, much to the delight of Tobias Merrion, the cook.

'I thank you, Dickon,' the ruddy faced cook said. 'Now there will at least be enough fare for dinner tonight. The Earl and his Council ate half the larder last night and I was thinking we would have to get the pantler to make the bread twice as thick this evening. Now, what about you? Which of this fine game would you care to sup on tonight? If you will, I shall prepare a special little feast for you and me. I have a flagon of fine cider that I have been keeping hid.'

'I thank you, Tobias, but I fear I have little appetite today. After Bunce's death and all.'

'You as well?' asked the cook. 'It seems that half the castle are in mourning for little Ned. And yet he was a frolicsome fellow and would not have wanted to see such long faces.'

'You may be right there, Tobias,' Dickon returned, trying to squeeze a smile. 'But can we have a rabbit, or a bit of hare. Anything but pigeon. I seem to have lost the taste for it.'

★　★　★

John de la Pole had gone to his chamber after the hunt and, as was his custom, practised his swordsmanship with his arming sword and buckler in front of the large mirror for fifteen minutes before making his ablutions and dressing before sitting down at his desk. He planned to write for an hour before dinner.

He had intended to pen some preliminary thoughts and snatches of verses that he had composed during the hunt, but his mind kept getting distracted by the conversation he had with Sir William Stanley. He could not help it; he simply did not trust the man. Yet his uncle had advised him to appoint him as a member of the Council of the North. It would, he felt, be another way of keeping a wary eye on the Stanley family and upon Margaret Beaufort, now Lady Stanley, the mother of Henry Tudor.

He heard the noise of someone shuffling outside his door and he immediately thought that it was Bunce, up to some jape or another. But then he chided himself, for poor Bunce was dead and would play the Fool no more.

'Who is there?' he called.

The shuffling stopped and he thought that he heard a rasping intake of breath.

'Come in!' he commanded.

He waited a moment, fully expecting someone to talk or try the door, but nothing happened. Instead he thought he heard the sound of a blade being unsheathed. Immediately he felt the prickle of hairs standing up on the back of his neck and he pushed back his chair as silently as he could, stood up and tiptoed over to his bed and picked up his sword and buckler shield.

Then swiftly, he crossed the room and threw the door open, immediately falling into a defensive position.

There was no one there.

He sprang through the doorway, spinning round as he did to meet anyone who might have been pressed against the wall. Seeing no one, he turned again and checked the stairwell.

It was only as he was returning to his chamber that he fancied that the tapestry outside his chamber was not in its usual place. He went back inside and tossed his sword and buckler back on the bed.

'Lincoln, you have started imagining things!' he said to himself. He wiped his brow and was surprised to find his hand come away moist. He sat down behind his desk and picking up his quill started to write.

'Now come, use that imagination to write this poem in memory of my Fool.'

* * *

Sir Roger Harrington was feeling fatigued after his day's hunting, for physical activity was not his favoured occupation. He was lying propped up on cushions on his bed with a cup of mead in his hand, when he heard a soft yet insistent rap of knuckles on the door of his chamber in the east tower.

'Who is it?' he called.

He recognized the wheeze that preceded the speech. 'It is I, Abbot Mallory of Monk Bretton. I would have a word, Sir Roger.'

Sir Roger scowled, then crossed to the door and transformed his expression from one of dismay to that of welcoming smile.

'Come in, your Grace,' he said, holding open the door and pointing to the flask of mead with his own cup. 'Will you join me in a cup of mead? It is my family's own secret recipe.'

The abbot shook his head at first, then seemed to think differently. 'Well perhaps a small drink for companionship, Sir Roger.'

Moments later, with cups charged, they saluted one another and sipped.

'An excellent brew, Sir Roger,' said Abbot Mallory. 'But if I might — ' He hesitated as if suddenly at a loss for words.

'Speak freely,' Sir Roger urged.

The abbot's mouth hardened as if some internal doubt was causing him great anxiety which he had determined to overcome. 'I want to seek your advice, Sir Roger. It is a delicate matter, for I have grave concerns about the Council of the North. I fear that there could be treachery afoot.'

Sir Roger almost choked on his mead. He spluttered and coughed for a few moments, then recovered himself.

'Tell me what is on your mind, your Grace. We live in treacherous times, but I for one have no desire to suffer from the treachery of others. What do you know?'

The abbot bit his lip. 'I pride myself in being a good judge of character, Sir Roger. I like and trust you. That is more than I can say about some of our fellow members.'

'Do you refer to our absent member, the Earl of Northumberland?'

'He is one, and I do not want to name other names as yet. But I think that we are all skirting one of the main issues that face England at the moment.'

'You mean the threat of rebellion?'

'Aye, Sir Roger. And also one of the reasons why we may be on the verge of rebellion. I am talking about the fate of the two princes in the tower.'

Sir Roger stared at the abbot for a moment then put a finger to his lips. He took two steps to the door and silently opened it to look outside. Then he quietly closed it and led the way across the chamber to the far wall.

'Let us be careful in what we say here, your Grace. I would not wish prying ears to misinterpret what you say as being in any way treasonable.'

* * *

Father Edmund was looking hot and red in the face as he crossed the drawbridge to enter the castle. He was making his way across the bailey courtyard towards the mews when he saw Will Holland come out of the barbican. Changing direction, he picked up the bottom of his cassock and trotted over to meet him.

'You look hot, Father Edmund,' said Will.

'That is true, Master Will,' replied the chaplain. 'I have walked far this afternoon. To Wakefield and back on some pastoral visits. Yet I am concerned about what has happened to Bunce.'

Will looked perplexed. 'Well, of course, we are all concerned about Bunce's death, I am sure.'

'It was not just about his death that I meant, Master Will. I am concerned about what I believe may have happened to him,

113

and about what may happen to his immortal soul.'

'I do not follow you, Father,' Will replied.

Father Edmund's eyes widened with the zeal of a truly godfearing priest. 'I understand from Dickon the falconer that his body was taken to the dungeon this morning. And I have heard that a hearing is to be called at the Manor Court in Wakefield tomorrow.'

'You heard correctly. I myself sent a message to the bailiff of the court.'

'I have also heard from some of the guards that Dr Musgrave was down there with Sir Giles for some hours.'

'That is true, Father. And I also was down there later on.'

'Has his body been desecrated?'

Will blushed and hesitated before speaking. Then:

'His body has been examined for legal purposes, Father. I am not permitted to say more.'

'Why has he not had holy rites said over him? His soul is at stake.'

'I cannot say, Father Burke.'

The chaplain's body seemed to shake and his face grew dark. 'I fear that evil has been set loose this day. You had best tell Sir Giles that he should allow me to see poor Bunce. I must save his soul.' He eyed Will askance. 'I do not wish to bring the matter up with the Earl himself.'

With that he stomped off across the bailey.

Will stood watching his retreating back. Although he had not said anything, he was all too aware that evil had been done, but soon Sir Giles would see that everyone would know about it.

★　★　★

Dr Musgrave had felt fatigued after his work in the dungeon. After completing an examination of the two dead rats he had placed Bunce's body in the small wooden coffin which the castle carpenters had built upon Sir Giles's instructions, then gone for a full ablution before eating lunch on his own. After a short rest he had attempted to divert his mind from the mysteries that had risen from Bunce's death by continuing his astrological studies in his workroom.

It was a subject which fascinated him and he soon lost himself in his contemplation of the stars and the cosmos. It was only when he heard the outer door open and his daughter's step in the corridor that he recalled how vexed he had been to find her gone when he had returned for lunch. He looked up from his astrolabe and sat back in his chair, tapping his fingertips against one another.

'I missed you, Alice,' he said as she came into the room with a great basket on her arm, from which a dozen different smells emanated. 'Where have you been?'

She raised her eyebrows questioningly. 'I have been out gathering herbs and flowers, father. Some of our stocks are low.' She held the basket out, indicating the various blooms and herbs. 'I have fresh comfrey, monkshood, lavender and — '

'Who did you go with, Alice?'

'Why, I was by myself, father.'

'You should not have gone without — '

' — without your permission!' she exclaimed. 'But father, I am a grown woman now. Need I must ask when I can go gathering plants?'

Dr Musgrave raised a hand. 'You misunderstand me. I was going to say, without a companion. Someone to protect you, should the need arise.'

Alice laid the basket down upon the desk. 'To protect me? From what, father? I have been going to collect herbs around the castle for months and you have never asked me to take a companion with me before.'

'We live in changing times, my dear. I have your interests at heart.'

'But what has changed, father. I know as well as any that there is a continuous threat of some sort of uprising against the King, but what danger is there here at Sandal when his majesty is in far-off Coventry or Nottingham? I can see for miles around when I am close by the castle on a day such as this.'

'It is not that which I was thinking about.'

'Then what, father?'

He gave a sigh of resignation. 'I had not intended to tell you of it, but you will hear soon enough. As you know, I made an examination of poor Ned Bunce's body this morning.'

Alice grimaced. 'Yes father, Will told me about it. You cut open his stomach to see if he had drunk so much wine that he fell into the moat.'

'We found that was not the cause of his death. He had been poisoned.'

Alice gasped in horror and raised a hand to cover her mouth. 'By whom?'

Dr Musgrave shrugged his shoulders. 'That is something that Sir Giles is determined to discover. But now do you see why I was so concerned, my daughter. If someone deliberately poisoned him then there is a murderer on the loose somewhere. And so, in future, please do not go anywhere on your own. Either wait for me, or get Will Holland or one of the Earl's men to accompany you.'

'You do not mind me going with Will?'

The physician tugged at his beard. 'I do not mind him as a companion, Alice. He is a smart enough fellow, the son of a gentleman, I believe.' His eyes narrowed. 'But have you it in mind that he may be marriageable?'

Alice stiffened and she stood up straight, her chin rising a fraction in defiance. 'Would that be so bad?'

'I do not know, Alice. I would need to know of his prospects. He is Sir Giles's assistant, but does he have plans — or the means — to become a sergeant-at-law, or a judge, like Sir Giles?'

'Oh father!' Alice exclaimed. 'What difference does it make how much wealth he has, if I love him?'

'Do you love him?'

Alice smiled demurely and nodded her head.

'In that case I need to know about his prospects.' He smiled as her face fell. 'I have your interests at heart, my sweet child.'

Her reaction surprised him.

Tears had welled up in her eyes, yet she did not sob. He saw the tightening of her jaw muscles. How like her mother she was.

'Are you sure, father?'

'Of course I am sure, Alice.'

She shook her head. 'No, I don't think it is my interests that you are worried about. I think you may have more concern that you may lose the assistant for your experiments.'

She curtsied and turned, then flounced out of the room.

The physician absently ran a finger over his astrolabe. He found himself wondering whether she had not been correct. He had long valued her abilities as an assistant. He reflected that there were several reasons why he would not wish to lose her.

* * *

Dickon was busy weighing the birds one by one in the mews, to determine which would need feeding after the hunt, and how much each bird should receive. He spun round at the sound of a foot on the straw.

'Sir Giles!' he exclaimed. 'I was thinking about you, and Bunce. Have you any news of my friend?'

Giles moved his head non-committally. 'I have begun an investigation, Dickon. And that is why I am here to speak with you. I need to know how that pigeon you caught yesterday tasted. You were going to have it for dinner, I believe you said.'

Dickon gave a wry smile. 'I was, Sir Giles. And looking forward to it as well. But it was stolen before I sat down.'

'Who could have stolen it? Do you have any idea?'

Dickon stared back, his shrewd eyes narrowing. 'I suspect it could have been Bunce. Why, my lord?'

Giles did not reply at once. He bit his lip. 'I suspected it was so.'

'Is it important, Sir Giles? I have lost many a meal and many a flagon of ale to that light-fingered little Fool.' He quickly crossed himself. 'May the Lord rest his soul.'

'There will be a hearing about his death at the Manor Court in Wakefield tomorrow. You will need to be there, Dickon.'

The falconer bowed and Giles left. It took some minutes before Dickon's heart stopped racing.

★ ★ ★

The Great Hall was a welcoming place that evening. Despite the warm summer evening a roaring fire burned in the hearth, light still streamed in through the three great mullioned windows and the castle quartet filled the air with music and song from the minstrel gallery high above the diners.

The feast that was set before the Council that evening was a triumph of Tobias Merrion's art. It was served by a veritable army of servants, marshalled by Smead, the Earl of Lincoln's steward of the household.

First the ewerer and his assistants passed along the tables with pitchers of rose-scented water, bowls and towels. Then the pantler and three robust serving women followed, distributing small half-loaves on to plates. Following them came the butler and his cupbearers with wine. When all had drink before them, Lincoln stood and raised his cup and toasted first his majesty, King Richard, then wished them all good health. Then, before they sat down, he raised his cup again.

'And in memory of my poor Fool, Ned Bunce, whose juggling, merry japes and antics at table will be no more. May the Lord look after his soul.'

When everyone had drunk to his memory, Lincoln gestured to Father Burke. 'Would you say a prayer for him, chaplain?'

Father Burke nodded gravely and led the gathering in a solemn-sounding prayer mumbled in Latin.

'And now let us enjoy the fruits of our hunt,' Lincoln said with a good-humoured smile.

Over the *entrement*, the first course designed to prepare the stomach, a leek poached in white wine, the Earl encouraged the assembly to recount their individual successes with their birds. The anecdotes were delivered in a variety of manners. Some, such as Sir William Stanley, barely gave a list of the prey they had caught, while others were natural storytellers.

Sir Roger Harrington was one of the latter, who did not mind poking fun at himself. He gave a flowery description of his bird's flight, embellishing his tale with a story of how his hawk had somehow supped from his cup of mead, which his servant had freshly poured in order to perk him up during the hunt, and of how he was sure it had seen double as a result, so that it had flown after the wrong rabbit and flown down a rabbit hole.

'Dash it if I didn't have to rescue the bird myself,' he ended with a flourish. 'And so, I ended up with a paltry total of one rabbit and one pigeon, my lord.'

His tale was followed by general hilarity. Once it settled, Smead the steward shrewdly divined it was appropriate time to clear the table and begin serving fresh trenchers. The diners chatted among themselves as a procession of servants entered with feathered woodcock adorned with saffron, roasted conies, and a roasted suckling pig, with a huge apple in its mouth.

While the carvers served the food, Sir Giles, sitting halfway down Lincoln's table alongside Dr Musgrave, took the opportunity to speak up. He leaned forward and addressed the Earl of Lincoln.

'With your leave, your Grace, may I report on the death of Ned Bunce?'

Sir Roger Harrington stopped with a piece of meat halfway to his mouth. 'Good heavens, Sir Giles, are you determined to put us off our meal? Can this not wait until later?'

But the Earl of Lincoln thought otherwise. 'I am keen to know what you and Dr Musgrave learned, Sir Giles. Proceed if you will.'

'My feeling is that the examination posed many questions that need close investigation. I am not in a position to say at this time exactly how Bunce died, except to say that I am not happy about the manner of his death. Accordingly, there is a need to hold a full hearing about it tomorrow at a special session of the Manor Court in Wakefield. It will have to be done properly, according to the law.'

'Of course,' Lincoln replied.

'That means that I must ask all of the Council to attend the Manor Court tomorrow morning.'

Lord Scrope of Masham was the first to react. 'The members of the Council of the North, attend a Manor Court? Ridiculous!'

Others noisily declared their agreement with much shouting, cursing and thumping of tables.

'Think of our positions!'

'It is disrespectful to us!'

It was Lincoln who silenced the tumult.

'Sir Giles is correct! A man has died in unusual circumstances and by law his death must be investigated. It shall be done properly, which means that we shall all attend the court, myself included.'

'Thank you, my lord,' Giles replied, gratefully.

Lincoln pursed his lips. 'Yet I fear you may have ruined everyone's appetite tonight, Giles.' He picked up his goblet and signed for it to be refilled. 'Have you any idea what happened to my poor Fool?'

'I cannot say as yet, my lord,' Giles replied, eyeing the gathering. 'But let me just say, his death raises many questions. Many unpleasant questions.'

* * *

It had seemed an interminably long day and he had not dared to leave the sanctuary of All Saints, the parish church beside the Bull Ring, until with the failing light his nerves finally got the better of him. He felt the need of two or three mugs of spiced wine.

The tavern was a dark and smoky place, already busy with a motley crowd of locals. He was pleased to see that no one took any real notice of him, dressed anonymously as he was in a travelling cloak and with his cap pulled down to shade his eyes. He sat in a corner drinking as casually as he could, yet keeping a sharp eye on the door and on anyone who entered.

With his ears straining to pick up any bits of conversation that might be useful, his eyes widened when he heard a fellow in the uniform of the watch swill back a free mug of ale then inform the entire tavern in a voice that slurred slightly, that their attendance would be required on the morrow at the Manor Court.

'What the hell for?' growled the potman.

'It's a special hearing called by the judge, Sir Giles Beeston. The bailiff has sent us to tell everyone to be there in the morning at ten o'clock. There has been a death at the castle.'

'So what's so special about that?' someone cried. 'Folk die every day around here.'

'This was special. It was the Earl of Lincoln's own Fool.' He belched, and then guffawed with laughter.

The news was greeted with much ribaldry and jokes in ill taste.

But he did not think the news funny in the least. He waited until the man of the watch had gone, presumably to another tavern and another free mug of ale, then he drained his own drink and chose his moment to leave.

The sitting of the Manor Court could be the very opportunity that he needed.

6

The Manor Court

Sir Giles sent Will Holland to Wakefield shortly after cock-crow, to organize with Master Crowther the bailiff for the setting up of the Manor Court. The town constables of the four quarters mobilized their men to ensure that everyone that should attend the court did so. By ten o'clock, when Giles arrived there was already a gathering of some two hundred people waiting inside the Wodehall.

Giles went into the Rolls Office and found Will waiting for him.

'Is the Earl on the road yet?' Will asked.

'He is, together with the whole Council, albeit most of them are reluctant attendees.'

'I have arranged for seats to be brought in for them, Sir Giles.'

'Well done. It will, I think, be a salutary lesson for many of them, for the sin of pride rests easy on nobility.' He smiled. 'Apart from the Earl himself. Like his uncle, the King, he has the common touch and sees nothing wrong in sitting in a law court. Especially a

127

court that is intent upon finding out who killed his Fool.'

'What made you think that someone had killed Bunce, in the first place?'

Giles sat down and sifted through a pile of parchments that Master Crowther had set out for his perusal before the Court opened.

'It was the quiet,' he replied as he read.

'I beg your pardon, my lord. I do not understand.'

'The quiet,' Giles repeated. 'No one noticed that he had fallen into the moat. That is odd, don't you think? If he had been drunk and simply slipped and fallen into the moat then he would undoubtedly have thrashed and splashed around and made an almighty noise to alert someone. People don't go to their death by drowning that easily. Yet the guards were up on the battlement walk and no one reported hearing anything. Even if he had drunk himself senseless it would be likely that the cold water would have revived him and he would have struggled and made some sort of noise.' Giles looked up and shook his head. 'But there was nothing, he just went quietly to his death. That does not make sense, so the only other conclusion is that he was already dead before he entered the water. If that is the case then someone put him there and they did it quietly while none of the guards was in a position to spot it happening. Again, it leads to the conclusion that he was — '

' — murdered! I see, my lord. And your examination with Dr Musgrave confirmed that. What will happen to his body?'

'Dr Musgrave and Dickon the falconer are bringing it in Dickon's cart. We will be looking at it in the Court this morning.'

Will's jaw dropped and he was about to ask another question when there was a tap on the door and Master Crowther entered.

'One of the constables has just reported that the Earl of Lincoln and his entourage from Sandal Castle have just crossed the bridge over the River Calder, Sir Giles.'

'I shall be with you presently,' Giles replied, opening the small chest and taking out his coif. 'I shall meet him as he comes into court. Have you selected twelve men for the jury?'

'I have and they are standing by their stools.'

Giles put on and adjusted his coif. 'We will follow you, Master Crowther.' Then with a nod to Will. 'Stay close Will. This may be a case that has more to it than is at first apparent.'

★   ★   ★

Dickon's cart trundled over the bridge and past the Chantry Chapel of St Mary the Virgin.

Dickon looked aside at his companion, Dr Musgrave, the bottom half of his face covered with a scarf.

'It is a sad day, Dr Musgrave,' said Dickon. 'I never thought that I would be playing the part of corpse bearer for Ned Bunce.' He snorted ruefully. 'He would have laughed to see you and me carrying him to the Manor Court.'

Dr Musgrave pointed at the Chantry Chapel. 'Perhaps his spirit is still with us. Perhaps it is there, in God's Chapel, watching us passing.'

Dickon shivered and quickly made the sign of the cross. 'Ah, but it is no laughing matter, is it. Not with his body starting to go ripe in this heat. I hope that we will soon be able to lay his body to rest.'

'Let us hope so, Dickon. Although they say that the souls of those slain can never be free until their slayer is brought to justice.'

Dickon clicked his tongue at his piebald pony as they began the trek up the Kirkgate hill towards the town.

'Come on, old lad, we had best be quick,' he said, coaxing the pony onwards. 'My lord, the Earl of Lincoln, is probably already at the

Wodehall. We don't want to be late or we'll be in trouble.'

'Have no fear, Dickon,' said the physician. 'I think that Bunce's appearance in the court may be crucial. I fancy that he will be making an even greater stir at this gathering than he ever did in life.'

Dickon shivered again, despite himself. He was not a particularly nervous man, yet he worried about Bunce's spirit hovering around them. He shook the reins, urging greater speed from the piebald pony.

★ ★ ★

For the people of Wakefield the appearance at the Wodehall of not only the Earl of Lincoln, but the entire Council of the North and an armed guard of the Earl's own men was a spectacle that they had never expected to see. Dressed splendidly in various colours and fashions, all of them stood out as people of importance. But of them all, the Earl himself attracted the most attention, especially from the ladies.

Sir Giles and Will met them at the door, with Adam Crowther, the bailiff, standing a couple of steps back and to the side.

'My lords, it is an honour that you do the Manor Court this day,' said Giles, bowing.

'It is our duty as true Englishmen,' returned Lincoln. 'Everyone in the land must expect fair law, so it is up to myself and the Council of the North to give our utmost backing to you as our appointed judge and constable. Lead on, Sir Giles.'

In turn, Giles held out a hand towards the bailiff and instructed him:

'Master Crowther, please show the Earl and the Council members to their seats.'

And the crowd shuffled further apart to allow the nobles ample room to pass. They walked down to the front of the hall and took up seats which had been set up behind Sir Giles along the back of the dais. When they had all sat down Giles himself took his seat at his desk and rapped the gavel in front of him.

'People of Wakefield and of the Manor of Wakefield, this is a special hearing convened urgently to investigate the sudden and unexpected death of one Ned Bunce, the official jester to his Grace, The Earl of Lincoln.'

There were a few mumblings and mutterings from around the crowd, but they were swiftly silenced by a rap of Giles's gavel. 'There will be order and due respect shown in this court. Any unseemly behaviour will not be tolerated.' He looked slowly around the hall, aware as he did that many present were intimidated by his eye patch. He went on:

'We are honoured to have the Earl of Lincoln himself here today, together with the members of the Council of the North. They are here to witness the process of law and to assist.'

Giles was aware of shuffling in the seats behind him and realized that he had perhaps taken some of the illustrious Council members by surprise when he suggested that they may actually be called upon to take part in the proceedings. He looked round and was encouraged to see the Earl nod affirmatively.

'Master Crowther,' he said, addressing the bailiff. 'Please swear in the jury. Their function today is also to observe, but if needs be I may call upon them to make a decision.' He rapped his gavel as he spoke, to emphasize his next remark:

'Their full attention is demanded and any who fall asleep may be considered to have held the court in contempt. This will result in a fine.'

And while the bailiff went about his business of getting each jury member to swear on the Bible, Giles ran through his notes. Finally, with the jurors seated on their stools, all determined to be alert, he opened the case.

'The body of Ned Bunce the jester was found in the early hours after midnight yesterday, floating face down in the inner moat of Sandal Castle. Three people saw the body: Dr Musgrave, the Earl's physician, and two men of the guard. We will hear the guard's accounts first.'

Then to Master Crowther: 'Call Guardsmen Mason and Jarman. We shall interview Guardsman Jarman first.'

The two guards approached the bench and Master Crowther directed Jarman, the elder of the two, to stand in the three-sided witness pen and swear on the Bible.

Jarman clearly thought that he was going to enjoy the attention that he was going to receive, since he had not been reticent in informing people at the castle and in a couple of the local taverns of how he had spotted the body in the moat.

Giles asked him to give his version of the discovery of Bunce's body.

Jarman stroked his stubbly chin and grinned at the audience. 'It was dark, an hour or so after midnight. Me and Mason there was doing the watch by the eastern wall. I have been teaching the lad the ways of the watch, him being newish to guarding and all. Well, it was cloudy, but as soon as the moon came up I scanned the outside of the castle, then like I always do I checked on the inside of the castle. I checked the bailey courtyard and then the inside moat.' He beamed proudly, revealing a couple of gaps in his teeth. 'I have about the best eyes in the castle for seeing at night, if I say so myself. And I saw him bobbing up and down in the water. I knew it was a body, sir.'

'You knew it was a human body.'

'I had a right good idea that it was a little one, sir. Then I knew it had to be the Fool.'

'And what did you do then?' Giles asked.

'I told Mason that we best get him out of the water.'

Giles looked across at Master Adam Crowther. 'Have you got all of that, Master Crowther?'

When the bailiff nodded assent, Giles looked dispassionately at Jarman, before turning to address the crowd and the jurors. 'Ordinarily, I would have the witness sign his testimony, but I am going to hear the other witnesses first, because the preliminary accounts that have been collected by my assistant, Master William Holland, do not tally with this witness's statement.' Again he turned to Jarman. 'Is there anything about your statement that you would like to alter?'

The guard swallowed hard, as if his mouth had suddenly dried up. He shook his head.

'Then you may stand down, but stay close,' Giles instructed. Then to the bailiff: 'Call Guardsman Mason.'

The younger guard glanced nervously at his comrade as he took his place in the witness pen and took the oath. Giles told him to give his account.

'Well, Sir Giles, it was a bit like Jarman said, only . . . only — '

'Only what?' Giles prompted.

'Only, Jarman didn't see him first. I did.'

'Indeed?' Giles said with surprise in his voice.

'Yes sir, but I wouldn't have seen him if I hadn't seen Dr Musgrave up on top of the south tower. He was . . . he was . . . doing some of his strange stuff.'

'What strange stuff, Guardsman Mason?'

'Looking at the stars and writing things about them. It seems strange stuff to me.' He looked sheepish. 'But I am not much of one for learning, not like the doctor.'

'And what did Dr Musgrave do that was relevant to this case?'

'He saw something in the water and it was him that started shouting and pointing to this shape in the water. And . . . and it was him who came down from the tower and made us get him out of the water.'

'Did you do this straight away?'

Mason shook his head. 'We couldn't, Sir Giles. We was on the watch. We are not allowed to leave, so I went and got the sergeant of the watch and he told us to go and get him out while the south wall watch split up and they covered our section.'

'I see. Is there anything you want to add to this?'

Guardsman Mason's face was almost bright red. He looked nervously at Jarman, and then shook his head. 'No, Sir Giles, I have nothing to add.'

'Then you will be asked to sign your statement soon,' Giles said. 'After we have heard Dr Musgrave's account.'

The physician took his place in the witness pen and proved to be a far more credible and confident witness.

'Dr Musgrave, do you agree with the testimony of the last two witnesses?' Giles asked.

'The second of the two witnesses gave a reasonable version,' Dr Musgrave replied. 'I had wished that they had been quicker in getting him out of the water, for I thought that it might have been possible for him to revive. I have known cases of people having water pumped out of their lungs and coming back to life. By the time he was taken out, it was too late.' He looked meaningfully at Giles and added: 'But the results of the examination tell us that — '

'That will do for now, Dr Musgrave,' Giles interrupted. 'You may stand down, but stay close, for I will call you back shortly. Remember that you are still under oath.'

There was a murmuring from the crowd at this sharp dismissal of the doctor, but it was silenced by a rap of Giles's gavel.

'Call the two guardsmen again — they will take the witness pen together.'

The two guards took their place in the witness pen and stood nervously as Giles scrutinized them.

'Guardsman Jarman, what have you to say about the difference between your account and that of your fellow guard, Mason, and that of Dr Musgrave?' Giles demanded sharply.

The guardsman shuffled and perspired visibly. 'I . . . I may have made a mistake, Sir Giles.'

Giles slapped the bench. 'You made a very large mistake! This is a court of law, the purpose of which is to find out the truth about this poor man's death. You, by trying to gain favour and respect by pretending to have first seen the body, and then denying Dr Musgrave's part in it, could have seriously jeopardized any chance of arriving at that truth. You will be fined thirteen pence.' He turned to Adam Crowther. 'Make a note of that, Bailiff.'

He waited for Master Crowther to make the note, then he turned to both guardsmen again. 'Did either of you hear anything during your watch? Any noise of someone falling into water, or anyone crying out as they struggled in water?'

The two guardsmen vigorously shook their heads.

'In that case, you may both stand down,' Giles said. Then to Master Crowther: 'And note that down, Bailiff. No one heard anything.'

He leaned forward and addressed the jury. 'And my assistant questioned the other guards of the watch and no one heard anything. That is, I believe, highly significant.'

Giles waited a moment then stood up and turned to face the Earl of Lincoln and the assembled Council of the North. He bowed.

'And now my lord, I think it would be helpful to the court if we could have some background about Ned Bunce. Would your Grace be prepared to talk in front of this court?'

'Sir Giles, this is outrageous!' Lord Scrope of Masham exclaimed angrily. 'This is precisely why I did not feel this hearing was appropriate. It is not seemly for the heir presumptive to the throne of England to speak in a common court. It is not — '

But he was silenced by the Earl of Lincoln himself. 'That will do, Lord Scrope. My uncle, the King, is adamant that he wants the law of this land to be fair to all. We, the members of the Council of the North, have a duty to lead by example and demonstrate our respect for the law and the courts of the land.' He looked pointedly at Lord Scrope. 'The Manor Court of Wakefield has a long and honoured tradition and I assure you that I am perfectly happy to be questioned under oath today, here in front of the good people of Wakefield. I owe it to Ned Bunce.'

'I thank you, your Grace,' said Giles. He gestured to the bailiff. 'The Earl of Lincoln can give his testimony from where he sits, but please, Master Crowther, administer the oath if you will.'

There were gasps of astonishment and admiration from all around the court as the Earl stood and took the oath. Then Giles began asking questions.

'How long had you known Ned Bunce, your Grace?'

Lincoln stroked his chin. 'Ten years, I think. He was employed by my father when I was thirteen. He was one of a troop of travelling jongleurs, a performing family actually, who regularly performed at the local fair. They did acrobatics, juggling, clowning and a bit of conjuring. Ned was the smallest of them and they used to throw him about, toss him to the top of a human pyramid, that sort of thing. Until one time they tossed him too far and he went up over the pyramid and broke his arm in a fall. My father took pity on him and let him stay at the castle, while the rest of the troop took to the road, the idea being that they would come back for him at the next fair day. But by the time they came back Bunce's arm had healed, and he had somehow inveigled himself in the affections of the family.' He grinned. 'Mine especially, as it happens. That came about when I went down with a sickness when I was about fourteen. They thought I might die, but Bunce kept appearing from nowhere and made me laugh. I rather think he saved my life.'

'And how long has he been in your own employ, your grace?'

'Six years, ever since I took to travelling on my own, to my own estates.'

'Did you enjoy his pranks, my lord?'

Lincoln gave a short laugh. 'Mostly. Sometimes he could get a bit too personal.' He waved his hand dismissively. 'But that is part of the function of a Fool. To be amusing,

141

annoying, unpredictable.'

'Has he ever had another patron than yourself or your family?'

'No. Yet I was approached six months ago at the last meeting of the Council of the North. Henry Percy, the Earl of Northumberland, seemed to find him exceedingly amusing and asked me if I would sell him.' He gave a derisive laugh. 'Sell Bunce? I told him that my Fool was not for sale.'

'Did Bunce know of this?'

Lincoln shrugged. 'Why should he? It was not a matter up for discussion.'

Giles nodded. 'Would you say that Bunce was a clumsy fellow?'

Lincoln laughed. 'He was an acrobat. He was small and looked odd, but he was really incredibly graceful and had perfect balance. He used to walk a tightrope at the fairs.'

Giles hummed. 'So it is unlikely that he would just have fallen into the moat. Not if he was sober, at any rate. Which leads me to the question, did he drink a lot, your Grace?'

'Like a fish, as we all know.'

'Could he swim?'

'Apparently not.'

'But can you say that with certainty?'

Lincoln scratched his chin. 'I suppose not.'

Giles felt a spasm of pain in his temple and gently massaged it. Then: 'I have just one more question, your Grace. Was Bunce unhappy or given to moods of melancholy?'

Lincoln was swift in his reply. 'There never was a merrier fellow. My Fool truly loved his work.'

Giles smiled. 'Then that will be all that I need to know for now, your Grace. Thank you.'

Giles turned back to face the main court. 'Yesterday, my assistant pieced together as best as he could the movements of Ned Bunce at the castle. It does not cover his entire movements, yet it gives an idea of whom he saw throughout the day. For this reason, the first person I would like to call to the witness pen is Father Edmund Burke, the chaplain of the castle.'

The castle chaplain took his place and was sworn in. He stood with his tonsured head half bent as he awaited Giles's opening question.

'How long have you been the chaplain at Sandal Castle, Father Burke?'

'One month, Sir Giles.'

'And before that, where did you serve?'

'I was a monk at Monk Bretton Priory, Sir Giles.'

Giles noticed the chaplain dart a glance at Abbot Mallory.

'And how did you obtain this position?'

'My Abbot advanced me, my lord.'

'And have you been happy at the castle?'

'Extremely, Sir Giles. It has been an honour to serve the Earl of Lincoln and his household.'

'And what of Ned Bunce, the court jester? What did you think of him?'

Father Burke made the sign of the cross in front of him. 'He was a cheerful fellow, Sir Giles. He was always amusing people.'

'And how did he amuse you the morning before last?'

'He . . . he splattered my head with dung, Sir Giles.'

'And that was amusing?'

The chaplain winced as one or two of the crowd suppressed chuckles. 'I was not amused, Sir Giles. But I forgave him. I always forgave him. He was doing his job and I did mine by forgiving him.'

'I understand that you wished to see him after his death?'

'To my knowledge he has not been blessed. I feel that his soul may be at risk, Sir Giles.'

Giles nodded. 'Then you may have the opportunity to do so soon enough. You may stand down, Father Burke, but stay close.'

When the chaplain had joined the throng Giles went on. 'The morning before last I and my assistant went to break our fast in the refectory and we met Bunce. He himself told us of the prank he had played on Father Edmund, and he told us of a tapestry that he said had been moved over the Earl of Lincoln's door. We believed that Bunce had moved it there as a joke. My assistant went to move it back while I talked with Bunce. Then we were joined by Dickon of Methley, the falconer. We shall now hear from Dickon of Methley.'

The falconer had been standing at the back and as he made his way through the crowd it was clear from the muttered greetings and patting on his shoulders and back that he was well known in Wakefield.

'Dickon of Methley, do you recall our meeting in the refectory the morning before last? And do you recall what you said to Bunce?'

'I remember being angry with him, Sir Giles. He had been interfering with my birds. He had untied them and thought to make mischief for me. But one of them took a fancy to his finger.'

There was general amusement at this, which Giles did nothing to suppress.

'Did you threaten Bunce?'

Dickon looked taken aback at this. 'I . . . er . . . may have, Sir Giles. But not seriously. I think I said I would tie him up.'

'And you cuffed his ear.'

Dickon coloured. 'I did, Sir Giles, but it was just the usual banter. I didn't mean anything by it.'

Giles looked over at Master Crowther. 'Record all of this, bailiff. And record that Dickon the falconer denies any malicious intent.' He turned back to Dickon. 'That is all for now, Dickon of Methley, but I may call you back soon. Stand down, but stay close.'

Somewhat bemused, and with more than a trace of anxiety, Dickon bowed and stood down.

'Later in the afternoon Bunce was found in the cellars by Edric, the second cook's assistant. He and Peter Griddle, the second cook, both declare that Bunce had stolen a flagon of the Earl's wine and was drunk. I have questioned them both and not deemed their presence necessary today. Make a note of that, Master Bailiff.'

Giles looked round, his eye resting on the Abbot of Monk Bretton.

'Abbot Mallory, I would like to ask a few questions. Would you take the oath?' Giles noted the look of exasperation that the abbot gave him, then added: 'You may of course, stay where you are seated.'

The abbot raspily repeated the oath on the Bible.

'We have heard that you advanced Father Burke to the position of chaplain at Sandal Castle. Why was that?'

'He is a good and capable priest.'

Giles nodded. 'But we are here to talk of Ned Bunce. You did not like the jester, did you, your Grace?'

'I found him irritating. He put worms in my bed.'

For the benefit of the court, Giles recounted the events at the feast, which had culminated in Bunce pretending to fall asleep.

'When we all left the Hall after dinner, did you notice if Bunce was still there? Was he still asleep?'

The abbot knitted his brows together. 'I do not remember. I think so.'

Giles turned to the Council. 'Does anyone remember seeing if Bunce was still there?'

Lord Scrope was the first to speak. 'I believe he was. Still rolled up in a ball. I thought he was faking it.'

The Earl of Lincoln agreed. 'It was play-acting, I am sure. But yes, I think we just walked round him.'

'But he could have been asleep?' Giles pressed the Abbot.

The Abbot concurred, reluctantly.

Giles watched as Adam Crowther, the

bailiff, made notes on the vellum parchment. Then he addressed him:

'Master Crowther, have the body brought in. It is appropriate that we should view it now.'

The small coffin had been delivered by Dr Musgrave and Dickon into the hands of the duty town constables, Tom Toliver and Bartholomew Crofton, who had locked it in one of the cells of the Tolbooth, opposite the Wodehall. Some minutes later, they brought it in.

The crowd parted noiselessly to allow them through.

'Lay the coffin in front of the bench,' Giles directed, 'and remove the lid.'

Constable Toliver, the shorter of the two prised the lid free then immediately covered his nose with his sleeve, as a waft of putrefaction escaped.

The crowd surged forward as people jostled to get a view of the body within. There were gasps and several exclamations of horror and disgust.

Ned Bunce's purple tongue was protruding from his black lips. The signs of Dr Musgrave's examination were not visible, for his torso was covered with a blanket.

Dr Musgrave had already been called back to the witness pen. At a sign from Giles he advanced to stand before the bench as Giles addressed the court.

'Yesterday, in my presence, Dr Musgrave performed a post-mortem examination on the body of Ned Bunce. That is, he cut the chest and belly open to look at the lungs and the stomach. It had been assumed that the jester had died by drowning, possibly after having drunk a large amount of wine which resulted in him falling senseless into the moat and drowning. I myself made notes of the examination as it occurred. I give these now to the bailiff, so that they can be entered into the Court Rolls.' He summoned Will with a gesture and handed him the sheaf of papers.

'The conclusion was that he had not drowned, because there was no water in his lungs, as one would expect. Secondly, when the doctor opened the stomach to find out whether he had drunk enough wine to have fallen into the moat, the doctor was able to confirm that Bunce had drunk some wine, but it was impossible to say how much he had drunk.' He looked around the court, allowing his words to register with people. Then he added: 'Yet you were able to prove something else, were you not, Dr Musgrave?'

'I was, Sir Giles. The food remnants inside the stomach were poisoned.'

There were gasps of astonishment and

disbelief from the crowd and from several members of the Council of the North.

The Earl of Lincoln leaned forward, much interested. 'And how did you know this?'

Giles nodded to the doctor. 'Show us, Doctor.'

Dr Musgrave peeled back the blanket to reveal Bunce's bare torso. A line of heavy stitching showed where his body had been opened and subsequently closed. Sight of this occasioned several shrieks and sharp intakes of breath from around the crowd. The physician reached into the coffin and drew out the bodies of the two dead rats. He held them up by their long naked tails.

'These rats were fed the contents of the stomach and they died instantly,' Dr Musgrave volunteered.

'And horribly,' Giles added. 'They died in considerable pain and started thrashing about in fits.'

Lord Scrope sniffed noisily. 'What sort of poison was this?'

Giles nodded encouragingly for the physician to answer.

Dr Musgrave laid the dead rats back in the coffin. 'It is hard to say, except that it was a very speedy one. That fact and the appearance of the corpse, which I must admit I had not noticed straight away, would make *dwale* a likely culprit.'

'Please explain what this *dwale* is,' Giles urged.

'It is a poison made from a common enough plant, Sir Giles. It grows in the woodland around here. Some call it deadly nightshade.'

'Would anyone use it for anything except poison?' Giles asked.

'Indeed, Sir Giles. Any physician or apothecary would tell you that it is a potent medicine in small doses against St Vitus's dance and the scarlet fever.'

'Do you have some of this dwale?' Giles asked.

The physician was cautious in his reply. 'I have tinctures of deadly nightshade and some dried plants and berries. I use them for their medical powers.'

'And could anyone get hold of your supplies?'

The physician shook his head. 'I keep these locked in a special cupboard. Only I have the key.'

Giles nodded to the physician. 'I thank you, Dr Musgrave, you may stand down.'

Then turning to the Earl of Lincoln: 'With your permission, your Grace, we shall permit Father Burke to say holy rites over the body, and then it can be released for burial. I understand that you have specific plans.'

Lincoln assented. 'I do, but I would also like to be present when prayers are said over his body. I suggest that you have his body taken to the Church of All Saints on the other side of the Bull Ring and we shall go there and honour him before we return to Sandal Castle.'

'As you wish, your Grace,' Giles replied.

He turned to the bailiff. 'Is the local priest of All Saints here in court?'

Adam Crowther consulted his records then shook his head. 'He is not in the town at the moment, Sir Giles. He is making a pilgrimage to Kirkstall Abbey.'

'In that case, Father Burke can take the service,' said Sir Giles. Then he turned to the Council of the North and spied Abbot Mallory: 'And if your Grace would also like to say something I am sure that would be appreciated.'

Abbot Mallory gave a curt nod. 'It will be my pleasure,' he rasped.

'That is arranged then,' Giles said, and he turned back and issued orders to the bailiff who arranged for the coffin to be solemnly taken away.

'And now,' Giles went on, returning briskly to his task: 'Call Dickon of Methley back to the witness pen. There are a few serious questions that I would have him answer.'

7

Cat Among the Pigeons

Dickon the falconer was not a craven fellow by any means, yet his brow perspired visibly as he took his place again in the witness pen. Ever since Sir Giles had been appointed as Constable of Sandal Castle Dickon had considered him to be both fair-minded and friendly, which seemed at total variance with his attitude in the court so far. He had watched him humiliate Guardsman Jarman, and he had felt the coldness in his tone when he had been dismissed earlier with the warning that he was to be recalled. It had been terrible to see Ned Bunce's body displayed in front of the whole of Wakefield, especially with those awful stitched-up wounds which showed where Dr Musgrave had cut out his organs and fed stuff from his stomach to the rats. Now he had a bad feeling as to where this further questioning was going to go.

'What do you think about this poisoning, Dickon of Methley?' Sir Giles suddenly demanded.

'I . . . I think it is a horrible thought, Sir Giles. Ned Bunce was my friend and I don't like to think of him dying that way.'

'You think it is worse than him drowning?'

'I think it is upsetting that someone might have killed him.'

'Who could have done that, do you think?'

'I do not know, Sir Giles,' Dickon replied earnestly, with a shake of his head.

'It is important that we find out,' Giles returned, coldly. 'Tell me, what did you have for supper last night?'

Comprehension suddenly dawned on the falconer. He had wondered what the purpose of Sir Giles' visit to him was the night before.

'I had no supper, Sir Giles. I was going to have roast pigeon. A pigeon that you had seen yourself, sir.'

'What do you mean you were going to have it?'

'Someone stole my supper, Sir Giles.'

'Could it have been Ned Bunce the jester?'

Dickon swallowed hard. 'I . . . I think it could, Sir Giles.'

To Dickon's surprise, Sir Giles dismissed him without any further questions.

'Dr Musgrave,' Giles went on, addressing the physician where he stood. 'Please tell the court what the poisoned food was that you removed from Bunce's stomach.'

'It looked like fowl of some sort, Sir Giles. I suspect it was roast pigeon.'

'I thank you, Dr Musgrave. You too may stand down.' Giles turned to the jury. 'The question we must now consider is how was this poison administered? Was this an accidental death? Did the pigeon eat these deadly nightshade berries before it died? Would that have resulted in poisoning the meat of the pigeon, even after it was cooked? Or . . . ' he looked around the hall at the crowd, 'was poison added to the pigeon after it had been cooked?'

Lord Scrope was the first to answer. 'I do not think it is possible that a bird could have eaten enough of these berries to kill a man without it killing itself.'

Sir Roger Harrington concurred. 'But I do not like the idea that someone deliberately poisoned the Fool. Why should they do that?'

The Earl of Lincoln leaned forward. 'Tell me, Sir Giles, is this pigeon the same one that you told us about the other night?'

Giles bowed his head to the earl. 'With your indulgence, your Grace, that is not a matter that I wish to disclose at this juncture.'

Lincoln held Giles in regard for a moment, then nodded comprehendingly. 'Then I leave this matter in your hands.' He leaned back, steepling his fingers pensively.

Giles sought out Dickon. 'Dickon of Methley, you may answer this last question from where you are. In your opinion as a bird expert, could a pigeon have eaten berries enough to kill a man?'

Dickon bit his lip. 'Pigeons will eat anything, Sir Giles. Contrary to what the good lords have said, I believe a pigeon could have eaten poison berries without being ill.'

Giles stared at him for a moment. 'Do you now?' he said slowly. Then to the bailiff: 'Record Dickon of Methley's opinion.' He waited for the bailiff to write down his notes.

'Now tell me, Master Crowther, are there many folk in Wakefield or in the Manor of Wakefield who keep or who breed pigeons?'

The bailiff chewed the end of his quill for a moment, then:

'I think that question might be better answered by Daniel Jackson, the master of the Guild of Butchers.' He looked at Giles for permission then, after scanning the crowd, he called across the hall to a burly, red-faced man dressed in the scarlet livery of the Guild of Butchers.

A few moments later, after he had taken his place in the witness pen and taken the oath, Giles addressed him.

'This is just information I need, master

Jackson. Who in this town tends or trades in pigeons?'

'That be easy to answer, Sir Giles. We had two poulterers in our guild until last month, but one passed away and the other bought all of his stock. That makes Jasper Hirst the only dealer hereabouts.' He craned his thick neck back and forth. 'But he is not here today.'

Giles stiffened slightly. 'And why not? All of the guildsmen were instructed to be present today, were they not?'

Adam Crowther raised his hand. 'I sent the town constables to alert all of the guilds, burgers and townspeople last night, Sir Giles. I have to say that it is not like Jasper Hirst to fail to attend. I can only assume that he is unwell.'

'Then he should have sent word that he was ill,' Giles returned stiffly. He signalled Will over to the bench.

'Will, I want you to go to this Jasper Hirst's home with a couple of constables and unless the man is dying, bring him back here. There are a few questions that I need the answer to. Master Crowther here will detail two constables to accompany you and show you the way.'

Will bowed. 'Consider it done, my lord.'

When he had gone Giles turned to the Earl of Lincoln. 'Your Grace, I am going to adjourn the court for an hour, which will be time to bring this last witness before us.'

'A good idea, Sir Giles. Indeed, I would like to have a private word with you before you restart.'

Giles turned to the court and announced a break for one hour. He rapped his gavel and immediately left for the Rolls Office, where he awaited the arrival of the Earl.

★　★　★

Will was grateful to be out in the open air again. He was also grateful for a swig of wine from the leather bottle that Tom Toliver, the senior of the two constables detailed to take him to Jasper Hirst's house, proffered him once they had walked out of sight of the Wodehall. The Bull Ring was very quiet, since most of the stall owners were in attendance at the court, having left wives, sons or daughters to look after their livelihoods.

'It is an unpleasant business this death of the Fool,' Tom Toliver remarked. He waved the butt end of his pike at four urchins who had elected to follow the three men in the hope of getting them to part with a coin or two. Will winked at them and tossed a couple of coins over their heads, which sent them scrabbling in the dust for their reward.

The other constable, Bartholomew Crofton, wrinkled his nose as if to show that he felt there was a bad smell in the air. 'This case stinks almost as much as the poor Fool's corpse,' he said. 'Yet that master of yours seems the sort who will wheedle the truth of the matter from someone.'

Will laughed and took another swig of wine before passing the bottle back to Tom Toliver. 'He is the cleverest lawyer there is. He has smelled a rat, I am sure.'

'He is not the prettiest of coves, though, is he?' Bartholomew Crofton ventured. 'How did he lose that eye?'

'He lost it fighting for the King,' Will said proudly. 'His majesty thinks just as highly of him as does John de la Pole, the Earl of Lincoln.'

'And what about you, Master Holland?' Tom Toliver asked. 'What do you plan to be?'

Will beamed. 'I intend to be a lawyer like my master one day. I learn from him all the time. England needs good lawyers.'

'That it does, Master Holland,' Tom Toliver concurred, cheerfully clapping Will on the shoulder and offering him the bottle again. 'And when you are a high and mighty judge, don't you go forgetting your friends.'

'We all need friends sometimes,' agreed

Bartholomew Crofton with a wink.

Will refused another drink. 'Loyalty, my friends. That is what we should all hold as our guiding principle. If you are loyal to your friends and family you can expect that they will be loyal to you.'

Bartholomew Crofton looked back at him with a crooked smile and eyes that looked as if they were beginning to feel the effects of strong wine. They were walking up the hill along the Northgate. He staggered as his foot slipped on a heap of cow dung, but he quickly regained his balance. He raised the bottle. 'To loyalty!' he said.

Tom Toliver grinned. 'Don't you worry too much about him, sir. He never has been much good at holding his drink.' He snatched the bottle back from Bartholomew Crofton before he could drink again. He emphatically shoved home the bung with the flat of his hand. 'We'll make that a toast to sobriety, shall we, Bartholomew?'

Will laughed. 'Good advice. Now come, tell me how far is Jasper Hirst's house.'

'He lives in a large two-storeyed house not far outside the city. He has done well for himself and no mistaking. He isn't married, but he has no trouble attracting women, if you know what I mean, Master Will.'

'A good-looking fellow, is he?' Will asked innocently.

The two constables laughed in unison. 'He has the face of a pig, Master Will,' said Tom Toliver.

'But his purse is bigger and fuller than any that could be made out of a sow's ear,' added Bartholomew Crofton. 'The inside of his purse is the secret of his attraction to women.'

'Maybe that's what is keeping him from court today,' laughed Tom Toliver as they passed the Chantry Chapel of St John before leaving the town boundary by the north gate. 'Maybe he's cuddled up with a couple of buxom wenches.'

'He had better not be,' said Will, 'or my master may give him a day or two in the stocks to show him the evil of his ways.'

A mile further on, as the road dropped into a dell, the two-storeyed home of Jasper Hirst came into view. As the two constables had said, it was the home of a trader who had done well for himself. It was newly thatched and well cared for, with a cultivated garden that backed on to a small copse of pollarded willow trees. By the side were several chicken coops, a couple of pens with geese and a large stone-built pigeon house, almost as tall as his house.

161

Countless pigeons were sitting atop its flat roof.

As they approached the house a couple of sentinel geese started honking, and soon the whole flock were making more noise than a pack of dogs.

'He's either not at home or he's lying in bed,' said Tom Toliver.

'Aye, but who with?' Bartholomew Crofton added.

Will quickened his pace. 'I don't like this,' he said. 'I have a bad feeling that something is wrong here.'

They shouted out and banged on the door of the house then entered. But there was no one there.

The hens started clucking, adding to the general mêlée as they searched the chicken coops and the pens.

'That's what isn't right,' said Will, suddenly pointing to the pigeons atop the pigeon house. 'Why are they all outside the house?' Then before the two constables could answer he had charged the door and burst into the pigeon house.

Lying on the straw and guano-covered floor, dressed in the scarlet livery of the guild of butchers lay the body of a man. His head was twisted at an impossible angle and his sightless eyes were staring straight up at the ceiling. Scattered around him lay the bodies of several dead pigeons.

Will knelt down beside him, while Bartholomew Crofton bent double and began to vomit.

'My God, Master Holland,' gasped Tom Toliver. 'Some bastard has rung his neck.'

Will stood up with the body of one of the pigeons in his hand. He held it up to show Tom Toliver, letting its head dangle loosely from side to side. He flicked it to emphasize its looseness.

'Aye, and whoever did this also did the same to these birds.' He bit his lip in puzzlement, and then added tonelessly. 'It is just like a cat had got in among the pigeons.'

★ ★ ★

The Earl of Lincoln dismissed the bailiff who had seemed intent upon ushering him into the Rolls Office himself, then he closed the door behind him.

'Now, Sir Giles,' he said, advancing into the room to stand and face the Constable of Sandal Castle. 'I have sent the Council of the North to the Church of All Saints to witness the holy rites said over Bunce. I told them that I would be only a few minutes, which gives you time to explain what you think is

163

going on here. I am sure that I do not need to tell you that some of my fellow Council members are less than happy about being made to sit through a Manor Court session.'

Giles bowed and gestured to a chair, but Lincoln refused it.

'I understand their annoyance, your Grace, but quite simply I believe that Bunce died accidentally.'

'Accidentally?' Lincoln repeated, staring at Giles with narrowed eyes. 'So what is all this talk about poison? You are talking about murder, surely?'

Giles unconsciously reached to massage his temple, for it had started to throb again. 'I think that murder was definitely intended, your Grace. But Ned Bunce was not the intended victim.'

'Who then?'

'It looks as if Dickon the falconer was the target.'

'Dickon!' Lincoln exclaimed. 'Why would anyone want to murder my falconer?'

'That I cannot say as yet, my lord. But I fully intend to find out.'

'Do you have any suspicions?'

Giles nodded slowly. 'Indeed, my lord. Until I exclude people then everyone who was in the castle the night of his death is a suspect.'

'Everyone?'

Giles returned the Earl's regard. 'Indeed. At this moment, everyone is a suspect.'

A fire threatened to erupt in Lincoln's eyes, but after a moment it passed and the Earl gave a thin smile. 'In that case, Sir Giles, I believe that I chose well in appointing you to the post of Constable of the Castle and judge of the Manor Court. This is just as my uncle, the king, would have wished it. The law is for everyone and none is exempt from answering to the law or to its officers. Come now, join me at this service for my good and sad Fool, Ned Bunce.'

Six of the earl's men-at-arms were waiting for them outside the Rolls Office, much to Adam Crowther's anxiety. They stood briskly to attention as Lincoln and Giles came out and formed a guard as they walked out of the Wodehall and made their way to the Church of All Saints. Its great spire had been rebuilt in the last century and its great doors stood open. Soldiers of the guard had been organized into two columns on either side of the doors.

As they approached they became aware of a commotion from within.

'What is the matter?' Lincoln asked as he entered. Most of the members of the Council of the North were sitting in pews or standing by them. The sad coffin of Ned Bunce had been laid on the floor in front of the high altar. 'Why are voices being raised in God's house?'

Sir William Stanley of Holt pointed at a lone figure bent in supplication in front of the altar. 'Some praying oaf of a monk is ignoring that Father Burke of yours, my lord.'

'Perhaps he is deaf?' Lincoln replied. 'Besides, what harm is he doing by being there?'

Giles walked up the aisle and bent down beside the hooded figure of the praying monk. He whispered something close to him. Then he put a hand on his shoulder.

The hooded figure slowly collapsed sideways.

'He is not deaf, your Grace,' Giles said, bending over the figure now lying on its side. 'He is quite dead. And unless I am much mistaken, he has had his neck broken.'

* * *

'Should we go back and inform Sir Giles, your master?' Tom Toliver asked.

'Not all of us,' Will replied. He pointed to Bartholomew Crofton who had staggered outside, from whence the noise of his retching could still be heard. 'Give your

166

friend some water when he has finished turning his stomach inside out, then despatch him to tell Sir Giles. You and I shall stay to ensure that no one else is about to disturb this murder scene.'

'Who would want to come here and see such a thing?' Toliver asked.

'The murderer might still be around,' Will explained. 'We may have disturbed him, so we shall have to make sure that we are alone.'

Toliver's face paled and any effects of the wine he had consumed seemed to disappear all at once. He tightened his grip on his pikestaff so that his knuckles grew white. 'You can rely on me, Master Will. I'll go and get Crofton off back to Wakefield and then I'll do a proper search around. If that murdering dog is still about I'll spit him on this pike.'

'No!' Will exclaimed firmly. He put an arm about the guardsman's shoulders and dropped his voice to a whisper. 'If we find anyone we must just restrain him. It is not up to the likes of you and I to do the work of the law. We could catch an innocent soul and by killing him we would be adding an unnecessary death to the picture. It is up to Sir Giles and the Manor Court to decide if there is guilt.'

Toliver shivered and replied in a whisper. 'Why, the way you say it, it sounds like you expect us to find this murdering dog. I am starting to feel most uneasy.'

Will patted his shoulder. 'And that is how we should be, Master Toliver. Uneasy about this murder and wary in case the murderer is still about. Now go. I think that Crofton has stopped puking. Give him water then give him his commission to fetch Sir Giles.'

And when Toliver left, Will squatted down by the dead body of the poulterer and just looked about. He knew Sir Giles and his methods. He knew that he would want to examine the body himself and would not appreciate anything being moved. He stroked his chin as he tried to imagine what Sir Giles would do if he was there.

★　★　★

Upon hearing Giles's announcement, the inevitable happened. Everyone in the church surged forward to get a sight of the dead man lying slumped on his side before the altar.

Giles looked up and spotted Dr Musgrave at the back of the crowd. He beckoned for him to come forward. When he had emerged from the crowd and joined him, he asked:

'Am I right, Doctor? Has this man's neck been broken?'

Dr Musgrave frowned. 'I will have to move

him to find out. Do I have your permission?'

Giles nodded and shuffled back from the body. Dr Musgrave knelt down and gingerly rolled the body over so that he was lying on his back. Then he pushed back the hood of the travelling cloak to reveal the man's features.

He appeared to be in his thirties, with lank carrot-coloured hair, tonsured as a priest. His skin was slightly pock-marked and covered in freckles, with several days' growth of stubble on his jowls. His eyes were wide open, staring straight ahead with pupils so large that there seemed to be hardly any iris present. Most noticeable was the fixed expression on his face, as if he had been suddenly startled and died in that instant.

'Notice this blue discoloration about his neck,' Dr Musgrave said. 'There has been some bleeding into his neck after he died.' Then taking hold of the head in both hands he moved it back and forth. 'It moves too easily,' he said, as he laid it back on the floor and slid his hands under the neck to examine the spine. Finally, he withdrew his hands and wiped them on his sides.

'You are quite right, Sir Giles. His neck has been broken. He would have died instantly. I have seen several cases of such wanton violence and his appearance is typical of a broken neck. If he had been strangled then his bowels and bladder would have opened. You note that there is no such smell.' He raised his eyebrows. 'If you wish, I can make sure?'

Giles shook his head. 'That will not be necessary just yet, Doctor.'

The Earl of Lincoln had been standing over them. He turned to the crowd. 'Does anyone know this priest?'

'He is not of our order,' Abbot Mallory said. 'In fact, if it were not for his tonsure I would not have thought him to be a priest at all. His hands have the look of one who has led a harder life than one of devotion.'

'Do you think so, your Grace?' Giles asked curiously.

'His face looks familiar to me,' said Sir Roger Harrington. 'But I cannot quite place him.' He shrugged. 'It may come to me. If it does, I shall let you know, my lord.'

Lincoln bowed his head. 'Better still, you will let Sir Giles know.'

Giles stood up. 'Then with your permission, your Grace, I shall make further examination of the church before we move the body to the Tolbooth. I propose to call a further session of the court tomorrow instead of today. I will question the poulterer Jasper Hirst in private, when my assistant returns with him.'

'Then I and the Council shall return to Sandal. Is there anything that you would have me do, Sir Giles?'

'It would be a sensible precaution to have extra guards posted at the town gates, my lord. Indeed, apart from yourselves I would think it desirable to prevent anyone from leaving the town until I have finished my investigations today.'

'I shall leave enough men and give them orders to obey you.'

Abbot Mallory and Father Burke did not leave when Lincoln left with the rest of the Council. Instead, they advanced to within a couple of yards.

'I understand that you think you are doing the right thing, Sir Giles,' Abbot Mallory said in his stentorious voice, 'yet I must remind you that you are in one of the Lord's houses. It should not be used for any ungodly acts.'

Giles regarded him coldly. 'And this man, whoever he is — or was — was also one of God's children. Indeed, it looks as if he was one of God's servants, one of your fellow priests. I would think it only right that we should find out more about how and why he died. Now sirs, I would be grateful if you would both retire.'

The abbot looked at Father Burke for support, but the chaplain merely dropped his head and averted his eyes. The abbot snorted angrily, turned on his heel and stomped out. Father Burke looked up at Giles, shrugged his shoulders apologetically and jogged after his erstwhile superior.

'So now,' Giles said to Dr Musgrave, 'let us learn what we can.' With which he bent down beside the body and lifted one of the hands. 'The abbot noticed that his hands were not priestly. What do you think, Doctor?'

Dr Musgrave clicked his tongue. 'They do have calluses, but that does not necessarily mean a lot. Many of the monks under the abbot's care may have calluses from the manual work that they do when they are not doing the Lord's work.'

Giles lifted the other hand. 'That is just what I was thinking. And not all priests have been life-long priests. Some are called later in life. But look at this, a strange broad ring this priest is wearing.'

Dr Musgrave looked at the ring and nodded in agreement. It was a plain ring, but very broad, covering almost the whole lower segment of the man's middle finger between the knuckles. 'Perhaps it is something to do with whichever order he belonged to.'

Giles shrugged his shoulders and laid the hand down again.

He rose to his feet. 'We shall have the body

removed to the Tolbooth and I would be grateful if you would make a fuller inspection of it there.'

He looked about. 'But why was this priest here?' he asked himself. 'I wonder!'

Before Dr Musgrave could venture to say anything Giles had strode off, past the altar, into the sanctuary beyond. And indeed, in a far recess, beneath one of the pallet beds that were provided for the use of sanctuary-seekers he found a saddlebag, a sword and another travelling cloak.

'Now why would a priest be living in the sanctuary of a church like this?' he mused to himself.

'Perhaps he was — ' Dr Musgrave began.

But they were interrupted by a loud knock of the iron ring knocker on the church door. Then it was pushed open and a breathless and perspiration-covered constable rushed in together with two of the Earl's guards.

'Sir Giles, I am sent by Master Holland to fetch you as soon as possible!' Constable Bartholomew Crofton blurted out. 'There has been murder done.'

Without more ado he bent over and vomited on holy ground.

★　★　★

After overseeing the removal of the priest's body to the Tolbooth Giles sent for Dickon the falconer.

'Do you want me to take Bunce's coffin back to Sandal, Sir Giles?' Dickon immediately asked.

'Not yet, Dickon,' Giles replied. 'I fear that you will have another body to transport in your wagon before you take poor Bunce back to the castle.' And he told him of their intended destination.

The falconer's eyes narrowed. 'You have too many deaths occurring in these parts, Sir Giles.'

Giles stiffened. 'Have a care with your words, Master Dickon. I have not yet finished questioning you in court.'

Dickon's eyes opened wide in alarm. 'My lord, I did not mean — '

But Giles had turned his attention to Dr Musgrave.

'I would welcome your opinion further, Doctor. But I must investigate this latest reported death myself. I must go with Dickon here, but I am almost certain that I will be bringing another body back for you to examine. This may prove to be a long day, so I would like you to rest. I have arranged with Master Crowther to have a couch put up in the Rolls Office. Go and rest and I will have refreshments brought to you, then I will see you when I return.'

Ten minutes later with a subdued Dickon driving, Giles sat beside him on the driver's seat while Constable Crofton marched a pace or two in front of the pony, clearing a way through the crowd that thronged Northgate with gruff commands and threats with his pikestaff. News of the discovery of the priest's body had spread faster than the plague around the town. That coupled with the presence of the Earl of Lincoln's guards on the town gates had promulgated the spread of a myriad of rumours. The fact that the Manor Court judge was following one of the constables that he had recently sent to bring back the local poulterer, Jasper Hirst, caused the rumours to become ever more macabre.

Two men in dusty travelling cloaks stood at the back of the crowd watching the falconer's cart lumber up the Northgate hill.

'That judge might prove to be an impediment to our cause,' the taller of the two whispered to the other.

'A temporary impediment then,' opined the other. Then tugging his fellow's sleeve, 'I suspect that he will be gone some hour or two. It would be as well if we found a tavern with a quiet corner to sup some food and ale.'

He grinned as the other stifled a yawn. 'Aye, and mayhap some sleep. I think that we may yet have work to do before too long.'

'Amen,' agreed the other.

8

Hidden Messages

Giles stood at the entrance to the dovecote and looked down at the body. He had told Will about their discovery of the body of the priest.

Will shook his head. 'I had thought that Wakefield was a peaceful town until now, with this spate of murders.'

Giles rubbed his temple, for his head was beginning to throb. He pointed at the body.

'Is it definitely Jasper Hirst?'

'It is, my lord,' Will replied. 'Constable Toliver knew him well, as did Constable Crofton. They told me about him on the way here. He had a reputation with the ladies.' He made a clicking noise with his tongue and added: 'But without meaning to be disrespectful, my lord, I cannot see how. He was not a pretty fellow, as you can see.'

'And yet from what I have seen so far of his home, he was clearly a man who was doing well. There would appear to be money to be made from trading in birds.'

'I imagine that there lies the secret of his

success with women,' said Will.

Giles cleared his throat, for he found the smell of pigeon guano less than wholesome. 'So tell me, Will, what do you make of this scene?'

Will took a deep breath. 'I have looked over the man's home and examined the carnage that you see before us and I must admit to being perplexed, my lord.'

'About what exactly?'

'About it all. I am no doctor, but the position of the man's head makes it clear that he has had his neck broken.' He pointed to the dead pigeons that surrounded the body. 'Just as these poor birds met their end. They all had their necks wrung. The question is why.'

'And have you come to any conclusions?'

Will shrugged. 'I can see no point in this, my lord. Surely it is the work of a madman.'

Giles knelt down by the body and made a cursory inspection. After a few moments he rose. 'He has a full purse and he has a long dagger in its sheath. His body has not been robbed, if robbery was the motive.'

'Exactly, my lord,' Will went on. 'I found no obvious sign of any robbery in his house, although without having seen his house before there is no way of knowing if anything has been taken. But nothing was broken or forced open. That is what I mean about it being a pointless killing. Unless — '

'Unless what, Will?' Giles urged.

'Unless the killer wanted us to think it was the work of a madman. Perhaps that is why he wantonly killed those pigeons.'

Dickon had been standing behind them at the entrance. He coughed to attract their attention.

'Begging your pardon, Sir Giles,' he said deferentially, taking a step into the dovecote. 'But do you mind if I look at those dead birds? Birds are my — '

'Your business,' Giles said. 'Quite so. Please Dickon, give me your opinion.'

The falconer bent and picked up a pigeon corpse and examined it almost tenderly in his work-hardened hands. Then he replaced it on the ground, seemingly oblivious to the body of the dead man lying before him, and selected another.

'Whoever killed Jasper Hirst didn't just wring the necks of these pigeons,' he volunteered.

'Meaning what, Dickon?' Giles asked.

Dickon looked up, his eyes suddenly covered with a film of moisture. 'The bastard broke their legs.'

Giles looked quizzically at the falconer, then at Will.

'This just gets more and more curious,' he said. 'Take good notice of all this, Will, for I will need to write a report on it all later today. I will need you to read through it once I have finished, in case I miss anything myself. So now, lead the way and let us make sure that we do not miss anything of importance in the fellow's house.'

★ ★ ★

Dr Musgrave had eaten and drunk well from the refreshments brought to him in the Rolls Office before slumping on to the couch and falling into a deep and dream-filled sleep.

He awoke with a racing heart and a brow moist with perspiration. For a moment or two he looked about him in confusion, for he did not recognize the room and he felt disoriented. That in itself would not normally have worried him had it not been for the fact that he had just been dreaming about being in another unfamiliar room. It had been a most strange room, with straw on the floor, strange murals of small tumbling men on the walls. Most strange of all, his waking mind realized, was that he had been aware of someone laughing and taunting him from the shadows of the dream room. At first he had thought that it was Ned Bunce, but he had told himself that it could not be he, since he was dead, pecked to death by a pigeon, and then dropped into the castle moat.

He realized that his thinking was jumbled, that the dream images were fast fading, as dreams are want to do. Yet it was the anxiety he felt that puzzled him. Yet Bunce had no power to give him fear.

'Fool that you are,' he chided himself as he heaved himself up and poured a cup of wine. 'Are you thinking Bunce's ghost has visited your dream? Pah! I do not believe in ghosts. Not even dream ghosts.'

Yet he did not fool himself. The image of Bunce had somehow seemed real enough to cover him in sweat and speed up his heart. Despite himself, his mind fought to keep Bunce's image in his head. And as he did so he recalled the words that the dream Bunce had kept repeating between peels of mischievous laughter:

'It wasn't the Fool's folly, it was the folly of the King.'

Unaccountably, Dr Musgrave felt a shiver run up his spine.

★   ★   ★

Giles's head was throbbing badly by the time they arrived back with the body of Jasper

Hirst. The constables and Dickon laid it out in the only vacant cell in the bowels of the Tolbooth while Giles went across to the Wodehall.

When he entered the Rolls Office he found Dr Musgrave finishing a cup of wine, looking as pale and drawn as he himself felt.

'Are you unwell, Doctor?' he asked as he took a seat.

'A bad dream, nothing more,' the physician confessed. He eyed Giles with concern. 'Have you the pain in your head again, Sir Giles?'

When Giles affirmed his pain Dr Musgrave swung his pouch round and delved inside to produce a small vial of liquid. He poured a little wine into a fresh cup and added a dose of the potion to it. 'This will help to ease it, Sir Giles. You will, however, probably feel the need of sleep within an hour or so.'

'That will be no bad thing,' Giles returned, gratefully draining the draft. 'I think the pain is back partly because my mind is spinning with all these deaths that have suddenly assailed us.'

'You have more bad news then, Sir Giles?'

'We have brought back the body of the poulterer, Jasper Hirst. It appears that he had his neck wrung, like the priest.'

Dr Musgrave's thick eyebrows seemed to close together in a worried frown. 'This is sad news, Sir Giles. Do you have any idea who killed the poulterer?'

'Not yet,' Giles replied, raising a hand to massage his temple. 'There are things that bother me, but I cannot quite put my finger on what exactly.' He contemplated the cup in his hand then replaced it on the table and reluctantly stood up. 'And now, if you are agreeable and rested enough, I would value your opinion on these two bodies.'

Will and Dickon were waiting with the two constables outside the heavy iron-studded door of the Tolbooth.

'Will you need me further, my lord?' Dickon asked.

'A while longer, Master Falconer,' Giles replied. 'But not while we view these bodies. We will be an hour or so. Go therefore and eat and sup, then I would have you take Dr Musgrave and Bunce's coffin back to the castle.'

Will looked slightly crestfallen.

'Are we not yet returning to the castle, my lord?' he said haltingly. 'I had hoped that we would be back in time for me to visit — '

'To visit my daughter,' Dr Musgrave suddenly interrupted.

Both Will and Giles were slightly taken aback at the steel in the voice of the normally placid and calm physician. Will blushed.

'Well, yes indeed, sir. That is I had hoped to see Mistress Alice, with your permission, of course.'

The physician's expression softened and he bowed his head an inch or so. 'Which is gladly given, provided it is not too late. I ask only what any father would ask — consideration for the treasure of my life.'

Will averted his eyes to his hands and fiddled nervously with his ring, twisting it round and round his finger.

'I assure you, sir, that I want only the best for your daughter. I trust that you know that I hold her in the highest — '

Dr Musgrave patted his shoulder. 'I know, my boy, I know. Now come, it is not fitting that we should be having this discussion in front of Sir Giles in the first place.'

Giles gave a wan smile. 'Think nothing of it, Doctor. It is all a matter of honour. Something that we must all be guided by.' He suddenly stifled a yawn. 'That potion seems to be working already upon me. So let us go and look at these two poor wretches who have had their lives snuffed out before their natural ends.'

With a nod at Constable Toliver the Tolbooth door was unlocked, a torch prepared and flamed and the three descended the steps to the cells.

Will came down last. He let out an involuntary gasp as Constable Toliver clanged the door shut behind them and the heavy key rattled in the lock.

'Your pardon, my lords,' Will excused himself. 'I was just thinking that there will be three of us and three dead bodies down here. The locking of the door made me suddenly feel that I did not relish the thought of being locked up with them.'

Neither Giles nor Dr Musgrave said anything to reassure him.

★   ★   ★

On his way back to Sandal Castle the Earl of Lincoln halted as the road began a sharp climb up towards the gleaming ashlar stone of Sandal Castle. A stone's throw away was the copse of willow trees, in the midst of which was the cross that marked the spot where his grandfather had perished a quarter of a century before.

'My lords,' he cried out to his entourage, which consisted of the Council of the North and the rest of his armed guards. 'All of you proceed back to the castle. It has been a long day and I am sure that you are all as tired as I am.' He smiled wistfully. 'I have it in mind to pay my respects to my grandfather's memory and then to choose the spot where I wish to have the body of my Fool buried.'

'Your Grace, you must not tarry on your own,' said Sir Roger Harrington. 'I will accompany you, with your permission.'

His petition was followed by that of half a dozen of the Council.

The Abbot of Monk Bretton rasped, 'And I will willingly accompany you to bless your choice of ground, if you will it.'

Lincoln laughed as he shook his head. 'I am touched by the concern of everyone, but this is a task that I wish to do alone. Besides, what harm could befall me so close to my own Sandal Castle?'

Sir William Stanley of Holt urged his mount forward. 'With respect, your Grace. I fear that your grandfather, Richard the Duke of York, thought something similar when he sallied forth from the castle on that evil day.'

Lincoln scowled and it seemed as if Plantagenet ire would erupt. Yet the impression passed quickly and he smiled. 'Then I fear I must compromise. I will keep two guardsmen with me while you all go back. They will stay here on the road and so they will be able to watch over me.'

Then he reconsidered and bowed to Abbot Mallory. 'I will, however accept your kind offer, your Grace. I would be grateful if you would bless that spot where I choose to have him interred.'

The Abbot's face visibly paled, but he immediately bowed in his saddle.

'It is my honour, your Grace. But would it not be as well for the guards to accompany us. For protection.'

'Protection?' Lincoln repeated with a tinge of sarcasm. 'Do you not forget that this is my uncle, King Richard's kingdom? What is there for us to fear?'

No one said anything for a moment. Then Sir Roger Harrington leaned forward and said softly, 'Treachery, my lord. Simply treachery.'

Lincoln's face was impassive for a moment. Then two patches of colour appeared on his cheeks. When he spoke his voice was steady, but there was an unmistakable edge of anger in it.

'I repeat — this is my uncle's kingdom. I have no fear of good Englishmen. Now, I have a good sword at my side, two good guards on the road, and the holy office of my good Abbot Mallory here. What cause for fear have I?' He sat challenging reply. When none came back his lips curled slightly.

'So now all of you go. I will follow before too long. I go now to pay homage to my grandfather, then to look for a place to bury my poor Fool.'

From the expressions of several of the entourage, Lincoln perceived that several of them thought that Bunce was not the only fool. He did not care for their expressions, but he noted and remembered those particular faces.

★ ★ ★

In the flickering torchlight Dr Musgrave bent over the body of the priest. Will had helped him to undress the corpse in order to look for any signs of other injury or wounding. Apart from the hideous bruising about the neck there was little apparent.

'Nothing else, Sir Giles,' the physician said after conducting an extensive examination. 'He is a man in his mid-thirties, I would say. He has his hair tonsured, which indicates that he was a priest of some sort. He is lean, but the muscles are firm and fairly well developed. His face is unremarkable, apart from that look of surprise that we noted earlier.'

'And his hands?' Giles prompted. 'Is there anything that the calluses can tell us? Did he develop them from working with a hammer, from digging or working a plough? Is there any way of telling?'

Dr Musgrave had picked up one of the

hands and scrutinized it. 'It may be possible, Sir Giles, but I do not know of anyone who has studied such things. All I would say is that I think the calluses are old and do not reflect what he has been doing lately. It may have been several years ago that he did any serious work, which would be compatible with his being a priest now.'

Giles sighed. 'So we are not really any further forward. There is not a lot to go on.' He touched his eye patch and yawned, before shaking his head. 'What about his belongings? Let us see if they can illuminate us.' He nodded at Will and pointed to the saddlebags, the sword and the travelling cloak that he had found in the sanctuary of the church.

While the physician covered the dead man with a blanket from the bottom of the pallet bed Giles emptied the contents of the saddle bag on the floor.

'Bring the torch a little closer, Will,' he said, kneeling over them and prodding them with a finger. 'Nothing here to really suggest that he was a priest. No bible, no papers or prayers. Nothing but clothes, a purse with a few coins in it, some food and a flask of water.'

'Are you sure it is his saddle bag, my lord?' Will asked.

Giles darted a quick glance at his assistant.

'Good thinking, Will.' And selecting a pair of breeches he went to the pallet bed, pulled back the blanket and held the breeches over him. 'And unless I am much mistaken, these clothes do not belong to him. So what does that mean, do you think?'

'They may have been left in the sanctuary by someone else,' Dr Musgrave suggested.

'Or the man could be a thief,' Will proffered. 'To profess to be a priest is no insurance of honesty.'

'Indeed not,' agreed Giles. 'And what of the travelling cloak? That looks as if it could be anyone's. Perhaps not a bad thing to have if you are trying to go unnoticed.' He picked up the sword, hefting it in his hand.

'It is a short sword. It has a standard five-finger handle, a light guard and a well-sharpened, tapered blade.' He swished it through the air. 'It could stab or cut. It is one such as any traveller might carry for protection.'

'Or any thief or robber, my lord,' Will suggested. He brought the torch closer and peered at it himself. 'I rather think that it has seen action lately, my lord. It is a good-looking blade that has been well cared for.' He leaned closer and smelled the blade. 'I wager it has had blood on it in the last day or two and been wiped, but only hurriedly.'

'I think that you are correct,' said Giles, sniffing it himself and detecting the coppery odour of dried blood. 'I like this less and less.' He laid the sword back with the other things and rearranged the blanket over the body.

'So now, let us see what we can find out about the body of Jasper Hirst.'

They went through to the neighbouring cell where the poulterer's body had been laid.

'Shall we undress him, Sir Giles?' the physician asked, reaching to undo the livery of the Guild of Butchers.

Giles nodded, having already examined his clothing as he lay at the scene of his death. He watched as Dr Musgrave and Will carefully removed the clothing while he held the torch aloft.

When they had finished Will took the torch back and stood turning his ring around his finger with his thumb. 'I cannot say that handling these bodies is making me feel at all well, my lord.'

Giles gave him a reassuring smile. 'Your stomach will harden as you gain more experience,' he said. 'But a word of advice, Will. Stop fingering that ring or you will wear it away.'

Will immediately dropped his hand to his side and looked nervously aside at Dr Musgrave. He grimaced at Giles, who

191

immediately understood. He presumed that the physician was not yet aware that his daughter had made two rings and that she was wearing one to match that of Will's. Fortunately, the physician had been too preoccupied in his examination of the dead poulterer's naked body to notice the exchange between them.

'There is no doubt, Sir Giles,' Dr Musgrave volunteered. 'Jasper Hirst, if this is he, died in exactly the same way as did the priest. He also seems to have an expression of surprise etched on his face. His neck is broken.' He demonstrated and then pointed to the swelling and bruising about the neck. 'The bruising and discoloration have taken place at the time of his death, just as in the last case.'

'Can you tell anything else about him?' Giles asked.

'He is well fed, Sir Giles,' the physician returned. 'His hands have done work, and they are not clean, but he is not one who labours hard for a living. I would say he is, or was, enjoying a good amount of comfort and prosperity.'

'As is evidenced by his home and his possessions,' Giles commented dryly. 'Indeed, he seems to have been doing uncommonly well for one of his guild.'

'Do you think he had another source of

wealth, my lord?' Will asked. 'From what the constables told me he was a ladies man.'

Giles looked at the coarse features of the poulterer. He shook his head doubtfully. 'I cannot think that he would have charmed women into giving him money. No, perhaps he was successful with women because he had money from elsewhere.'

Will scratched his head. 'What sort of source could that be, my lord?'

Giles slowly shook his head. 'I have no idea, Will. Not yet, at any rate.' He looked down at the body, then he drew a sharp intake of breath. 'Pah! This sharp eye of mine has not been so sharp. Look at that ring on his finger.'

Dr Musgrave picked up the hand. 'Now that is curious. It is a plain ring, but I would almost swear that it is the match — '

'Of the one on the priest's hand!' exclaimed Giles. 'Well, we shall look at it in a moment.'

Giles knelt down by the body and tried to pull the ring free. 'It is stuck.'

'It will probably come, Sir Giles. I fancy that it is just because of the corpse stiffness of the finger joints.'

Giles tried again and pulled it past the first joint. 'Ah, it has come.' He let the hand flop down as he stood and held the ring up to the light of the torch. 'No, there is nothing here. It is but a strangely broad finger ring. Nothing else.' He knelt again to replace it.

'But what is this?' he mused, turning the hand palm upwards. There was a small mark on the pulp of the finger just beyond the palm crease. 'It looks like a burn. Unless I am mistaken it is a tiny brand in the shape of an animal.'

The others had bent close.

'I agree, Sir Giles,' the physician remarked. 'A cat of some sort, I should say.'

'Or a lion,' Will suggested.

Giles pushed the ring back over the brand. 'Perhaps that is the secret of the ring. It was a cover for this strange little brand. Come then, bring the torch and we shall see if the priest has a similar brand under his ring.'

* * *

An hour later Giles watched as Dr Musgrave climbed up on to the driver's seat of Dickon's cart.

'You will be back at the castle before night-fall,' Giles said to the physician. 'I would be grateful if you would inform the Earl of Lincoln that I am not going to call another session of the court just yet. I have more reflecting to do and further investigations to make.'

'Of course, Sir Giles,' Dr Musgrave replied. He turned and nodded his head at the interior of the cart, where Bunce's coffin had been stowed again. 'I imagine that his Grace may plan to have Bunce's funeral soon.'

Will was standing by his horse, his reins in one hand, ready to mount. 'I wish that you would come back with us, Sir Giles.'

Giles stifled a yawn. 'I told you, Will. I have to write my report while it is all fresh in my mind. Where better to do it than the Rolls Office, now that it has a couch and provisions. And I have my guard to watch over me.' He pointed to Constable Crofton who was standing beside the Wodehall door, his pike at his side.

Giles allowed himself a rare grin. 'Besides, this will give you the opportunity you so craved to visit Mistress Alice.'

Dr Musgrave gave Will a look of mock sternness. 'Providing it is not too late,' he said.

Will mounted swiftly. 'Then with your permission, sir, we should ride like the blazes.'

Dickon clicked his tongue and flicked his reins to start off. 'You can go as fast as you want, Master Holland, but we will travel with due dignity.'

And having seen them set off, Giles turned

and entered the Wodehall. 'See that I am not disturbed, won't you, Constable,' he said as the officer curtly came to attention, clicking the bottom of his pike on the ground.

'Don't worry about a thing, Sir Giles,' replied Constable Crofton. 'I will be here until midnight when Constable Toliver has arranged for me to be relieved.'

Giles went along the back corridor to the Rolls Office where a sconce of candles spluttered on his desk, illuminating his papers and writing paraphernalia. He sat down, rubbed his quill between his palms, then dipped it in the inkpot and began to write out his notes in his customary authoritative handwriting.

Once he had written down as much detail as he could, he lay the quill aside, leaned back and steepled his fingers together as he reflected on his findings.

The two dead men had identical rings, both covering identical brands.

'But why a cat?' he mused to himself. 'Or a lion? Either way it was a symbol of some kind signifying a strange connection. A secret society of some sort.' He tapped his teeth with his thumbnails. 'And if so, a secret society with what purpose?'

The candles spluttered noisily and he felt a shiver shoot up his spine. In the current climate of uncertainty, with so many rumours being whispered all over England: in the corridors of the great houses, in the cloisters of the holy houses, in the homes of the law-abiding people, and in the taverns and brothels of the revellers, all over the country there was an air of suspicion. King Richard had reigned for a mere two years, since the untimely and unexpected death of his brother, King Edward the fourth, yet in that time the rumours had been legion. Rumours and counter-rumours between the two houses of York and Lancaster.

There had been twelve years of peace after King Edward had won the battle of Towton. Then with his death the whole of England seemed to go mad. Robert Stillington, the Bishop of Bath, had declared to Richard, at that time still the Duke of Gloucester, that his brother's marriage to Elizabeth Woodville was invalid, because the King had previously married in secret. As a result, his two sons, Edward and Richard, were declared illegitimate and moved to the Tower of London for their supposed protection. What happened then was unknown. The King's supporters said that they were alive and well, which seemed to be borne out by their own mother's support for the King, for he had permitted her to come out of sanctuary and return to court. There were others, notably the Beaufort family, who averred that Richard had put the children to death. And equal to her in rumour-mongering there was Dr Morton, the Bishop of Ely. It was said that when the King gave Dr Morton into custody of Henry Stafford, the Duke of Buckingham, the wily old bishop had turned his mind and somehow persuaded him to turn against the King. Then when the Duke of Buckingham rebelled in 1483, gaining nothing but his own execution, Dr Morton absconded to France to join the court of Henry Tudor, the pretender to Richard's throne.

Giles had considered all of these rumours and been unimpressed with the arguments against the King. From all that he knew of him, his relationship to his elder brother Edward, his attitude to honour, the law and the welfare of the people of England, he could not bring himself to believe that he would have harmed so much as a hair on the heads of either of the two princes. Indeed, it would not have been remotely logical for him to do so, for their welfare would have been his own prime concern, the greatest protection for his crown.

On the other hand, he had no great liking for the Lady Margaret Beaufort, now Lady Stanley. She, he was sure, would do anything to have her son, Henry Tudor, proclaimed king. And again, King Richard's generosity in merely having her kept under house arrest by her own husband, Sir Thomas Stanley, surely showed that Richard's actions were those of a caring monarch.

Even the sad death of Richard's own son the previous year, followed by that of his Queen a few months later, had been followed by scurrilous rumours that were spawned in the cesspits of evil minds. It angered Giles that there were some who even suggested that his majesty planned to marry his own niece and that he had his queen poisoned in order to clear the way. The King had gone so far as to make a public declaration about it. He felt that it had been the best of all things for England when he had declared his own lord, John de la Pole, Earl of Lincoln, as his heir presumptive.

'Oh, for more years of peace!' Giles exclaimed, his head heavy from all his concentration and squinting his eye in the dim candlelight.

And yet he felt uneasy. There was no escaping the deaths that had occurred in the last few days. Ned Bunce had been poisoned, and two men had been killed by having their necks broken, presumably from behind.

'And why were the pigeons' legs broken?

Perhaps Will was right and it is the work of a madman?'

He leaned forward, picked up his quill and added some fresh notes to act as a future prompt in his investigations. Then with another yawn he sprinkled chalk on his writing and blew the excess dust away.

'A most wonderful potion that Dr Musgrave gave me,' he said with a smile as he poured a cup of wine and sipped it to clear his mouth. He fully intended rising and crossing to the couch, but such was his sudden fatigue that within moments he had fallen into a deep sleep.

★ ★ ★

The noise seemed like metal scraping on stone. Giles awoke with a start, noting immediately that the candles had burned down almost an inch. He waited, straining his ears.

But he could hear nothing. That worried him, since it could mean that the constable on guard duty had fallen asleep at his post, for the noise had been loud enough to reach Giles at the back of the Wodehall.

He picked up the sconce of candles and with them held high to illuminate his passage he let himself out of the Rolls Office and made his way along the corridor.

The great door was still closed. Then as he advanced he fancied that he could see something on the floor, just behind the door.

In the instant that he recognized that he was looking at a body he felt a thump on the back of his head and he tumbled forward, plummeting swiftly into a dark pool of unconsciousness.

9

Fool's Farewell

Alice came out of the garderobe with an earthenware jar of freshly passed urine. She was humming a cheerful tune despite feeling apprehensive about what she was about to do. The moon was just visible and she knew that it was a good time to water the seedlings.

'Oh my love, what I would do for you,' she said as she stood by the ledge beneath one of the slit windows of the south tower. Before her mind's eye she saw Will Holland, lying naked on the bed, just as he had been after their love-making. She sighed as she picked up the two small flowerpots that she had filled with earth and pushed three small seeds under the surface of each. 'In fact, how I wish that you were here right now, so that I could give myself to you again.'

She giggled at the thought, then immediately rebuked herself for her foolishness. 'It would be a disgrace if I fell with child,' she told herself. 'And that is why I must see. By planting these seeds by moonlight and nourishing them with my water, if I am pregnant the seeds will sprout before those that I give but plain water.' And so doing she soaked one with her urine, and the other with water from a pitcher.

She knelt on the floor and looked out of the window at the moon. 'Oh please, my lady, let it not be. At least not yet, until we are — '

She started as the door behind her creaked open and a man's voice whispered to her.

'Let what not be, mistress?'

Alice spun round and quickly stood up. She blushed to see Sir Roger Harrington standing at the threshold with a goblet of mead in his hand.

'My lord — it is Sir Roger, is it not? I . . . I fear that you are lost. This is not — '

'Oh I am not lost, mistress,' he purred, his voice slurred. 'I knew exactly where I should be going. And what do I find you doing, hmm? Some sort of magic, unless I am mistaken.'

Alice looked horrified. 'That is not so, sir. But as I said, you have come to the wrong part of the castle. This is where I live with my father.'

Sir Roger came in, shutting the door with his foot as he did so. He came across to her, his walk slightly erratic, his eyes red and his manner unpleasantly familiar.

'Yes, it is where you live, I know my dear. It

is where you live with your peculiar father, who gets up to all sorts of unusual practices.'

Alice stiffened. 'My father will be home shortly.'

'Oh, not for a while yet, I think. It will give you and I time to get better acquainted.' And he moved swiftly, his arm out to ensnare her waist.

But Alice moved nimbly aside. 'I shall scream if you come another step towards me,' she threatened.

'Oh, scream away, my pretty wench. And what will you say that I was doing? Me, a member of the King's Council of the North, and you the daughter of a witch.' He picked up the earthenware jar and sniffed it. His mouth grinned maliciously. 'Why, I caught you doing some strange spell with this jar of . . . piss! And then you started praying to the moon. To the witch goddess. I could have you declared a witch, too. And I expect you know what his majesty thinks about witchcraft. Everyone knows that he suspected that his son and his wife had been killed by witchcraft. And his own withered arm he is convinced was afflicted by the actions of a witch.'

Alice looked terrified.

'It was nothing like that, Sir Roger,' she began.

'It won't go any further than this,' he said, drawing close, his breath smelling strongly of mead. 'If you are kind to me.'

There was the sound of a foot upon the outside stairs and the handle of the door rattled then the door swung open.

'Why, Sir Roger,' Dr Musgrave said, entering and bowing. He looked up, at once taking in his daughter's look of horror and Sir Roger's guilty flush. 'Are you unwell?' he asked.

Sir Roger straightened and drained his goblet. 'On the contrary, good doctor, I am very well. I did have a slight pain in my back, no doubt from that tedious court sitting today, but your charming daughter here has taken it away.' He smiled benignly at her. 'Her conversation has quite removed any thought of pain and you see me restored.' He bowed to them both then made his way slowly out.

'Did he bother you, daughter?' Dr Musgrave asked a few moments later, as they heard the knight's heavy footsteps retreat down the stairs.

Alice took a deep breath then threw herself into her father's arms.

'He was horrible, father,' she sobbed. 'He let himself in while I was . . . was — '

Dr Musgrave's gaze settled on the pots on the ledge and his eyebrows rose, but he said nothing. Instead, he patted her shoulder reassuringly.

'Did he do anything, my dear?'

'He . . . he said that you were a witch and that I was one also. He said that he could make trouble for us and that I should be nice to him.'

Dr Musgrave's jaw muscles tightened. 'From now on you must bolt the door whenever I am out. No one must enter if I am not here. I shall have a word with Sir Giles about this.'

'But father, do you mean that I must not even allow Will Holland in?'

Her father looked again at the pots on the ledge and the earthenware jar. 'I shall think about it, daughter.'

★ ★ ★

Giles rose to consciousness and immediately felt a pounding in his head and a surge of nausea which made him want to retch. But as he tried to throw himself forward to vomit, he discovered that he could not reach out to steady himself. Worse, he was suddenly aware that something had been stuffed in his mouth and tied in a tight gag. He realized it was his own eyepatch.

He forced back the urge to vomit lest he

choke himself and gingerly opened his eye. Slowly, his vision cleared and he perceived that he was in the Rolls Office, bound to his chair. One of the candles had gone out so the room was dark beyond the ring of candlelight. Someone was laughing at his discomfiture from the shadows.

'So you are back with us are you, you dog's spittle of a judge?' a voice sneered rhetorically.

'But maybe not for long,' added another voice, from behind him.

A figure advanced from the shadows in front of him, repeatedly spinning a short dagger in his right hand. He was a man of middle height and build dressed in nondescript traveller's clothes, clean shaven, yet with a livid scar on his chin. In the uncertain light Giles estimated that he was somewhere in his early thirties. His dexterity with the dagger was suggestive that he was one well used to weaponry. Considering his position, it was not a pleasant conclusion for Giles.

The man stopped by the desk and picked up the paper with Giles's last set of notes from the desk.

'You seem to have been busy, Judge whatever-your-name is. And you seem to be more curious about things than is good for you.'

Another figure appeared from behind Giles similarly armed with a dagger. He was younger, taller and leaner. 'Stop pissing about, Henshaw. Either make the dog talk or just slit his throat. We can destroy his papers and get on the road.'

The threat of immediate death had three effects upon Giles. The first was a natural feeling of fear which caused his bowels to feel as if they wanted to squirt. This was closely followed by a surge of anger that swept the fear aside. Lastly, came an overwhelming curiosity as to why these two men were here. That they were trained assassins he had no doubt, but he dearly wanted to hear from their own lips why they had killed the priest and Jasper Hirst, the poulterer.

The one called Henshaw shot a venomous look at his fellow, then turned to Giles with a look of geniality. He crossed to Giles and reached out towards his face with the dagger. Giles felt perspiration run down his brow and he tried to move his head back as far as he could, but to no avail, for the dagger came slowly nearer. Then with a rapid movement Henshaw slipped the tip under the leather strap of the eyepatch that gagged him and sliced it in two.

Giles felt a sudden release of pressure from his mouth and dislodged the patch with his tongue. He coughed, spluttered and retched before finding his voice.

'Thank you for that, at least,' he gasped. 'Is my guard harmed?'

Henshaw shook his head and dangled the dagger in front of Giles. 'I ask the questions, Judge, and we will begin with your name.'

'I am Sir Giles Beeston, Constable of Sandal Castle and Judge to the Manor of Wakefield Court. And I ask again, is my guard harmed?'

'He is dead,' Henshaw replied glibly. 'Not that it is of any consequence. Now you listen. Your only chance of survival is to answer my questions quickly and clearly. If you so much as draw a deep breath to attempt to cry for help, then I'll cut your throat where you sit. Do you understand?'

'I understand,' Giles said, his mouth as dry as a bone.

The other man snorted disdainfully. 'Why are you playing with him, Henshaw? All he knows is written there. Just kill him and let us be gone.'

Henshaw glowered at him. 'We will go soon enough. As soon as he has told us who else knows about all this.'

'My assistant and the Earl of Lincoln's physician know everything. They have gone back to Sandal Castle and even at this moment the Earl is probably riding back here now with an armed guard. You will not be able to leave the town.'

The younger man waved his dagger menacingly. 'The dog has just signed his own death warrant. Let us do it and go.'

'Wait, I want to be sure,' Henshaw said. He still held Giles's paper in his hand. He raised it and with his other hand ran the tip of his dagger along the notes that Giles had made. As he did so Giles noted the ring on his hand. He darted a look at the other assassin's hand and noted that he also had a ring.

'My associate is right,' Henshaw remarked casually. 'You don't know anything. And I can't blame you for trying to bluff us. I would do the — '

'I know about the rings and the brands you wear beneath them,' Giles said quickly. 'I know about the Society and by now so too will my lord, the Earl of Lincoln.'

The two men stared at each other and Giles saw the alarm in their eyes.

'By God, he knows too much,' grated the younger man. 'We must go now.' He grabbed Giles's hair and yanked his head backwards to expose his throat. Giles strained with all his might against his bonds but it was to no avail. He saw the blade coming at him and he closed his eye as he braced himself for the mortal cut.

He felt a jolt as his head was shoved even further back, then he felt blood spurting over his face. Yet amazingly there was no pain. He opened his eye at the same time as he heard the bloodcurdling scream from his assassin. Then he realized that the blood that had spurted into his face was not his own, but that of the assassin who was at that moment starting to convulse. The end of a pike blade was protruding from the front of his chest, from which blood was gushing. As Giles watched in horrified relief he saw the skewered man stagger backwards towards the shadowed doorway as Will Holland attempted to dislodge him from the weapon. Through it all he screamed like a stuck pig.

'You will both die for this!' cried Henshaw, leaping towards Will with his dagger raised ready to slash or stab.

'Look out, Will!' Giles yelled.

Will instantly let go of the pike handle and the assassin slumped to the ground. His hand went to his sword, but he did not have time to draw it before Henshaw was on him, slashing in an arc with his weapon. Will ducked, then came up and closed with him, catching both wrists. For a few moments they struggled, then Henshaw feigned, dropped his weight and caught Will off balance. They fell, rolled over and over in the pool of blood that was fast covering the floor until Henshaw managed to wrench free. He got to his feet and prepared to launch himself again at Will.

He was within a few feet of Giles, who had managed to rock his chair hard enough to topple forward. 'We have him, Will,' he cried, in an attempt to distract Henshaw. He tumbled forward and managed to butt the back of Henshaw's left knee with his head. It was enough to make the assassin's knee buckle momentarily.

'You dog!' cried Henshaw. 'Your turn will come. After I — '

But his words died as Will grabbed the moment to draw his sword and lunge forward to stab the man through the heart.

Yet in his dying moments the assassin slashed out with his dagger and managed to rake it across Will's upper arm. Will cried out in pain, but flashed his hand to his belt and drew his own dagger, plunging it to the hilt in Henshaw's throat.

'Take that, you bastard! That is for mistreating and threatening my master.'

Will stood breathing heavily as Henshaw fell to the floor beside his fellow, blood gushing from his two mortal wounds, contributing to the gory pool that covered the floor.

'My lord, thank heaven that I made it back in time,' he gasped, as he knelt to cut through Giles's bonds and help him to his feet. 'I found poor Constable Crofton inside the door with his throat slit open. Thank goodness these vermin left his pike by his body.'

Giles seized Will's hand and pumped it with vigour. 'I thank you, good Will,' he said, examining Will's wound with concern. 'How come you came back, anyway?'

Will raised his hands, but winced as the action hurt his wounded arm. 'I just had a bad feeling, my lord.'

'Then I am glad that you have such feelings, Will. Now come, we will have to tend to this wound or it might fester.' He bent and retrieved his eyepatch. ''Tis just a pity that we could not take them alive to learn more of this society of theirs.'

'What society is this, my lord?'

'The rings, Will. These two killers wear rings as well.' He finished tying his patch back in place, then bent and picked up the ring hand of the younger man. He prised it up to reveal a tiny brand, just like the ones they had seen earlier. He laid the hand down again. 'And now let us see this one.

Henshaw is his name.'

'Will that help us, my lord?' Will asked, making way for Giles to get to the older assassin's body.

'Just as I thought,' Giles said a moment later after inspecting the man's ring and his hand. 'All identical, which proves that they are all in some society.' He stood up and scratched his nose.

'And yet it makes no sense,' he added. 'Unless there had been some sort of dispute and that these two had been sent to kill the priest and the poulterer. Yet why?'

Will had been holding his arm, blood trickling down his arm into his hand. 'My lord, do you mind if I sit a while. I begin to feel faint.'

Giles looked up quickly, seeing even by candlelight that his assistant had gone very pale. 'Of course! Sit and I will — '

There was a sudden roar of alarm from the end of the corridor, followed by several raised voices and cries, then by running feet coming both along the corridor and through the court hall itself.

'Don't let anyone pass!' a voice cried out. Then a moment later Constable Toliver's wide-eyed face appeared at the entrance, his pike before him. Two more men of the watch appeared behind him, their faces equally startled.

'My God!' Toliver exclaimed. 'Poor Bartholomew Crofton dead with his throat cut and now two more bodies. Are . . . are — ?'

'These are the two men who killed him, Constable Toliver. And they would have slain me had it not been for the timely return of Will Holland here.' He pointed at the two corpses on the blood-covered reed floor. 'Do you recognize either of them?'

Constable Toliver prodded first one then the other with his pike blade to ensure they were dead, then bent and scrutinized their faces. 'Neither of them is from hereabouts, as far as I can tell, Sir Giles.' He turned to the two men of the watch, who had been joined by the other who had come through the hall. 'Have any of you ever seen these two?'

They all shook their heads, staring with disgust and anger at the men who had apparently killed their fellow constable.

'In which case, have their bodies taken over to the Tolbooth and put them in a cell together. I will inspect their bodies and their belongings in the morning.'

'And with respect sir, what about poor Bartholomew's body? I would be grateful, sir, if I knew that he wasn't lying beside the dogs who killed him.'

'Of course,' Giles returned. 'I suggest that

he be laid out on this couch, then his family can — '

'He had no family, Sir Giles,' Toliver interrupted. 'Just us. We were the nearest he had to a family. And I thank you, sir, for although he was a bit rough at times, still he had respect for the law. He would like to think he was lying in the Court Rolls office. Sort of looking after the documents after death, if you see what I mean, sir?'

Giles nodded. 'In the meanwhile, Will and I shall go to a hostelry for the night and I will have this wound tended.'

'I'll send one of the men ahead to knock up the landlord of the White Boar Inn, Sir Giles. It is the best in the town. And his wife is skilled in dressing wounds.'

'I am obliged,' Giles replied. 'We will come back in the morning to view the bodies. Just one other thing.'

'My lord?'

'It would be as well if someone woke Master Crowther, the court bailiff, and alerted him to this tragedy. He will want to oversee the cleaning of this office.'

'I will do that myself, Sir Giles,' Toliver replied, standing to attention as Giles helped Will past. 'Although he can be an old windbag at times, Adam Crowther has a good heart. He will be sad to hear about poor

Bartholomew. Happen I will persuade him to bring his bible to say a few words over his body.'

Giles turned at the door. 'A commendable idea, Constable Toliver. One last thing I must impress upon you.' He looked at the other men of the watch. 'This includes all of you. A heinous crime has been committed here tonight, and thankfully we have killed the criminals. It is important that news of this does not get out of hand, for panic in Wakefield and the surrounding area would be the result. I will investigate this, but I must do it in my own way and in my own time. I do not want this to be discussed beyond the men of the watch and Master Crowther. Tell him that I will talk with him in the morning.'

Tom Toliver looked puzzled, but after a moment he nodded. 'As you wish, Sir Giles. You can rely on me and my men.'

★ ★ ★

Father Burke was praying in the Earl's Chapel in the west tower when he heard a rasping breath behind him. He opened his eyes and turned to see the Abbot Mallory standing at the door, breathless from the climb up the tower stairs.

'Your Grace, would you care to join me in

prayer,' Father Burke asked.

'No, my son,' the abbot replied, using the tone that he used to use when Edmund had been a junior monk under his care at Monk Bretton Priory. 'But I wanted to have a word with you.' He closed the door behind him. 'In private,' he added meaningfully.

Father Burke shuffled nervously. 'Is there something wrong, your Grace?'

'No, but I have fears that things are not as they should be. This funeral troubles me.'

'I do not understand you, I am afraid,' Father Burke replied. 'Which funeral are you talking about?'

The abbot took a deep breath, as if in consternation. 'Of the Fool, Bunce. He was an evil little fellow in life, making fools of his betters, and in death he seems to be taking up too much time.'

'I still do not understand, your Grace.'

'This blessing and this funeral. The Council of the North is supposed to be meeting to decide important policies, yet what have we been doing? We have been sitting in a common court listening to meaningless babble about pigeons and the death of a mangy Fool. It has to stop.'

'How can I help, your Grace?'

'You are the Earl of Lincoln's chaplain, are you not? You must get this funeral done quickly and you must persuade the Earl that it is not healthy to dwell over the death of a Fool.'

'I . . . I will do my best, your Grace,' Father Edmund replied, with as much assurance as he could muster.

'Good. Now I have disturbed your prayers long enough,' said Abbot Mallory, turning and opening the door. 'You always had the makings of a good priest,' he said as he stood on the threshold of the little chapel. 'I was right to have put my faith in you.'

Father Burke stared at the door after the abbot had left. He was unsure whether he entirely understood the purpose of the abbot's visit.

* * *

Giles and Will had a hearty breakfast at the White Boar Inn before going back to the Wodehall where they found Adam Crowther and Constable Toliver waiting for them. Both men had red eyes, which made Giles think that they had both wept for their dead friend and colleague. Master Crowther had somehow managed to have the Rolls Office cleaned, either by himself or aided by another. The body of Bartholomew Crofton had been laid on the couch, his horrible

219

wound concealed and his eyes closed so that it looked as if he had merely fallen asleep.

Then they had all gone to the Tolbooth, a place already smelling badly as the first two bodies had begun to produce the putrefying gases that followed death. But Giles's inspection of the two bodies revealed nothing tangible apart from the already known findings of the rings and the concealed brands. Similarly, their belongings, which Constable Toliver had somehow managed to track down to the Stableyard at the back of the Bull Ring along with their two horses, yielded no clues.

'Do you not think it odd that there was no sign of their identities, my lord?' Will asked as they rode down the hill from Wakefield to the Chantry Bridge over the River Calder.

'I would have been surprised if there had been anything,' Giles replied. 'These men were assassins. They would have nothing to connect them to a place, in case one or the other was caught. No Will, it was but chance that we found those brands beneath their rings.'

Will had been fingering his own ring and he held his hand towards Giles. 'This little ring of mine looks so slight in comparison to those large ones that those swine wore. Yet mine also has a hidden message from my loved one.'

Giles smiled. 'But that is where the similarity ends. Your message is one of love, their brands surely implied some sinister purpose. Besides, you have no brand on your fingers.'

Will gave a hollow laugh. 'So what do we do now, my lord? Look for all men wearing rings and ask to see what lies beneath?'

'If necessary, yes.'

Will shrugged. 'It would have been a painful thing to have a brand put on your finger. Especially there, where it would hurt so.'

'I imagine that the pain of the process would have been part of some oath that they said to bind them. The brands must have been to set these men apart, to show that they had a common purpose and that they were prepared to tolerate pain to show it.' He pointed at Will's bandaged arm. 'Does your wound pain you terribly?'

'Barely at all, my lord,' Will replied with a smile. 'Yet it may get more painful when I see Mistress Musgrave.'

'I am sure she will be more than sympathetic.'

They crossed the bridge and passed the open door of the Chantry Chapel.

'I do not like this crossing, my lord,' said Will. 'Ever since you told me of the murder of the Earl of Rutland by the Butcher Lord Clifford.'

'The Butcher Lord had just deserts at Ferrybridge on the eve of the Battle of Towton,' Giles returned. 'And his brother, Sir Roger Clifford, went to the block on the King's orders only a few months ago. Treason again.'

'A treacherous family, my lord,' Will commented distastefully.

'So it seems. Yet their treachery worked well for others. After the Battle of Towton the lands and grants around Skipton Castle, which had belonged to Lord John Clifford, were given by King Edward to Sir William Stanley.'

Will gasped. 'Sir William Stanley of Holt? He who sits on the Council of the North?'

'The same. He is at this moment at Sandal Castle. But he only gained the ownership of Holt Castle and the title that he now enjoys after Buckingham's rebellion two years ago. These he was given by King Richard.'

'So the Cliffords would have little love for him?'

Giles laughed. 'Between the two of us, Will, I think that Sir William is not one to readily inspire love.'

They trotted up the road, which began a meandering course beside the undulating fields of rhubarb, liquorice, oats and barley. On their way they passed several shepherds and swineherds taking their meagre flocks to Wakefield.

While still two miles from Sandal a rider in the livery of the Earl of Lincoln galloped towards them, waving his hat at them as he fast approached.

'Sir Giles,' the messenger said, as he drew to a sharp halt beside them. 'I am commanded to fetch you with speed to Sandal Castle by his Grace, the Earl of Lincoln. He wishes you to be present at the funeral of his good friend the Fool, Ned Bunce.'

'We come, already,' Giles replied. 'Return to the castle and tell his Grace that we are already well nigh returned.'

When he had gone, Giles looked quizzically at Will.

'I hate to admit it, Will, but I will be glad to see Bunce finally buried and blessed. It seems that his folly started this whole business.'

* * *

From one of the slit windows that overlooked the barbican and the bailey beyond, Alice looked out and felt relief to see Giles and Will ride over the drawbridge. She rushed down the stairs and entered the main keep, then ran across the first draw-bridge into the barbican, then down more stairs before crossing the drawbridge over the inner moat to arrive at the bailey courtyard just as Giles and Will had been relieved of their horses by one of the ostlers.

'May I request leave for a few minutes, my lord?' Will asked. He gave a mischievous smile and clutched his arm. 'My arm has started to pain me.'

Giles grinned back at him. 'I had better tell Mistress Alice how you came by the wound first. We shall simply say that I was attacked and that you came back in good time to help me. Remember that I do not want too much news about last night's events to become common knowledge as yet. It should be enough to know that you have been heroic.'

And after greeting Alice with a bow, Giles gave her an account that was carefully edited for her ears, yet which contained enough of the truth to cause her concern for Will's wound as well as building his heroism in her eyes.

'And so, it would be good if I could leave him in your care and ask you to let your father cast a look at the wound.'

When they had gone Giles waited a few moments then himself made his way to the north tower of the keep, to seek a private audience with the Earl of Lincoln. Mounting the stairs quickly, he arrived outside the Earl's chamber and was pleased to see that an armed guard had been stationed outside. In response to Giles's request, the guard beat out a prearranged staccato on the door and a few moments later a bolt was slid aside and Lincoln threw open the door.

A sheepish Dickon the falconer came out, his head bobbing up and down deferentially as he passed Giles.

'Ah, Sir Giles, welcome,' beamed Lincoln. 'You had my message about the funeral? I want this done today, within two hours. I have already started preparations. Now sit, I have written a poem to honour my good Bunce and I would value your opinion.'

Giles sat as he was bidden. He had no doubt that the poem would be good, for he was aware that the Earl was descended from the great Geoffrey Chaucer. He also decided that it would be as well to wait until after the funeral before he informed him of the recent events.

* * *

The funeral cortège assembled on the bailey courtyard. Ned Bunce's coffin had been placed on top of the roof of Dickon's cart. In front of it was a party of guards with halberds, two men with horns and two boys with side drums, ready to set off upon the Earl of Lincoln's order. Following behind were the Council of the North and many of the castle residents and servants.

'Wait!' called Lincoln, coming down the steps from the Great Hall. He walked past the ostler who was waiting with his horse saddled.

'I want no cart for my Fool. I will carry the coffin myself.'

'Your Grace, is that seemly?' Abbot Mallory asked.

'Most seemly,' Lincoln replied. 'He was my friend as well as my Fool.' He looked up at Dickon. 'Bring him down, Dickon. And prise off the lid, if you will. I would like to see his face again.'

Dickon took the coffin down and placed it on the ground. 'Begging your Grace's pardon,' he said. 'But are you sure? Poor Bunce will not look as he did, and he will smell less than wholesome now.'

Lincoln gave a rueful laugh. 'Do not worry, good Dickon. Just say that I have a hard stomach to go with a soft heart. Now come, let us see my poor Fool.'

Dickon did as he was bid and removed the coffin lid, releasing as he had predicted the bitter odour of putrefaction.

Lincoln looked down and flinched. Yet it was not through having his senses assaulted by the odour that troubled him. 'Where is the Fool's hat?'

Sir Giles was a pace behind. 'I cannot recall seeing it since he died, your Grace,' he volunteered.

'A pity! It would have been good to see him laid to rest in his hat.'

And bending, he picked up the coffin. 'Come my friend,' he said to the alabaster white face of Ned Bunce. 'Let us lay you to rest where I can see you.'

The drawbridge was lowered and the portcullis raised, then to the sound of horn and side drums the cortège left the castle and began the walk down the hill to the spot that Lincoln had chosen. There, Bunce was buried with full honours. The Earl of Lincoln read his poem, which moved several hearts and caused many tears to fall. Then Father Burke led the funeral service and the Abbot of Monk Bretton gave a blessing.

'And now falconer,' Lincoln said to Dickon. 'Have you the bird.'

Dickon advanced with a caged pigeon.

'Bunce liked pigeons,' Lincoln explained. 'It seems fitting, therefore, to release this pigeon. Let it fly heavenwards with his soul as it goes to heaven.'

Dickon opened the cage and the pigeon flew out and up into a clear blue sky.

The funeral party watched it fly higher and higher. Then from some distance off, another bird appeared. It was flying fast, gaining quickly on the pigeon. Its shape was unmistakeable. 'Whose falcon is that?' Lincoln thundered.

'It is not one of ours, your grace,' Dickon replied.

They watched as the falcon flew above the hapless pigeon then swooped and took it in mid air. Then it soared down, lost to sight beyond the copse of willow trees. No one said anything for several minutes, for it was clear that the earl was angry that his plans had been thwarted.

'Look, my lord!' one of the guards cried a few moments later. 'There comes a party of armed men with banners.'

And from the far side of the copse a mounted party of knights and soldiers approached. When they rode up, a knight dismounted, his gauntleted fist held in front of him, upon which perched a falcon. In his other hand he held the dead pigeon.

'It is Henry Percy, the Earl of Northumberland!' Sir Roger Harrington exclaimed. 'He looks less sick than his message would have had us believe.'

The Earl of Northumberland, a handsome man of about forty years, albeit with a weak chin, advanced with a grin. He bowed to Lincoln. 'Your grace, I received your letter and came as soon as I was able.' He held the pigeon towards John de la Pole, the Earl of Lincoln. 'Please accept this peace offering.' He looked about at his fellow Council members and the rest of the group. 'Is this a party I have joined?'

Lincoln glared at him, but accepted the pigeon. 'It is a funeral, my lord. The funeral of a friend of mine. My Fool.'

Northumberland looked surprised. 'A pity. A good Fool he was too. How sad.'

Will leaned close to Giles and whispered in his ear. 'This will be a funeral to remember for many a year, my lord.'

Giles did not reply immediately. Instead, he pointed to the Earl's banners. 'Look at Northumberland's cognizance. Does it look familiar?'

Will's eyes opened wide. 'Good grief, my lord. It is like a cat.'

10

King of the Cats

Alice and Will lay in each others arms in Will's small chamber in the barbican. They had arranged to meet there after the funeral.

'Does it hurt much, my love?' Alice asked, tenderly touching his arm and kissing his bare chest.

Will gave a rueful smile. 'Actually I think it hurt more when your father branded me.'

Alice gave him a playful bite. 'You rogue! He did not brand you, as you well know. He cauterized the wound with a hot iron to prevent further blood loss and stop any bad humours from getting into your blood. And I prepared the herb poultice myself.'

Will laughed. 'I was merely teasing. The pain is indeed bearable. It was a small price to pay for my master's life.'

'Does Sir Giles appreciate it?'

'Oh yes. He has always been good to me and I know that had our positions been reversed, he would have done the same for me.' He kissed her lips. 'But talking of brands, those that I told you about on the fingers of these men is troubling Sir Giles. He believes that they all belonged to a secret society of some sort.'

'But a society for what purpose?'

'That is the thing that he does not know. But England heaves with treachery and treason these days. The Duke of Buckingham and his rebellion. The Clifford family and their double-dealing.' He kissed her again, then disentangled his arm from about her and sat up on the edge of the bed. 'And worst of all, the Stanleys. They seemingly support his majesty, yet Lady Stanley, she that was Margaret Beaufort, is mother to the traitor, Henry Tudor.'

He clutched his head in his hands and ran his fingers through his hair. He stood up abruptly and stamped angrily. 'I hate treachery, Alice. I would have all traitors — '

Alice looked up concernedly, for she had not seen him lose his temper so swiftly.

'I am not sure that I trust all of the members of the Council of the North,' he went on. 'My master seems to think that there is much naked ambition among them. And now the Earl of Northumberland rides up and ruins the funeral of Ned Bunce. The Earl of Lincoln looked angry and upset when Northumberland's falcon took down the pigeon that Dickon had just set free.'

'And why should the Earl of Northumberland bother you, my sweet?' Alice asked, pulling the blanket about her and sitting on the edge of the bed herself.

Will sat down beside her. 'I think that Sir Giles suspects there may be some connection with this secret society.' And he told her about Northumberland's coat of arms. 'The brands on those men's fingers look like cats, too.' He punched a fist into the palm of his other hand. 'I do not like it, Alice. I have a bad feeling.'

Alice bit her lip. She had been about to tell him of the unwanted visit that Sir Roger Harrington had paid upon her, and of his threats. Yet Will's ire was such that she decided to say nothing.

★　★　★

John de la Pole had indeed been angry that his plans at the funeral of Ned Bunce had been thwarted. He had returned with the cortège and instructed the castle chamberlain to arrange for accommodation to be made ready for the Earl of Northumberland and his company. While that was being done he went to his own chamber to compose himself. He looked out of the window and nodded with some satisfaction to see that the top of the

232

cross that had been raised on Bunce's grave could be clearly seen. And beyond that was the copse of willows and his grandfather's memorial.

'You will be sadly missed, dear Fool,' he mused to himself. He stood pondering for a few minutes, then went to his desk and picked up a quill to write a letter to his wife, Lady Margaret FitzAlan. With a sigh, he realized how lonely he felt. How much he wanted to see her. 'Soon, my dearest,' he said as he began writing. 'Once this Council is over I will return to you and to our marriage bed.'

As he wrote he became aware of a strange prickling sensation in the back of his neck, as if hairs had begun to stand up. He spun round then came to his feet. Picking up his sword he approached the curtain that covered the entrance to his private garderobe and pulled it back swiftly.

There was no one there.

'Is that you, Bunce?' he asked the air, half jokingly. 'I seem to be sensing something these last few days since you left this place. Something bad.'

He laughed to dispel the gloomy thought and returned to his desk. 'You just keep watching over me, my Fool,' he said, 'just as I will watch over your grave.'

Giles had gone to lie down in his chamber after the funeral. His head ached and he took some more of Dr Musgrave's potion in a draught of wine that Will had left for him. Within several minutes he had fallen asleep.

The knock on the door roused him and, assuming that it was Will, he called out to enter. The door creaked open and he swung his feet on to the floor and adjusted his eyepatch. He had not expected Sir William Stanley to pay a visit on his own. He rose and bowed. 'An unexpected pleasure, Sir William. What service can I do for you?'

Sir William entered and went over to the window. 'A good view you have here,' he said absently, before turning and coughing, as if to move from pleasantries to some matter of importance. 'I seek no service, Sir Giles. I wanted to express my concerns. Concerns that I have already raised with his Grace, the Earl of Lincoln.'

'I am not privy to his Grace's thoughts, Sir William. Can you be more precise?'

'Loyalty, Sir Giles. I speak of loyalty and the need for loyalty.'

'You mean loyalty to whom in particular?'

Sir William frowned irritably. 'Pah! This is the trouble in speaking with lawyers; they question everything when it is already spoken in plain English. I talk of loyalty to the throne, Sir Giles. That means loyalty to King Richard and to his named heir, the Earl of Lincoln.'

'You are saying that you are loyal?'

'Of course I am loyal. It is as I said to his Grace himself. I and my family are loyal. It is a question about other people that concerns me.'

Giles felt that it was not unlike drawing a load through mud, yet it was difficult ground that they now covered. 'Who are you concerned about, my lord?'

'Northumberland, of course! Why has he been absent from the Council?'

'I understand that he had been ill.'

'Does he look ill? And what did you make of that little act of his with the pigeon and his falcon?'

'I made nothing in particular, Sir William. I do not think that he realized that he had stumbled upon a funeral. It could have been an innocent event.'

'It might have been, but so too it could have been Northumberland's way of telling his Grace that he was not to be sent letters.'

Giles nodded. 'Your reasoning is logical enough, Sir William, but you are without one thing.'

'What thing?'

'Proof! All that you say is mere speculation. The law does not allow for such a thing.'

'Pah! There is a time for law and there is a time for action.'

Giles drew himself up to his full height and fixed his gaze on Sir William. 'There is always time for the law, my lord. And you had better make no mistake about what you are saying. This is a highly serious matter, so let us be in no doubt about what you actually are saying. Is it your belief that Henry Percy, the Earl of Northumberland, is a traitor?'

Sir William Stanley of Holt glared at Giles for a moment, his lips twitching as if he had difficulty in reaching a decision of some sort. Then he shook his head.

'Pah! Lawyers! I said no such thing. I came to talk about concerns, nothing else. And if you have his Grace's ear, then you would be doing him a service to let him know that I and others have concerns, that is all.'

He stomped out of the room, leaving the door open.

Giles closed it and stood stroking his chin for a moment. He had to admit that he had concerns himself and planned to investigate matters further.

* * *

Dinner in the Great Hall was a lavish affair that evening. As befitted his rank, Henry Percy, the Earl of Northumberland, was seated on the left of the Earl of Lincoln on the high table atop the dais, while Lord Scrope of Masham sat upon Lincoln's other side. The castle's quartet of musicians played in the minstrel's gallery while Smead the steward of the household oversaw the serving of food and wine.

'This is a most excellent feast, your Grace,' Northumberland said, between mouthfuls of capon. 'Yet it is a pity that your Fool is no longer here. I found him a merry jackanapes. He was better than any physic at making a man laugh. A real tonic for melancholia.'

Lord Scrope gulped wine then lay his goblet upon the table and signalled to a servant to fill it up again. 'May the Lord look after his soul. Yet we did not all find him amusing, if I may say so. Ask Abbot Mallory of Monk Bretton what he thought of him.'

The abbot was sitting on one of the tables arranged at right angles to the high table. He looked up at Lord Scrope's words. 'I feel it would not be appropriate for me to speak ill of the Fool, especially since he has only just departed this earth and may not yet have arrived at his destination.'

'But surely it takes but moments after

death for a soul to rise to heaven,' Lincoln said.

'But if you please, your Grace,' Sir Roger Harrington interjected, his eyes already slightly pink-rimmed, undoubtedly from a few cups of mead in his chamber. 'It is possible that Bunce was not heading for heaven.'

Lincoln looked less than pleased at this exchange. 'Think you not, Sir Roger? Why so?'

'Well, I agree with Lord Scrope, my lord. He was always playing japes, like the one that he played on my Lord Abbot there.'

'Tell me what this prank was,' Northumberland said. 'You have made me most curious.'

At a gesture from Lincoln, Abbot Mallory recounted his finding of worms in his bed. Despite his obvious revulsion, the anecdote caused mild amusement among the Council and a belly-laugh from the Earl of Northumberland.

'It does not sound the sort of sin that would result in him going to hell and eternal damnation,' Northumberland said, once he had stopped laughing.

'I agree with you,' Lincoln said. 'Yet you clearly do not know all of the circumstances. Sir Giles Beeston, the Judge of the Manor

Court, is still investigating his death.' He leaned forward and nodded at Giles.

'Pray tell the Earl about your findings, Sir Giles.'

Giles gave a brief account of the finding of Bunce's body and the examination that had been done on his body. Throughout the entire tale the Earl looked more and more disgusted.

'Poor Fool that he was,' he said at last. Then turning to Lincoln: ''Tis a pity that you did not take up my offer the last time I was at Sandal, your Grace. Had you sold me the Fool and let him come into my employ the chances are that he would still be alive.'

There was the sudden metallic noise of a goblet falling to the floor and everyone looked round to see Sir Roger Harrington staring at the Earl of Northumberland.

'That's it!' he exclaimed. 'Talking about the Fool and employing him just reminded me.' He thumped the table, almost upsetting Sir William Stanley's goblet in the process. 'I have just remembered where I saw that priest before.'

'What priest do you mean, Sir Roger?' Giles asked.

'The dead one, of course! Only he wasn't a priest then. He was a soldier of some sort serving in his Grace, the Earl of Northumberland's army.'

* * *

Dickon was busy checking on the birds in the falconry when he was alerted by several of them to the presence of someone or something nearby. With their superior hearing they had instantly heard movement outside in the mews moments before he heard a footstep. In his current state of wariness his hand went to his belt, to hover over his hunting dagger in case of attack.

'Dickon?' came a familiar voice.

The falconer relaxed upon recognizing Will's voice. 'Hush, Master Will,' he said softly. 'I am settling the birds down. I will come out.'

Will was leaning against the wall, nursing his arm.

'There have been rumours that you have been injured,' Dickon remarked. 'Is that true?'

Will gave a dismissive smile. 'I and Sir Giles had an encounter last night in Wakefield. I am permitted to say no more.'

Dickon pulled out a piece of fresh straw from a bale and chewed it thoughtfully. 'I saw you charge off last night and thought that something must have been amiss.' He pointed at Will's arm. 'I would have gone with you had you asked. I have been known to be useful in a fight.'

Will grinned. 'I had a bad feeling about my master staying on his own. And I was right. Keep this to yourself for now, Dickon, but two men tried to murder Sir Giles. They killed Bartholomew Crofton, one of the town constables.'

Dickon's eyes widened in horror. 'The vermin! What happened to them?'

'They are dead. I believe that Sir Giles is planning to hold a special session of the Manor Court tomorrow. It could be gruesome, since he will want to show the bodies. They are not a pretty sight.'

'There have been too many people killed lately,' Dickon said wearily. 'But I just hope those bastards who killed poor Bartholomew Crofton are now begging for water in the fires of hell.'

Will nodded. 'I think they will be, Dickon. But before I forget, I wanted to ask your opinion about the Earl of Northumberland's bird.'

'His falcon? From what I saw of it, it looks to be a well-trained creature.'

'That is what I thought. And what of the way he handled his bird?'

'Very well, which is hardly surprising for a man of his station. He will be well used to hunting.'

'Why do you think he let his bird loose at almost the exact time that you let loose the pigeon at the funeral. It seems curious, don't you think.'

Dickon spat the chewed straw from his mouth. 'I had been thinking much the same, Master Will.'

★   ★   ★

The Earl of Northumberland stopped with his goblet halfway to his lips. He looked at Giles then at Sir Roger Harrington. 'A dead priest, did you say? And he used to be a soldier in my service.'

Giles nodded. 'I was going to talk about this after the meal, but with your Grace's permission — ?' He looked at Lincoln for approval, then proceeded.

'I told you that we are already investigating the death of Ned Bunce. The case has yet to be concluded. Compounding this, however, during the investigation there have been two more deaths. Both murders!'

Abbot Mallory rasped: 'You will have to put a stop to these murders, Sir Giles. Is that not your task?'

Giles stared coldly at the abbot. 'I will stop them when I discover who is behind them, your Grace.'

'How were these men murdered?' Northumberland asked.

'Their necks were wrung, your Grace. Just as you would wring a chicken's neck.'

Northumberland paled. 'And am I to believe from Sir Roger that one of these bodies is a priest or a soldier and that he was in my service?'

Giles shrugged his shoulders. 'This is news to me, your Grace. It is information that Sir Roger has only just given me.'

Sir Roger's face had gone purple. He spluttered with sudden embarrassment. 'Why I think . . . that is, I thought that I remembered the fellow.'

'And should I remember him?' Northumberland asked, his jaw muscles tensing. 'Is there any reason that I should? Is it of importance?'

'I believe it could be of immeasurable importance, your Grace,' Giles replied. 'There is a possibility that all of these deaths could be linked.'

Lincoln leaned forward and rested his chin on his cupped hands. 'This becomes ever more sinister, Sir Giles. Do you think it has anything to do with the Council of the North?'

'That I do not know, your Grace. Yet the story is more complex than this. There have been three more deaths last night in Wakefield.'

'Ye Gods!' exclaimed Lord Scrope. 'More murders?'

'One murder and two deaths occasioned through self-defence.' And he told the Council of the death of Constable Crofton and his own imprisonment and rescue by Will Holland.

'I would have been dead by now had he not shown up,' he concluded. 'And the case would have been closed, at least temporarily.'

'I shall reward the good Will Holland,' said Lincoln. 'But what do you propose now, Sir Giles?'

'I propose to hold a court session tomorrow morning at Wakefield. And I will require all of the Council to attend.'

Lord Scrope slapped the table in ire. 'Not again! How humiliating.'

'I shall not be attending this court of yours,' said Northumberland.

'Indeed you will, my lord,' said Lincoln in a voice that would brook no argument.

Giles watched and saw the look of cold fury that Northumberland gave his fellow peer. Clearly, there was no love lost between them, but Lincoln, as heir to the throne, held supremacy.

'It would be a great service to me in solving this matter if you would come, your Grace,' he said. 'It may be that only you are able to supply us with this missing information. Who this priest was.'

* * *

Adam Crowther, the bailiff, had the court ready in the morning. The body of Bartholomew Crofton had been moved to lie in the home of Thomas Toliver, having had prayers said over him by the bailiff before being moved.

'We will bring his body into court if you need it, Sir Giles,' Constable Toliver said, as Giles sat down at his desk to go over his papers before the court began. He and Will had ridden from Sandal Castle without waiting for breakfast in order to have an hour or so to prepare before the Earl of Lincoln and the Council of the North arrived for the start of the session.

'I thank you, Constable,' Giles replied. 'There will be no need to view Constable Crofton's body in public. I shall spare his memory that indignity. You may make provisions for his burial.'

The constable thanked him and started to depart with the bailiff.

'We will, however, be viewing the other bodies during the session,' Giles said. 'Please have four tables set up before the witness pen. It may be a harrowing morning for many of the townsfolk, but we must get things cleared up as soon as possible.'

'That will be good, Sir Giles,' Adam Crowther, the bailiff, returned. 'There is much panic among people in town. News of these brutal deaths has spread round the town and people are fearful of their own lives.'

When they were on their own Will asked, 'Are you going to tell the court everything that we know, Sir Giles?'

'About the brands and the secret society, you mean?' Giles shook his head. 'I shall say nothing about the brands at this time. It is information that could cause ever greater panic and alarm.'

Will nodded. 'Do you think that his Grace, the Earl of Northumberland, will be able to identify the priest?'

Giles shrugged his shoulders. 'Who can say? He did not seem overkeen on attending court today. It is thanks to the Earl of Lincoln that he is doing so.'

'There does not seem to be overmuch love lost between them, my lord.'

'No. The Earl of Northumberland is considerably older and thought that he should have been appointed as president of the Council of the North. His family have been powerful in the realm for generations and I am sure that he feels slighted.'

He sat for a moment and stroked his chin pensively. He himself wondered if Northumberland would be able to throw any light on the darkness.

★ ★ ★

As usual, Giles waited until the hall had filled up before opening his small chest and putting on his lawyer's silk coif.

There was a tap on the door and Adam Crowther entered. 'Their Graces the Earls of Lincoln and Northumberland and the Council of the North have arrived, Sir Giles.'

'Have they taken their seats?'

'As before, on the dais,' Adam Crowther replied. 'With the Earl of Northumberland coming, I am afraid that there was not room for all of the Council to sit upon the dais.' He seemed to shiver, as if he had performed an unpleasant duty. 'I have had to ask the Abbot of Monk Bretton to sit at the end of your table, if that is agreeable to you, Sir Giles?'

Will suppressed a laugh and was rewarded with a stern glance from Giles. 'What did the abbot himself say?' Giles asked.

'He was not amused, Sir Giles. I suspect he felt that I was not being respectful of his position. But I thought that his ... er ... rank was below that of the lords and knights.' He mopped his brow with his sleeve. 'I hope that I did the correct thing, Sir Giles.'

'Quite correct,' Giles replied reassuringly. 'I am sure that Sir Roger Harrington was pleased.'

'He did seem to be smiling at something, Sir Giles.'

Giles stood up. 'There will probably be little cause for smiling as this morning progresses. Let us go now.'

As before, Giles welcomed the Council of the North for attending and asked Lincoln's permission to begin.

He gave it and Giles duly instructed the bailiff to swear in the jurors. While this was being done the Earl of Northumberland rapped his fist on the arm of his chair to gain Giles's attention.

'Enough of this rigmarole, Sir Giles. You asked us to come to see this body, so where is it?'

Giles turned in his chair. 'We shall see the body in due course, your Grace. But this is an investigation and the viewing of the body will be done at the correct time.'

'That does not suit me,' Northumberland replied tartly. 'I have no wish to spend more time than I need in this common place. Now kindly have this body brought here and let me see it.'

Giles opened his mouth to reply, but was beaten by the Earl of Lincoln. 'Patience, your Grace, patience.' His tone was calm, but decisive. 'The Council has other business, that is true, but this is a matter of the law. My uncle, the King, is adamant that the law of the land shall be upheld and its officers accorded the necessary powers to carry out the law. Sir Giles is the Judge of the Manor Court and it is up to him how he conducts his court. We the Council must support him, and if that means that we stay until he says otherwise, then so be it. I for one am happy about the way he has conducted the investigation into the death of my Fool, Ned Bunce. And I am happy to sit and listen to the rest of the case.'

There were calls of support from other Council members and several of the crowd began to applaud and cheer.

Northumberland scowled and two points of red appeared on his cheeks. He stared at Lincoln with narrowed eyes for a moment, then his face burst into a smile and he leaned back with a sigh of seeming good humour. 'So be it. Indeed, we must do as our King would have us do.' He bowed to Lincoln. 'You are young in years but carry a wise head on your shoulders. Excuse my impatience, I shall sit and follow your Grace's example.'

Giles gave Lincoln a nod of gratitude and proceeded with the session. He addressed the court.

'The last court session was adjourned while we sent for the poulterer, Jasper Hirst. As I am sure everyone here has heard, the body of Jasper Hirst was found in his dovecote. We shall now view his body.'

Adam Crowther signalled to Constable Toliver, who marched down the hall and left, returning shortly afterwards with two other constables carrying a body on a stretcher.

The crowd shuffled uneasily as the blanket-covered body was borne down the hall and laid upon one of the four trestle tables. Giles signalled for Constable Toliver to remove the blanket.

There was a collective gasp from the audience as many recognized the dead poulterer.

Giles nodded to Dr Musgrave, who was standing at the front of the crowd. 'Dr Musgrave, please come forward and examine the body for us,' Giles said, pointing to the table.

The physician approached the body and with the help of one of the constables undressed it. He then spent some minutes feeling the body before turning it over to inspect for any signs of wounding.

'This is the body of a man of about thirty-five,' he said at last, turning to face Giles. 'He was killed by having his neck broken. Twisted as one would wring a bird's neck.'

There were more gasps and utterances of horror from the audience and one woman swooned. Adam Crowther arranged for her to be carried from the hall.

Will had taken his usual stance to the side of Giles's desk in case he was needed. He wondered how much his master was going to tell.

'There did not seem to be any robbery committed,' Giles went on, 'but whoever murdered him seemed to have gone mad in the dovecote. The bodies of several pigeons were lying about him, also with their necks wrung.'

Giles peered at the audience, looking for reactions. He spotted Dickon and added: 'And with their legs broken.'

Abbot Mallory, sitting at the end of Giles's table, wheezed. 'The work of a madman, without a doubt. Killing god's creatures without cause.'

Giles addressed the jurors. 'We do not know whether this was the work of a

251

madman, but it is a possibility.' Then he turned to Adam Crowther who was busily making notes at his small desk. 'We shall now see the second body. Please arrange it, Bailiff.'

And while Constable Toliver and his constables left the hall to bring in the second body, Giles informed the court of how the body of an unknown man, dressed like a priest, had been found in the Church of All Saints, when the Earl of Lincoln and the Council of the North had gone to witness a blessing being said over the coffin of Ned Bunce.

The constables laid the second body on the adjacent trestle table. At a sign from Giles they pulled back the blanket to reveal him.

'Ye Gods!' exclaimed the Earl of Northumberland, coming swiftly to his feet. He crossed the dais and leaped down to stand over the corpse. His face registered shock, and then he turned and stared at Giles angrily. 'Is this some sick jest? Do you make sport with me, Sir Giles! I know this man only too well.'

Giles had hoped that the Earl would recognize the priest, but he had not expected such a powerful reaction.

'Would your Grace care to tell us how you know this man?' he asked.

Northumberland ignored the question, instead barking out one of his own. 'How did he die?'

'We will find out as soon as Dr Musgrave has had a chance to examine him,' Giles replied.

'Then get him to do so!' Northumberland ordered truculently.

Had anyone else addressed him in such a manner, Giles would have reprimanded them, but Northumberland was one of the most powerful nobles in the land. He therefore suppressed his personal anger and requested the physician to examine the body.

Once again, the doctor undressed the body with the help of one of the constables. Then he went through the same examination that he had performed on Jasper Hirst's body. It took about ten minutes, at the end of which he wiped his hands on the blanket and turned to face Giles.

'This is the body of a man of some thirty or so years. He was as you know dressed in the fashion of a travelling priest. His hands are unblistered, free of calluses, yet they look as if they had known hard toil of some sort before.'

He looked quizzically at Giles. 'Do you wish me to talk about his personal jewellery, Sir Giles?'

'That is not necessary at this stage,' Giles said casually. He turned to the bailiff and added: 'State in the record that both men were wearing rings.' And as Adam Crowther duly wrote this additional note, he told Dr Musgrave to continue.

'Like the other case, the man died of a broken neck. I imagine that his head had been twisted from behind.' And he demonstrated on an imaginary body in front of him.

Giles nodded to the bailiff to record these findings, then turned in his chair and addressed the Earl of Northumberland.

'And now, your Grace, you said that you recognized the man. Can you enlighten the court?'

Northumberland gave a half-snort, then a shrug of resignation. 'His name was Gideon Longbridge and he was a member of my staff at Alnwick Castle for several years. He had been a soldier, a damned good one, I can testify to that myself. But he had some learning, he'd been an apprentice of some sort and had an aptitude for clerking. And he had a decidedly devout side to his nature. He asked to be released from my troops and take up the cloth.'

'You mean he wanted to become a priest?' Giles asked for the sake of clarification.

'That's what I said,' the Earl replied

254

irritably. 'Anyway, I gave him a small curacy in one of my manors. He did that for two years until I sent him to Henry Stafford.'

The Earl of Lincoln stiffened at mention of the name. 'You sent him to the Duke of Buckingham? Why?'

Northumberland took a sharp breath. 'I am not sure that this information should be bandied around in a Manor Court.'

Lincoln disagreed. 'I think that it should, your Grace. This is an important case and we must support the process of the law. Please enlighten us further.'

Northumberland sighed and continued. 'This was all before Henry Stafford turned traitor and raised his rebellion.'

'The traitor got what he deserved!' interjected Sir Roger Harrington. 'God save the King!'

There was a great cheer from the crowd and Giles allowed it to run its course before rapping his gavel for order.

Northumberland continued. 'It was when Dr Morton, the Bishop of Ely, was put under house arrest under the Duke of Buckingham's pleasure. Buckingham approached me if I knew of anyone suitable to look after the bishop. I felt that since he needed a man able to handle himself physically, yet with a developed spiritual sense, the ideal person was Gideon Longbridge, one of my curates.' He looked at the naked body lying on the trestle table. 'It is a shock to see him thus.'

'I thank, your Grace,' Giles said. 'And now, Master Crowther, please have the other two bodies brought in.'

And, while the constables brought in the bodies and lay them down on the vacant tables, Giles explained to the assembly that he had been attacked the night before last and that the two men had slain Constable Crofton. He also recounted how Will Holland had rescued him and in hand-to-hand combat had managed to despatch both men.

Once more Dr Musgrave examined the bodies and reported on the horrific injuries that had caused their deaths.

'But do not feel remorse for these fellows,' Giles announced as many of the crowd made the sign of the cross in front of them. 'They were common cut-throats, of that I have no doubt.'

Sir Roger Harrington gave a hollow laugh. 'But they have their just rewards.'

There was a general muttering and mumbling from the crowd. Giles rapped his gavel for order.

'Does anyone here in this court recognize either of these men?'

There was no response.

'Record that, if you will,' he instructed Adam Crowther. 'The presence of these two cut-throats is a mystery.'

The Earl of Lincoln tapped his chair to gain Giles's attention. 'Have you come to any conclusions, Sir Giles?'

'I have, your Grace,' Giles replied. 'And I will now outline my theory and lay it before the jurors.'

He turned to look at the twelve men of the jury. 'I am fairly certain that Jasper Hirst and this man, whom we now know to be named Gideon Longbridge, were both killed by the man called Henshaw and his accomplice. It is likely that robbery was the reason they were both killed. Then they killed one of the watch, Constable Crofton, and tried to kill me, presumably to create a disturbance and furore, during which they planned to escape from Wakefield.'

The Earl of Lincoln did not look convinced. 'And what of the death that started all of this investigation. What about my Fool, Ned Bunce?'

Giles nodded. 'I was coming to that, your Grace. First of all, I need to recall Dickon of Methley.' He turned and nodded to Adam Crowther, the bailiff, who called the falconer.

Dickon's mouth felt as dry as a bone and he was aware of his heart beginning to race as he took the stand.

'Master falconer,' Giles began. 'I confess that at the start of this investigation I was concerned that Ned Bunce had been poisoned. The fact that he, a trained acrobat, could have gotten drunk and fallen quietly into the moat seemed unlikely to me. Dr Musgrave's examination of his lungs showed that there was no water in them, so he did not drown. That means that he must have been dead before he slipped into the water. And that means that either the poison overcame him rapidly and he slipped, or he had been put in the moat by someone else.'

Dickon swallowed hard. 'I . . . I don't know what you mean, Sir Giles.'

'I have not finished,' Giles said coldly. 'Then we heard that Bunce had stolen your dinner, a roast pigeon. And the meat that was in Bunce's stomach was pigeon and it was poisonous enough to kill two rats.'

Dickon stood looking horrified. He shook his head.

'Upon hearing this, several of the Council of the North declared that a pigeon could not have eaten the berries of deadly nightshade and lived. Yet you declared, and we have your opinion recorded, that a pigeon could eat such things and be unaffected.'

'I . . . I believe that to be true, Sir Giles,'

Dickon stammered.

There were murmurs from all over the audience and several of the Council of the North leaned forward in their seats. Dickon looked anxiously about, sensing hostility towards him from the crowd.

Giles rapped his gavel for silence.

'I asked Dr Musgrave to put this to the test,' Giles went on. 'Yesterday he fed two caged pigeons deadly nightshade berries and they seemed unharmed. He then killed them, roasted them in his kiln and fed the meat to two more rats from the Castle dungeon.'

He sought the physician and asked: 'What was the result, Doctor?'

'The rats died instantly,' Dr Musgrave replied.

'Indeed,' Giles went on. 'And this being the case, Dickon of Methley's testimony is accepted by the court. It appears that the pigeon he was preparing to eat that night was poisoned with deadly nightshade berries that it had eaten.' He looked at Dickon and nodded. 'It appears that you had a narrow escape from the poison that killed Ned Bunce. You were fortunate that he stole your dinner. It was his folly to do so. You may stand down.'

Giles waited for the audience to settle down, and then went on. 'My conclusion is therefore this. I think that Ned Bunce, the Earl of Lincoln's Fool, died by unhappy chance after eating a pigeon that had poison in its system from having eaten deadly nightshade berries. The murders of Jasper Hirst and the priest were unconnected to his death, but brought about by these two killers.' He pointed to the two bodies lying in front of him. 'It is fortunate that the two men have been killed, so I do not feel that there is any cause for further alarm among the good people of Wakefield. I ask the jury to consider this now and give me their opinion shortly.'

There was a collective sigh and an obvious feeling of relief from the people of the town upon hearing Giles's summing up. Ten minutes later, after the jury delivered their agreement with his assessment, the hall was cleared.

The Earl of Lincoln suggested that the Council of the North should return to Sandal, a suggestion which was eagerly accepted by them all. Before he himself left, the Earl of Lincoln arranged for Giles to call upon him as soon as he arrived back at the castle.

'My lord,' Will said, once he and Giles were alone in the Rolls Office. 'Do you really believe that the deaths were unconnected?'

Giles rested a hand on Will's shoulder and

shook his head. 'Of course not, Will. I am sure that there is more to these Wakefield deaths than I can put my finger on. But I need time to think about it. That is why I have closed the case. I need everyone to believe that it is all finished. I think that his Grace, the Earl of Lincoln, understood this, which is why he wants to talk with me at Sandal.'

He bit his lip. 'But in truth, it gives me little joy to think about it. I have a bad feeling about it all, Will. I think that there is something truly sinister at work here and I am determined to find out what.'

11

An Unexpected Visitor

Alice had been busily compounding medicines and potions for her father all morning. He had left instructions for her to brew a decoction of hawthorn root in order to replenish the stock bottle of his special dropsy remedy, prepare an ointment to treat the piles of one of the guards, then make up a tonic of brash water from the blacksmith's quenching bath. All of these tasks had necessitated heating various flasks and jars, the result being that she was both parched with thirst and uncomfortable from excess perspiration. The former she could tolerate but the latter felt unseemly to her.

'Thank goodness that Will cannot see me thus,' she said to herself as she dabbed her forehead with her kerchief.

Then she smiled as her mind's eye conjured up the image of the last time she had been bathed in perspiration from her exertions. Only that time it had been pleasurable exertion and neither she nor Will had been wearing any clothes at all.

'Oh, you silly maid!' she chided herself. 'What foolish risks you have taken.' And so thinking she rushed through to look at the plant pots on the window ledge in the neighbouring room. Scooping them up she explored the surfaces for any signs of germination.

'Please, blessed Virgin,' she whispered, shutting her eyes tightly as she did so, 'let there be no growth.' She bit her lower lip anxiously, since she knew only too well that if there was early sprouting of the seeds watered with her own urine, it would almost certainly mean that she was with child.

Her eyes narrowed, for in the dim light she thought that there was a minute shoot breaking the surface of the soil.

'More light! I need to see better,' she told herself. 'But I cannot go where anyone can see what I am about.'

Then she snapped her fingers. 'I must go to the top of the tower.'

And after placing the pots in a basket which she looped over her right arm and gathering up the hem of her gown with her left hand she scurried up the stairs to the top of the tower.

A few moments later atop the tower she almost fell to her knees. 'Oh thank you, my lady,' she sighed with relief upon finding the soil unbroken.

She looked about her, revelling in the slight breeze that was inevitable from the highest point for miles around. And feeling happy and free, she found herself dancing, spinning round and round. Then she saw movement from the south. She shielded her eyes from the sun and focused on the horizon. There was movement and a slight cloud. Gradually it became clear that a large detachment of men on horses was advancing towards the castle. A horn sounded from the battlements below, followed by a drum beat. Then voices were calling, summoning the sergeant of the watch.

'A party approaches,' she heard a guard bluster, when the sergeant came rushing towards him along the battlement walk.

'My God!' the sergeant, a ruddy faced middle-aged fellow gasped. 'It cannot be!'

But from her vantage point, with young unfettered vision, Alice had already seen what bothered the sergeant. She saw the cognizance on the banners fluttering from the raised halberds of several of the leading riders. 'The white boar,' she whispered to herself. 'His Majesty the King himself approaches.'

Despite herself she felt her heart begin to flutter, though she was unsure whether it was from excitement or from fear. What would they do, since there was no one of any rank left in the castle to greet their sovereign?

'My lady,' the sergeant called up to her. 'What do you think we should do? I am given orders to admit no one that I do not recognize.' Anxiety was written in every line on his face. 'But it is the King himself!'

Alice was unsure of what to say. She had no status within the castle, for she was merely the daughter of the Earl of Lincoln's physician. Nevertheless, she found herself replying. 'Let down the drawbridge, but do not raise the portcullis until you have made absolutely sure that it is indeed the King.'

* * *

Alice stood on the bailey courtyard, her mouth threatening to fall open in awe at the spectacle of the King's entourage trotting over the drawbridge, the guards in royal livery and with the royal banners hanging from shining halberds.

King Richard dismounted nimbly and advanced towards her. He was dressed in fine riding clothes with a capuchon hat upon his head, his long brown hair just brushing his shoulders. He was of average height, well muscled as befitted the man of action that he was known as, with sharp features and with a lower lip that seemed to tremble, as if he was in the habit of chewing it. But his eyes made the deepest impression upon her. They seemed shrewd, penetrating even, yet shrouded in such sadness. And as she thought this, she chided herself, for had not the King the right to be sad, having lost his son and his wife in the space of a year.

'Welcome to our castle, Your Majesty,' she said, dropping into a curtsy, and hoping that her voice did not betray the fear that she felt overcoming her.

The King graced her with an indulgent smile, then he raised an eyebrow. 'Your castle, my lady?' He gave a look of mock surprise. 'Sandal Castle has been in my family's possession for four generations. It was my father, the Duke of York's favourite castle in the north and I remember it well from my youth. The last I heard, it still belonged to the crown, with my nephew, the Earl of Lincoln, as its president.'

Alice gasped and covered her mouth and dropped into another curtsy. 'Your Majesty, I . . . I . . . meant no offence. It was just — '

King Richard gave a short chuckle, pulled off a gauntlet and, taking her hand gently, raised her to her feet. 'Forgive me, I was but teasing you.'

Alice averted her eyes, conscious of the

amusement that the encounter seemed to have generated among the knights and men who had remained mounted behind the King.

'Now tell me where is my nephew, the Council of the North and the rest of his household?' King Richard asked, his eyes darting about as if searching the castle lest he be taken unawares. 'I was not expected, I know, yet I had not thought to find a royal castle unoccupied and so scantily guarded.'

Alice felt another surge of anxiety, unsure as she was about how to take the King's question. She was uncertain as to whether he was angered to find the castle thus.

But then again he smiled, his lip twitching slightly. 'But you have me at a disadvantage, my lady. You are — ?'

'Alice Musgrave, Your Majesty. I am only the daughter of his Grace, the Earl of Lincoln's physician. His Grace and the Council of the North are attending the Manor Court. Sir Giles Beeston, the judge, is conducting an investigation into the death of Ned Bunce, the Earl's Fool.'

The King's eyes widened. 'The Fool is dead?' Then his face again registered the sadness that she had noticed at first. She felt her heart go out to him. 'Perhaps it was folly for me to come to Sandal after all,' he added, almost as a whisper, as if he was no longer conscious of her presence before him.

★ ★ ★

The Earl of Lincoln approached the castle at the head of his entourage and the Council of the North. He felt bemused to see the flag fluttering from the pole atop the north tower of the keep. Scarcely believing his eyes, he noted that it was not his own arms, but that of the white boar.

'Uncle!' he cried a few minutes later as he galloped across the drawbridge and saw the figure of the King surrounded by his knights and men at arms. He was talking to Alice Musgrave. He dismounted, passed between the knights and immediately knelt before his king, his head bent in supplication.

'Rise, good nephew,' King Richard said. 'I appreciate that you were not expecting me. I have come to seek your counsel and to have a little diversion from the cares of the crown.'

The sound of numerous horses crossing the drawbridge was followed by the appearance of several members of the Council of the North. There were gasps of astonishment as the leading riders recognized the King. There was a flurry of dismounting, bowing and expressions of surprise.

Sir William Stanley was one of the first to pay his respects in person. 'Your Majesty, we did not expect such a blessing as your visit.'

'I trust that your majesty is in good health?' Lord Scrope queried, deferentially.

The Earl of Northumberland arrived and immediately joined the mêlée. 'Your Majesty,' he cried, dismounting and bowing. 'You honour us with your presence. It is a meeting well made, for I would count it a favour to have words with you in private.'

King Richard's lower lip seemed to twitch and he twisted a ring on his hand. 'Perhaps later, my lord Northumberland,' he said. Then turning to the rest of the gathered knights and lords he raised his hands for silence.

'My good subjects, I thank you all. I am well, and I have been welcomed most delicately by this good lady here.'

'By Mistress Alice?' Lincoln repeated, his eyes falling on the physician's daughter. Alice immediately blushed and dropped into a curtsy before the Earl.

Lincoln laughed. 'Aye, Your Majesty. Mistress Alice is a rare jewel, much as is her father, my physician. What would I do without either of them? They keep me and my household well.' He bowed to her. 'I thank you, Mistress Alice, for greeting my uncle, the

269

King. It should have been my duty to do so.'

King Richard linked his arm through Lincoln's. As he did so, Alice noticed that his right shoulder seemed slightly higher than the other, which had led to the rumour that he was affected by a humpback and a withered arm. Her practiced eye told her that it was not so. Likely that it was simply more developed from years of sword and arms practice.

'Let us talk in private a while, nephew,' he said as he allowed Lincoln to lead the way to his chamber. 'I understand that you are in mourning.'

'In mourning, Your Majesty?'

'Your Fool! I heard from Mistress Alice that Ned Bunce is dead. I would like you to tell me about it.'

Two guards and one of the king's servants bearing a medium-sized chest accompanied them to Lincoln's private chamber. The guards took up a position outside the door while the servant followed them inside.

'I have brought gifts for you, nephew,' said King Richard, snapping his fingers at the manservant, who lay the chest down on a table. At another gesture from the King he opened it, and then retreated from the chamber.

'I bring you two books newly printed by

William Caxton,' King Richard said, lifting out two leather-bound volumes and handing the top one to Lincoln. 'First, Le Morte d'Arthur by Sir Thomas Malory. It is about King Arthur and the Knights of the Round Table and their quest for the Holy Grail. And secondly, to show my affection for you, the great text by your ancestor.'

Lincoln stood admiring both volumes. Then he laid the first down and opened the second. His face registered first amazement then utter delight. 'Uncle, they are magnificent.' He ran his fingertips almost reverentially over the cover then opened the book and gingerly and respect-fully turned the pages. 'The Canterbury Tales by Geoffrey Chaucer.' He laughed with delight. 'My grandmother's grandfather. Why, it is a wonderfully thought gift, Your Majesty. But I do not deserve it.'

The King placed his hands on both of Lincoln's shoulders and gave him a gentle shake. 'Enough of that, nephew. You are the most important member of my family, now that my son and my dearest wife Anne have gone.' His eyes filmed over with tears. 'So why should I not make a gift to my appointed heir?' He chewed his lower lip for a moment then with a snort to stifle any further threat of tears he strode to the other side of the chamber and stood looking out of the large slit window. 'I like the changes that you have made to Sandal Castle, John. The new facing on this tower has greatly improved its appearance.'

'I am glad that you approve, Your Majesty. It has been given five faces to make it both more appealing to the eye, and better for defence. By next summer the other three towers will be similarly faced.'

The King nodded. Then he pointed out of the window. 'I can see the willow copse where my father, your grandfather, fought until his last. But what is that other cross just beyond the rise, before you come to the willows?'

Lincoln joined him at the window. 'It is the cross that marks the grave of Ned Bunce, uncle. We buried my poor Fool yesterday.'

King Richard looked sidewards at his nephew, recognizing the grief in his face and voice. 'It hurts, does it not? Losing someone close. And a good Fool is like a prized hound or a favourite horse. You still feel the pain of the loss.' He chewed his lip again. 'I can feel your pain, John. I understand completely, having lost so many people myself.'

Suddenly, Lincoln became aware that his uncle was trembling, fidgeting with his hands at the rings on his fingers. He had seen him act so when under pressure before, yet this time it seemed that the movements, the fidgeting was magnified several-fold.

'Where did it all go so horribly wrong, John?' he asked, slumping into a chair and pulling off his cap to run his fingers through his hair.

'My lord, what has gone wrong? Your crown is secure; your people love you and are both well fed and well governed.'

The King looked up at his nephew, his eyes heavy with anguish. 'But the people do not love me, John. I was popular when my dear brother Edward was on the throne, and I was popular while I was still the Lord Protector. The truth of the matter is that I never wanted to be king. It was circumstances that forced it upon me.'

Lincoln had never seen his uncle in such a state. Even after the death of his wife earlier that year he had still presented the demeanour of a strong and resilient king. 'My lord, I do not understand.'

'When I discovered from Stillington, the Bishop of Bath, about my brother's previous wedding, I had no choice but to declare that his children were illegitimate.'

Lincoln nodded. 'I agree, sir. You had no

choice. And parliament agreed with you when Titulus Regius[1] was made law.'

'I had to keep my brother's children in custody for their own safety.'

'And they are still well in the Tower, are they not, your majesty?'

The king let out a deep sigh. 'They were the last report I had. But to tell you the truth John, I do not enjoy seeing them, and have not seen them these two years gone. Ever since Buckingham rebelled two years hence I have relied upon reports from Sir Robert Brackenbury.' He gave a short ironic laugh. 'I have let their mother, Elizabeth Woodville, out of sanctuary and she has returned to court. She receives almost daily reports.'

He stood up and struck the back of the chair with his fist. 'But still I have to put up with the rumours spread about by the malicious Dr Morton, that scoundrel, the traitorous Bishop of Ely.'

He looked at his nephew with ire starting to show in his expression. 'Do you know that

---

[1] Titulus Regius, a statute of Parliament issued in 1483 by which the title of King of England was bestowed upon Richard, Duke of Gloucester. It was an official declaration that found Edward IV's marriage to Elizabeth Woodville to be invalid and their children illegitimate.

274

I had to stand before parliament and declare that I had no intention of marrying Elizabeth of York?'

'So I understood, my lord.'

Bells were starting to ring in Lincoln's mind at this talk of the Bishop of Ely, Dr John Morton. His mind went back to the Manor Court, to the news that the priest that they had found murdered in the Church of All Saints had been in Northumberland's employ, then was sent to Buckingham to look after Morton. He wondered if there could be some link. But how to broach it with the king in his present state. He decided to be circumspect for a while.

'But my lord, you are surrounded by men who are totally loyal.'

Richard laughed. 'You are a good and honest nephew, John, and I have no doubts about your loyalty. But take the Council of the North, how many of the members are truly loyal to me?'

Lincoln thought for a moment. 'They have all expressed their loyalty to you, sire.'

'And I would expect that some have been more vociferous in doing so than others,' the king replied.

'That is true, my lord. Sir William Stanley, Lord Scrope and Sir Roger Harington have all been at pains to emphasize their allegiance to our house.' He bit his lip and added: 'The Earl of Northumberland too.'

King Richard laughed heartily. 'Of course they do. That is partly the reason why I put all of their names forward to be members of the Council of the North. Keep your friends close, John, but keep your enemies even closer. But sometimes it is hard to know which is which.'

He turned and peered out of the window. 'Is that not Sir Giles Beeston I see down there?' Then before Lincoln could reply he turned and said: 'I heard that he is investigating the death of your Fool. Why is this, nephew? Was there something suspicious about his death?' His eyes narrowed and his eyes darted from side to side, as if he suddenly felt uneasy or suspected that ears were listening to their words. 'How did he die?'

'He was found in the moat, Your Majesty. But it appears he was poisoned.'

The King's eyes widened in horror. 'Poisoned? Then let us hear what Sir Giles thinks. Have him brought up and we will talk.'

★ ★ ★

Giles and Will were watching Dickon issue instructions to a couple of the Earl of

Northumberland's men who were trying to kennel several of the Earl's hunting hounds into a spare building at the end of the mews.

'They will need to be muzzled and kept quiet,' Dickon told the men.

'And how do you keep hounds quiet, master,' one of the men returned. 'These are hunting animals and they are highly strung.'

'That's your problem,' Dickon replied. 'But if they upset my birds, then I will be your problem!'

The two men, swarthy looking fellows who could probably have given a good account of themselves, backed off when they saw Sir Giles and Will Holland advance upon them.

'We'll do our best,' replied the one who had spoken. And he and his colleague bustled about, chivvying the hounds along with one or two yanks on the chains that they were leading the hounds with.

'Can I help you, Sir Giles?' Dickon asked.

Giles was about to reply when he heard his name called and turned to see one of Lincoln's men come running across the barbican drawbridge. 'Your presence is wanted, Sir Giles. The King and the Earl of Lincoln wish you to attend on them straight away.'

Giles followed him up back through the barbican then through the drum towers to the stairs leading up to the north tower of the keep. Two guards were stationed outside Lincoln's chamber, but at his approach the door opened and the Earl himself came out.

'A word with you, Sir Giles,' he said, leading him up the stairs out of earshot of the guards and the servant. 'His Majesty wishes to talk about your investigation. He is concerned about poison. I think he has a fear of poisons.' He hesitated, and then went on, as if deciding to take Giles into his deepest confidence. 'His Majesty is not himself at the moment, Sir Giles. He is suspicious of most people and I think that the cares of state are weighing heavier upon him than usual. So come, talk with us, but I pray you, be careful of upsetting him. I am concerned for his health.'

Giles bowed hastily. 'His Majesty's health and your own, my lord, are my prime concern. Indeed, I had looked forward to our discussion, but perhaps we had better wait until I have satisfied his majesty, or otherwise.'

Lincoln looked at him askance. 'I pray let it not be otherwise, Giles. I wish His Majesty to enjoy his time here at Sandal. I will do all in my power to make it so.'

And with a nod of acquiescence, Giles followed the Earl back down to his chamber to see his sovereign.

King Richard spun round at their entry, his hand hovering above his sword. At sight of his nephew and Giles he smiled and held out his hand to Giles. Giles bowed low and kissed his sovereign's hand.

'I hear from my nephew that you have been conducting an inquiry into the death of his Fool, Ned Bunce. I did not like to hear that there was suspicion of poisoning.'

Lincoln had gone to the table behind the King and began pouring wine into goblets. Giles noted his slow shake of the head.

He is serious, he thought. He does not wish me to alarm his majesty at all.

'It is true, Your Majesty,' he said. 'I have been carrying out an investigation in the Manor Court. I concluded that poor Ned Bunce died accidentally.'

'Accidentally?' the King repeated.

'Yes, my lord. It is likely that he ate a pigeon that had been diseased. Poisoned from eating deadly nightshade berries. Dr Musgrave was able to confirm for me that pigeons will not die from consuming them.'

Giles noticed Lincoln's smile of satisfaction and nod of approval as he handed him a goblet.

'I was conducting the case as part of a

greater investigation,' Giles went on. 'I have to report that there have been several other deaths in Wakefield of late. Rather suspicious deaths, Your Majesty.'

The King's eyes widened.

'But I concluded that these were unconnected with Bunce's demise,' Giles added. He noted Lincoln's slight shake of the head and the look of worry that flitted across his face. 'I mention them merely because one of the dead men may once have been in the service of his Grace, the Earl of Northumberland.'

Giles waited for King Richard to drink some wine before continuing.

'I thought it best that you should be aware of this before dinner, Your Majesty. In case the subject comes up.'

Lincoln took a gulp of wine. 'Sir Giles seems to have it all well in hand, Uncle.'

The King's lips stretched into a thin smile and he gestured for Giles to drink. 'I am relieved to hear this, Sir Giles. You alarmed me, I admit, with talk of poison. It is one of my greatest fears.'

He slumped down in the chair behind the Earl of Lincoln's desk and moved some papers aside in order to make space for his goblet. 'A poisoner can introduce death when people are protected from every form of violence. Take my — '

The King seemed to be peering into the distance, beyond the walls of the Castle. He suddenly hesitated and dashed a glance at Giles and his nephew.

'Your Majesty — ?' Lincoln urged.

But the King waved his hand. 'It is of no matter.' He grabbed the goblet and drank deeply. Then he sat staring pensively at the vessel as he swirled the dregs in the bottom. 'There are many poisons that can be used against a king, did you know that?'

He gave a short, humourless laugh, and then continued before either Giles or Lincoln could reply: 'There is the poison that can be used to kill the body.' He took out an ornate horn-handled knife from his belt and let it lie in the flat of his hand for them to see. 'The handle of this knife is said to be made from the horn of a unicorn. If poison is present in food it becomes moist.' He resheathed it. 'You should know, nephew, that there have been three such attempts recently to murder me.'

And as Lincoln stiffened, his mouth dropping open in alarm, the King went on reassuringly. 'All three plots were discovered and the perpetrators caught, punished and then executed.'

'Did the torture reveal anything, my Lord?' Giles asked.

'Did it reveal a connection, do you mean?' King Richard asked. He shook his head. 'They were all working alone.' He breathed deeply, as if to emphasize that he had finished with the subject. 'And then there is the poison of witchcraft. It is all around. I am sure that bitch woman, Lady Margaret Beaufort, is a witch. She and that dog son of hers, Henry Tudor. They are continually plotting to kill me and make me ill.'

Giles noted how he clenched his fists and then his teeth as he talked about them.

'My son Edward, the Prince of Wales, my dear wife, Queen Anne! I believe that somehow their deaths — ' His voice trailed away and he drank the rest of his wine before taking another deep breath, then he started again: 'And then there is the poison that they use on the minds of my people. The rumours, damn them!'

Giles was all too aware of the many rumours that abounded. The rumours that Richard had himself poisoned his wife. The rumour that he had either killed or had his nephews killed in the Tower of London. Giles had heard all of these and had come to the conclusion that they were nothing but scurrilous rumours. He had come to the conclusion through logic, not merely through blind loyalty, for it was obvious that the King had nothing to gain by the deaths of his nephews, but everything to gain by keeping them well and healthy.

Since he was already king, and Titulus Regius had been passed by parliament, he had no reason to wish them dead. They could pose no threat. Had he wished them dead then he could easily have made up some story and made it public about them having died of some illness or malady, as his own son had died.

The King went on. 'And then there is the poison that they use to demean me! Me, the rightful King of England! Last year that Tudor lackey, the dog William Collingbourne, pinned that piece of doggerel on the door of St Paul's Cathedral.' His eyes seemed to smoulder with rage as he recited the piece:

'*The Cat, the Rat and Lovell our dog,*
Rule all England under the hog.'

He sighed. 'That was a devilish reference to my friends Sir Richard Ratcliffe, Sir William Catesby, good Francis, Viscount Lovell and me.' His face had gone grim first, then progressively paler as his fury rose.

Lincoln attempted to calm his uncle. 'And Collingbourne was tried for sedition, found guilty and justifiably hanged.'

The King nodded. 'Aye, and this year there have been several other traitors who have followed him.' He stood up and began pacing the chamber, ticking off names on his fingers. ' . . . Sir Digby Herbert, Lord Percy Welles, Sir Roger Clifford. Traitors all. But though I cut off their heads, like that Hydra monster in the Greek legends, two more spring up. And everywhere I see the influence of that witch, Margaret Beaufort, and her traitorous son, Henry Tudor. Thank God that I had the foresight to put her under house arrest with her husband Lord Stanley.'

Giles ventured a question. 'Do you trust the Stanley family, Your Majesty?'

The King smiled. 'I have told my nephew before, keep your friends close, but your enemies closer. The Stanleys have too much to lose by crossing me or by choosing the road of treason. So too, I might add, has my lord the Earl of Northumberland. My main concern is Henry Tudor and his faction who all now live happily in France.'

'Is the Bishop of Ely, Dr Morton, in France with him, Your Majesty?' Giles asked.

'He is,' the King replied. 'He fled after Buckingham rebelled against us.'

Giles nodded, but said no more. There had been much that the King had said which intrigued him. He needed time to think it all through.

'I came here to take a break from the cares

of the crown,' Richard said. 'I have left my friends — the Cat, the Rat and the Dog,' he added sarcastically. 'They are in Nottingham waiting for any news of Tudor. They did not care to see me take my leave of them, but I needed to see and have some time with my nephew and heir.' He took two steps and clapped Lincoln on the shoulders. 'So let us feast well this evening, then tomorrow you can divert me. I take it that the Old Park is still full of wild boar?'

Lincoln nodded enthusiastically. 'It is, my Lord. You shall have a hunt such as you have never enjoyed before.'

Giles felt a shiver run up his spine. He had done as Lincoln had wanted and revealed little to the King. Yet he was not sure that was the most sensible option.

* * *

An hour later Will tapped on Giles's chamber door and waited until he was bidden entry.

'Did you enjoy your audience with the King, my Lord?'

'Not entirely, Will. I fear that His Majesty is feeling under great strain. That is why he has come to Sandal, to get away from the great cares of state.'

'But the events that have occurred here will

hardly give him respite from care,' Will pointed out.

Giles shook his head. 'He does not really know what has happened here, Will. The Earl of Lincoln does not want him to be bothered with extra woe. For that reason, I told him that I have concluded that Ned Bunce died accidentally from eating a diseased pigeon.'

Will nodded without comment.

Giles grimaced. 'Yet I am uneasy about everything that has happened. Indeed, His Majesty said something that made me think twice. He talked about poison and was on the verge of telling us about something that bothered him.'

'What about, my lord?' Will asked, his curiosity roused.

'I think that he may have been referring to the princes in the Tower. But I was unable to pursue it, for he changed the subject.'

'You mean they may have been poisoned, my lord?' Will asked, aghast. 'Murdered?'

'It is possible, Will. But if they were, and it would still only be a possibility, then I am convinced that His Majesty had nothing to do with it.'

'But who could have done such a thing?'

Giles bit his lip. 'I have a suspicion that it could have something to do with Dr Morton, the Bishop of Ely, and the Duke of

Buckingham. It would seem to fit. Buckingham rebelled and, when the rebellion failed, Dr Morton absconded to France.'

He suddenly felt a spasm of pain and rubbed his temple. 'Gah, this pain is back again. How it clouds my thinking at times.' He massaged it for some moments then went on: 'But he also talked about that piece of doggerel that was circulating last year. About the Cat, the Rat and the dog Lovell, and the hog.'

'I remember it vaguely, my lord. It referred to some of the great lords and the King himself.'

'Precisely,' replied Giles. 'Catesby, Ratcliffe and Lovell. And all of them have always been close to the King. He has left them in charge of the Council in Nottingham.' He suddenly pointed to Will's ring. 'Remember the rings, Will. And the brands.'

'The brand of a cat,' Will returned. 'And you said that you think that it has something to do with a secret society, my lord.'

'Possibly, Will. But it might not be a cat. It was a pretty indistinct brand on all of them. It could have been a cat, or a dog. Or perhaps even a rat.'

Will's eyes opened wide as he considered this. 'Do you mean that it could have referred to one of the three names in that poem?'

Giles creased his brows. 'I don't know, Will. I may be chasing straws in the wind. But those dead rats struck a cord. And perhaps there could be a conspiracy between the three.'

'Treason, my lord?'

Giles gave a slow nod. 'That is what worries me about the King's sudden appearance here. I fear that it may have been folly for him to come to Sandal Castle — especially as we have all of these suspicious deaths.'

'But the Earl of Lincoln — '

Giles nodded. 'I know. He made me keep things from the King. And that is another thing, Will. Lincoln's cognizance is that of a lion.'

'Another cat, my lord!'

Giles nodded grimly. 'Another cat!'

Will looked pensive for a moment then snapped his fingers. 'I completely forgot, my lord. Dickon wondered what it was that you wanted to ask him.'

But Giles did not answer. He rubbed his temple as if it was suddenly causing him great pain. 'How I wish that the King had not come to Sandal, Will.' He sighed. 'I fear for him. I fear for England.'

12

A Maiden in Distress

Giles was woken early the next morning by an insistent knocking on his door.

'Sir Giles, I have Dickon with me,' came Will's voice from the other side of the door. 'May we be admitted?'

Yawning as he adjusted his eye patch, Giles threw back his cover and walked barefoot to open the door. 'What hour is it?' he asked.

'Not yet cockcrow,' replied Will. 'Dickon woke me with the news and I thought that I — '

'What news?'

Dickon was a pace behind Will. 'I was up as usual to check and weigh my birds, Sir Giles,' he explained. 'And one of the ostlers came and sought me with one of the Earl of Northumberland's men. They found two of his Grace's hounds dead, sir. They had froth at their mouths and they smelled of garlic.'

'Meaning what? Poison?' Giles asked.

Dickon nodded diffidently. 'I am supposing so, Sir Giles.'

'What have you done with them?'

The falconer looked uncomfortable. 'Nothing, Sir Giles. I thought that you might want to see them.'

Giles turned to his clerk. 'Have you seen them?'

'I have, Sir Giles. They were dead as Dickon said and they smelled of garlic as he told you.'

Giles nodded. 'Then I do not need to see them. I suggest that you tell the Earl's man to inform his Grace himself.' He yawned again. 'I thank you for letting me know. And now it is still early, I must get back to bed. I will see you after breakfast.'

He closed the door, leaving Will and Dickon to stare at each other. Sir Giles's reaction had not been as they had expected.

But indeed, had they been able to see his expression as he returned to lie on his bed, they would have realized that the news of the dogs' deaths was puzzling him greatly. It was for this reason that he felt the need to lie down and think.

★ ★ ★

The Earl of Northumberland's man did not relish the task of personally telling his master, so he waited until after cockcrow and relayed the information to one of the Earl's squires.

290

Having thus discharged his duty, he retreated again to the kennels in the mews and removed the other hounds and tethered them outside, where they began to howl in unison for their dead fellows, until they were whipped into silence.

When the Earl finally heard the news himself he became infuriated.

'Poisoned!' he exclaimed upon visiting the kennels in person and viewing the corpses. 'Get the Castle Constable at once!'

But Giles had made his way as soon as he spied the Earl crossing the bailey.

'I am here, your Grace. Can I say that — '

'You damned well better tell me how this happened!' Northumberland exclaimed. 'And I want to know who did it. I will have his head, whoever he is!'

'I imagine that will be difficult, your Grace.'

The Earl's face went puce with rage. 'Difficult? Don't play with me, Sir Giles Beeston. What do you mean?'

'I mean that the culprit — if culprit there is — will have made sure he cannot be detected. Besides, the Earl of Lincoln has made it clear to me that His Majesty must not be distressed in any way.'

Northumberland's brows beetled. 'What has His Majesty to do with this?'

'Nothing, as far as I am aware, your Grace. But he has an aversion to the idea of poison.' Giles adjusted his eye patch. 'But I am glad that I find you here. I would like to ask you a question about the priest that was killed.'

'Gideon Longbridge? What of him?'

'You said that he was in your army. Was he just a fighting soldier or did he have any particular skills?'

'I told you that he had a sense of spirituality.' The Earl considered for a moment, then: 'I believe he also had some skills with herbs and physic. He had been an apothecary's apprentice or some such before enlisting in my army.'

'An apothecary's apprentice,' Giles repeated. He bowed. 'I thank your Grace. I will arrange for the bodies of the dogs to be removed and then checked by Dr Musgrave.' He leaned closer and said in a lower voice. 'And may I ask that you say nothing of this to His Majesty?'

The Earl scowled. 'I and Sir William Stanley are going hunting in his party this morning. I shall say nothing about this to either of them.'

Giles bowed again. 'I thank your Grace. And I will do my utmost to find the culprit.'

'But you said you would not be able to find him?'

'I said that it would be difficult, your Grace, but hopefully not impossible.'

Giles took his leave, turned and retraced his steps to the barbican, feeling a lot less confident than he had just tried to sound.

★   ★   ★

The Earl of Lincoln was already up and had completed his ablutions when Giles approached his chamber and asked his guards to seek a meeting. Some minutes later he was shown in and was greeted by the Earl, who stood with a quill in one hand.

'I was just about to pen a few lines,' he explained, holding up the quill and shrugging his shoulders. 'Sadly, inspiration will not come this morning.' He crossed to his desk and tapped the two volumes lying beside his papers. 'My great, great grandfather's work makes me realize how devoid of art I really am.'

Giles was about to protest, but the Earl waved him to a seat. 'I presume you have come for that meeting we were not able to have?'

'I have indeed, your Grace,' Giles replied. 'And I must confess that with His Majesty's unexpected arrival I have become quite concerned.'

'About what?'

'His safety, your Grace. It is my belief that there is a conspiracy of some sort afoot.'

He told the Earl of his finding of the brands beneath the rings worn by the four dead men. 'The brand is of some sort of animal. I had thought that it was a cat, but it could equally have been a rat, a cat or a dog.'

Lincoln stared shrewdly at him. 'Do you mean that it could be linked to that piece of doggerel written by William Collingbourne? The one that my uncle, the King, referred to yesterday?'

'Yes, your Grace. Collingbourne was a poet, like yourself.'

Lincoln's eyes narrowed. 'Like me? Are you implying something, Sir Giles?'

'Forgive me, your Grace. I meant no such thing,' Giles replied emphatically. 'Yet from what His Majesty himself said yesterday, he seems to have so many enemies that he may not be able to trust even his best friends. Perhaps not even the Cat, the Rat and the Dog.'

'Do you really believe that?'

Giles shook his head. 'Actually, no, your Grace. But last night I had the impression that His Majesty trusts no one — except for you.' He took a deep breath, and then added: 'I confess that I am worried for him. I talked with the Earl of Northumberland and he told me that the priest who was killed, Gideon Longbridge, had some training at some time in the apothecary's art before be became a soldier. And then after that, he became a priest.'

'And so?'

'So therefore he may have had some knowledge of poisons.'

'And where does that take us?'

Giles shook his head uncertainly. 'Perhaps nowhere, your Grace. But I am concerned in case there is a link to the Lady Margaret Beaufort. In that case there may be a link to Lord Stanley. And if that is the case, then possibly to Sir William Stanley.'

Lincoln's brows furrowed even deeper and he sat down and began toying absently with the quill. 'I am not sure that I see the link?'

'I am not sure that there is one, your Grace. Except that the priest was being employed to look after Dr Morton, the Bishop of Ely, when he was under the care of the Duke of Buckingham. Dr Morton and the Lady Margaret Beaufort have a long association.'

An expression of understanding appeared on the Earl's face. He sat forward. 'You do know that Margaret Beaufort, Henry Tudor's mother, was married to my father when they were children?'

Giles nodded. 'And I am also aware of Sir William Stanley's allegiance to his brother, Lord Stanley. I must confess that I am slightly concerned that His Majesty will be in the same hunting party as the Earl of Northumberland and Sir William Stanley, this morning.'

Lincoln gave a silent curse. 'I understand what you say, Sir Giles, but it was my uncle's express wish to hunt with them. I am unable to arrange it otherwise.'

'I understand, your Grace. Will you be going with another hunting party?'

Lincoln shook his head. 'There are four other parties going, but I have already asked permission from the King to be excused. I want to write a poem to mark his majesty's visit to Sandal on this day.' He raised his quill. 'As you can see, I have made a poor start.'

Giles smiled benignly. 'Is there some way that we could ensure that your uncle, King Richard, is fully protected?'

'My uncle is a warrior, Sir Giles. If he thought that he was in any physical danger he would have taken suitable steps. Both Northumberland and Stanley are bound to him and would ensure his safety. Besides, he has five of his personal guard with him.'

Giles was thinking of an assassin's arrow or crossbow bolt, but he said no more. He had it in mind that perhaps he and Will would ride out after them.

'I thank you for your time, your Grace,' he said. He bowed and retreated to the door. 'There was yet one other strange event, your Grace. This morning two of the Earl of Northumberland's hounds were poisoned. The Earl is understandably cross, but I have asked him to say nothing to the King. He agreed and said that he would say nothing to Sir William Stanley either.'

Lincoln clicked his tongue. 'Curious indeed. I take it that you are taking measures to find the rogue?'

'I will do what I can, my Lord, but I confess to being puzzled. If I could see a reason for the act then I might know where to start.'

'Malice, do you think?' the Earl suggested. 'His Grace the Earl of Northumberland is not a man known to make friends.'

★ ★ ★

Giles's head had been hurting since he awoke. It often did if he was roused from

297

sleep, as if it was a sleeping demon that reacted grumpily to being stirred before it was ready. And it had gradually worsened, so that by the time he had left the Earl of Lincoln's chamber he was tempted to return to his own chamber to seek the solace of a pillow and the dark. Yet he did not succumb for there were too many things to do. His stock of potion had been used up already, so his only resort was to seek a fresh supply from Dr Musgrave.

'It will take me about an hour to prepare it, Sir Giles,' the physician told him. 'But I can give you a different remedy which I already have made up. It will work quicker and will ease the pain, but I warn you it will make you drowsy very quickly.'

Giles pressed his hand to his throbbing temple. 'Then take it I must,' he replied. And he sat and waited as the physician poured a powder into a goblet of watered wine. Dr Musgrave swirled it round to disperse the powder then handed it to Giles.

'I had a look at those hounds, Sir Giles,' he said. 'It does indeed look as if they were poisoned with dwale, which smells like garlic, as you know. And hounds will guzzle anything, so it would not have been hard to poison them.' He stood tugging at his beard. 'But why poison hounds?'

'A question that has puzzled me, Doctor,' Giles said, as he drained his goblet.

★ ★ ★

Will had taken the opportunity to pay a visit upon Alice. She had been making up her father's prescriptions, but had broken off to share kisses and embraces with Will.

'It is exciting to have His Majesty stay with us, Will,' she said, intertwining her hand with his and turning them back and forth to admire their two rings. She sighed. 'It seems like a blessing. As if our love, our union, is somehow sanctified by the King's presence.' She squeezed his hand. 'Will it be long before we can declare our love properly before my father?'

Will winced and reached for his arm. 'Forgive me, my love. My wound still pains me at times.' His face clouded. 'But alas, until I can become a proper lawyer I do not think that your father would consider me suitable for your hand. He has as good as said that to me already.'

Alice stiffened, her eyes becoming round as little anger lines formed on her brow. 'Did he indeed? I shall — '

'You shall say nothing, my love. It is up to me to show my worth. If I can assist my master in the problems he has, then all will be well. I am sure that he will advance my case.'

'What problems?' Alice queried.

Will bit his lower lip. 'The problems posed by these murders. I sense that he has some idea, yet he will not fully confide his thoughts to me. I think that he has doubts about some of the Council of the North and their loyalty to the King. But we shall see.'

Alice kissed the back of his hand then gently touched his wounded arm. 'You worry me, Will. It sounds as if there may be danger. I do not want any harm to come to you.'

Will brushed her lips with his. 'Have no fear, my love. No harm will come to me.'

Alice hugged him. She was not entirely reassured.

★   ★   ★

Dickon trundled his cart across the drawbridge in the wake of King Richard and his hunting party. His wagon was devoid of birds for on this occasion his function in the proceedings was to be the carrier of the spoils of the hunt. Boar hunting was not exactly what he considered proper hunting, yet who was he to question the preference of a king.

Ahead of him the kennelers went on foot, hauling back on the chains of the hounds.

And indeed, as he followed the royal party he felt a growing sense of uneasiness. He was falling further and further behind. His hand went to his belt to check that he had all his usual things in place. He touched his catapult and his long hunting knife and felt somewhat reassured. He flicked the reins to speed the pony up.

'Quicker, old lad. We must get as close as possible to the King.'

★ ★ ★

The Earl of Lincoln was feeling woefully inadequate. He had struggled to write five lines of what he considered to be reasonable poetry, before he became stuck. Then in an attempt to stimulate himself he had turned to Caxton's latest copy of The Canterbury Tales by his ancestor, Geoffrey Chaucer.

It was, he quietly concluded, a mistake.

'He was a genius!' he exclaimed aloud, rising from his chair and stamping across the chamber. 'Whereas I am merely a writer of doggerel. Heavens, I wish my sweet Margaret was here. Perhaps in a day or two I shall be able to go to Lincoln and see her.'

He picked up his sword from on top of the cabinet by his bed and hefted it in his hand. 'Whatever made me think that I could write an adequate poem for my uncle?' And so saying, he felt his temper begin to rise. Almost mechanically he began to go through his usual sequence of practice moves. Then he repeated them, only faster and more vigorously.

'A doggerel writer, that's what I am. Like that traitor William Collinbourne! Pah!'

With that exclamation he realized how angry he had become. And times like that were when he felt the loss of Ned Bunce most acutely, for he could make his Plantagenet ire disappear and replace it with merriment as quickly as it took him to turn a cartwheel, tell some appalling joke, or recount a recent jest.

He crossed to the window and looked out towards the recently erected memorial to his Fool.

His eyes suddenly blazed and his jaw muscles tightened.

'Infamy!' he thundered.

In five strides he bounded across the chamber and threw open the door.

'My Lord? Can we do — ' began one of the two guards, uncertainly.

'Stay here!' the Earl snapped. 'Allow no one into my chamber.'

The two guards stared in amazement as their master rushed down the stairs, his sword scraping the stones as he ran.

Giles felt as if he was swimming in a dark pool when a sudden booming noise rang out from all around him. He struggled to clear his mind, feeling disorientated about where he was. There was something familiar about his surroundings and the situation, yet it did not become immediately clear to him.

And then with another booming he realized that he was abed, as he had been an hour or two before when Will Holland had woken him with a pounding on the door. And then he heard Will's voice calling to him from behind the door.

'Come!' he called, pushing himself up on his elbows and reaching to secure his eye patch.

'My Lord, you must come,' Will cried as he unlatched and pushed open the door. 'There has been murder done.'

Giles shook his head, for he was still having difficulty thinking. Then he realized the reason. It was the drug that Dr Musgrave had given him. He had warned him that he would feel drowsy, but he had not expected the reaction to be so severe. It had forced him to lie down in his chamber.

'Murder, you say?' Giles repeated, forcing his tongue to articulate the words. 'Who has been murdered, Will?'

'The gatekeeper, my Lord. I had been waiting outside your chamber, as I always do when you sleep. Then I heard the noise of someone galloping across the bailey. Then I heard a scream and dashed to the window just in time to see a horse disappear over the drawbridge.' He gulped, for his breathing was laboured and his brow damp with perspiration. 'I thought it odd that no one had challenged the rider, so I ran out and found the bailey deserted. I think almost all of the nobles, except for a handful have gone hunting with the King, and the castle servants are either at work or taking mass. But I could not see any of the guards.'

'None?'

Will shook his head emphatically. 'Then I saw one lying on the battlement walk with a crossbow bolt in his back. It was one of the guards who found Bunce's body. Jarman was his name. I ran to the gatehouse and found the guard on gatekeeper duty, his friend Miller, with a bolt in his chest. He was near to death, but he tried to tell me who the rider was.'

'Out with it, Will!' Giles demanded as he saw the look of despair on his clerk's face.

'He said, 'The Councillor shot me as he rode out.' ' Will swallowed hard. 'And he said he had a prisoner with him. Sir Giles, it was Alice!'

Giles's head cleared at this news. He swung his feet off the bed and rubbed his temple. 'Have you checked Alice's chamber?'

Will shook his head. 'I came straight here, my lord. I thought you should know first.'

Giles was on his feet. 'Then come, we must see if her father can give us any help.'

They rushed to the physician's chambers in the south tower. They found the physician lying on the floor, his head surrounded by a small pool of blood. Giles bent over him and listened for the noise of breathing. 'He is alive,' he announced, 'but only just. I fear he has been struck from behind, so it is unlikely that he will be able to identify his attacker. There is no time to be lost, Will. You must go after the villain and save her. I will send guards after you. Get a horse from the mews and go now. I guess that the villain has gone south on the London road.'

Will's mouth twitched and he seemed to unsuccessfully search for words. Then he nodded and left at a run.

'God pray that he is not too late,' Giles mumbled as he lifted the physician and carried him to his bed. 'My old friend, I must leave you a while longer,' he said to the unconscious doctor. 'Your wound is no longer bleeding and it will heal well, I am sure. I fear that a conspiracy is being played out here and I must attend to His Majesty.'

Leaving Dr Musgrave, he started towards the barbican with the intention of getting a horse himself and mustering however many guards he could to help in the pursuit of the Councillor, whichever of them it was. Then he stopped himself with a rejoinder that he must think logically. He recalled that there were just a handful of the Council who had declared that they would not be hunting. The Earl of Lincoln, he knew, was planning to stay to write a poem. And then there was Lord Scrope and Abbot Mallory, both of whom disliked riding and hunting. The aged Lord Danvers of Hull was too infirm to sit a horse. And Sir Roger Harrington had complained about a pain in his foot. Gout, he had suspected, from his love of his wine and mead.

'Sir Roger Harrington, the lecher!' Giles said aloud, remembering Dr Musgrave's tale of him making lude advances to Alice. He had been careful not to tell Will of that. Suddenly, he felt a stab of guilt, for if he had said something, then perhaps this situation would not have arisen.

'You are getting ahead of yourself,' he chided himself. 'It may not be Sir Roger.'

And with that in mind, he decided to search the knight's chamber first to see if there were any clues.

The sight that greeted him a few minutes later when he pushed open the door was not as he had expected.

Sir Roger Harrington was sitting slumped in a chair, a goblet still clutched in his hand, but the contents spilled out on the floor. His face was a ghastly pale colour, at variance with the livid slash mark across his throat and the blood-soaked tunic below.

'So it was not you, my friend,' Giles mused. 'Then who?'

He left the chamber and made his way towards the room allocated by Lord Scrope. He was about to knock on the door when he heard footsteps behind him. He spun round and found Father Burke and the abbot of Monk Bretton coming towards him along the corridor.

'How now, Sir Giles,' said the abbot. 'You look like a man in a rush.'

Giles decided that explanations would take too long. 'You have been at mass, I perceive. Was Lord Scrope with you?'

The two clerics shook their heads

'I will explain later then,' Giles said. 'I would ask you both to go to the Great Hall and wait there.'

He ignored their questions and let himself into Lord Scrope's chamber. It was in a state of disarray, as if the occupant had left in a hurry.

In a corner was a blood-stained knife. Giles imagined it to be the weapon that had recently slit the throat of Sir Roger Harrington.

The thought of a conspiracy became more likely and he felt that he needed to discuss his thoughts with the Earl of Lincoln. Time was marching on and the paramount concern had to be the safety of the King.

He began to wish that he had not sent Will off in pursuit of the Councillor and Alice, when his brawn and fighting skills might be more use if there was an unfolding plot to kill the King.

He ran as fast as he could to the north tower and mounted the steps three at a time. The entrance to the Earl's chamber was blocked by his two guards.

'We are ordered to let no one into his chamber, Sir Giles,' the elder of the two said. 'The Earl said so himself.'

'Where is he?' Giles demanded.

The guards stared at one another and shook their heads. 'We know not. He just came rushing out in a rage and ordered us to stay here and let no one in.'

'Right! I am giving you new orders. Now listen! Go and get as many of the other guards as you can and make a search of the castle for any of the Council of the North members. Take them and all of the castle servants to the Great Hall, where the abbot of Monk Bretton and Father Burke will already be waiting. Keep them there until I say otherwise. There has been bloody murder here today and two of your fellow guards have been slain.'

The guards hesitated, but Giles shouted again and they departed.

Giles let himself into the Earl's chamber and looked around.

'Now what could have made him take off on his own?' he asked himself. He searched the room, checked the desk and papers, the half-written poem. 'Perhaps it was something that he saw?' And as he said it he crossed to the window and looked out. In the distance he saw the top of Ned Bunce's memorial. Fluttering slightly in the breeze, atop it he saw the missing three-liripiped jester's hat.

'The Fool!' Giles gasped. He struck his forehead with the flat of his hand. 'Jesu! What a fool I have been!'

13

A Woman Scorned

The bailey was deserted when Giles reached it, since the guards had already begun their search and were gathering everyone they found into the Great Hall. He thought of taking a horse from the mews, but quickly decided against it. There was no time to saddle up. Besides which, he felt that it was imperative that he make as little noise as possible.

Holding his sword at his side to steady it he ran over the drawbridge then ducked his head down and ran as nimbly as he could down the hill towards the grave of Ned Bunce. He kept looking right and left, fully aware that even running crouched as low as possible he could be a target for a crossbow bolt at any moment.

The land rose and then fell in a gentle slope towards the memorial that marked Bunce's grave. Giles stopped running as he approached the rise and then continued stealthily. Close to the top he stopped and inched his way onwards, bent as low as possible to peer over the top.

There was no one there, yet the sight of the grave alarmed him. Ned Bunce's jester cap had been stuck on top of the memorial, just as he thought he saw it from the Castle window. The grave itself had been desecrated. The flowers that had been laid at the funeral had been kicked aside and the ground over the grave looked as though it had been churned up with a sword. Clods of soil and turf had been tossed about.

As Giles advanced over the rise he saw that a trail of the clods seemed to lead in the direction of the hollow with the copse of willows a hundred or so yards distant. From where he was he could just see the top of the cross among the willows which marked the spot where the Duke of York had fought and died a quarter of a century before.

The hairs on the back of his neck prickled and he gripped the sword tighter.

'What a fool I was to send Will off like that,' he thought as he advanced slowly towards the copse of willows, all too aware that he was alone.

★ ★ ★

Dickon had to admire the skills of the King. He rode as well as any of his knights, having

311

learned to ride, hunt and use all manner of weapon during his happy youth at Middleham Castle. He had gone after his boar and killed it cleanly.

'A good omen,' King Richard had cried gleefully. 'The white boar has taken the forest's finest. What do you think of that, Northumberland?'

Sir William Stanley rode up to the King. 'I am afraid that the Earl of Northumberland asked me to send his apologies, Your Majesty. He suddenly felt indisposed again. He had been suffering from a malady for some days and had come from his sickbed to attend the Council of the North.' He coughed, as people do when they wish to speak confidentially. 'I must confess that I thought he looked well when he came to the castle yesterday, but even I thought he looked ill this afternoon. Your nephew, the Earl of Lincoln, may have mentioned to you that he had sent a message to him, requesting his presence.'

King Richard frowned. 'So he did. But that is a pity. I would have enjoyed seeing his face when he saw my quarry. Still,' he said, beckoning Dickon to attend to the boar's corpse, 'perhaps I will dedicate this kill to him. That should cheer him up at dinner this night.'

One of the Earl of Northumberland's

squires rode up, doffing his cap and dismounting to bow to his King. He deferentially gave the King virtually the same message that Sir William had just delivered.

'It seems that the Earl of Northumberland is eager for me to know that he has returned indisposed to the castle,' the King said with a short laugh. He wheeled about on his horse, noting with satisfaction that he was surrounded by so many of his personal guard.

'Your pardon, Your Majesty,' Dickon ventured. 'Shall I take the boar back to the castle now? I could get the cook to prepare the beast for your feast this evening.'

King Richard stared at Dickon for a moment, as if he might suddenly erupt at having been addressed by a servant without having spoken first. But instead his face softened and he tossed his head back and laughed cheerfully.

'A good idea, Master falconer. A good feast should restore all of our spirits.'

Dickon bowed and backed away. He sought the aid of two of the King's men to manhandle the boar's body into his wagon. He did so quickly for he was anxious to be off, for he had earlier noted the Earl of Northumberland and most of his party leaving and he had felt unable to relax. He wanted to get back ahead of the King.

*   *   *

The Earl of Lincoln felt as if he had been hit on the head with a mace. He felt a searing pain as he struggled to regain consciousness, but yet he was unable to move his arms to reach for his head. He realized that he was lying on his back with some sort of sack over his head and with a gag tied tightly over his mouth. He struggled to move against the ropes that bound his hands.

There was the noise of wind moving leaves. He moved his head back and forth to try and locate some sound that might help him to place where he was. Despite himself he felt panic begin to seize him and grip his heart. That he had fallen into a trap was obvious, as was the realization that at any moment death might come. He cursed himself for a fool.

A peel of mocking laughter made his heart race and he lay stock still, tensing his muscles in the expectation of some sort of a blow.

His head was suddenly yanked upwards and the bag was pulled roughly from him. He blinked as the sunlight blinded him for a few moments. Then as his vision cleared he saw that he was lying in the middle of a clearing in the copse of willows that surrounded his grandfather's memorial stone.

A shadow passed over his face and he

turned to see the outline of a man standing before him with a sword in his hand. Screwing his eyes up against the sun he saw that the man was wearing a leather executioner's mask.

'Welcome back to the living, you usurping dog-head!' the figure snarled. 'Enjoy your last few moments of this world before you journey to hell.' The voice trailed off and the man began to chuckle malevolently. Then: 'Do you not find this an appropriate place for an execution? Within a few feet of where your grandfather was hacked down and beheaded!'

★ ★ ★

Giles had reached the edge of the willows and moved from tree to tree until he saw the clearing and the memorial cross to the Duke of York. Then he saw the body of the Earl of Lincoln lying on the ground before it.

His heart began to pound and he felt a trickle of sweat run down his spine. Grasping his sword tightly, but yet with his wrist flexed and ready for action, he edged towards the clearing.

The Earl suddenly turned his head in his direction and he saw that he had been gagged. Giles saw the warning in his eyes a moment too late. Before he could turn he felt

315

a sharp blow on the back of his head and then he was being propelled forward to fall on his face beside the Earl.

* * *

Giles had a vague impression of countless horses trotting close by. For a moment he imagined that he was lying face down in the mud on the battlefield at Berwick upon Tweed after he had been unhorsed by a pikeman.

Then he remembered where he was and how he had gotten there. He had seen the Earl of Lincoln lying bound and gagged, recalled seeing the look of warning on the Earl's face, then the thump on the back of his head, and then no more.

The noise of the horses receded into the distance and he tried to move, becoming aware that he could not do so, for something was pressing on the back of his neck, pinning him down and holding his face in the mud.

A coarse chuckle preceded a disdainful voice. 'One false move and my sword will part your head from your neck, Sir Giles. No one can help you here.'

A foot was removed from his neck, then: 'Roll over, but make no attempt to do more than that. I had not expected to catch two rats in my little trap.'

Giles saw first the Earl of Lincoln lying bound beside him, then their captor standing above them, a sword poised and ready to strike. He realized immediately that he would have no chance to fend off a sword thrust and no chance to reach his own sword, which had been tossed on the far side of the Earl.

'You are just in time to witness the execution of the Earl of Lincoln — before your own demise!'

Giles pointed at the mask. 'Why bother with the mask, Will? That false voice betrays you enough.'

The man in the executioner's mask laughed. 'Ha! You don't even sound surprised, Sir Giles.'

'I am disgusted more than surprised, Will. Disgusted at myself for taking so long to realize that I would find you here.'

'I imagine that you found Sir Roger. I thought you might take the bait.'

Giles nodded. 'I also found the knife that you used and left so conveniently in Lord Scrope's chamber. Did you kill him too?'

Will Holland chuckled again. 'You are actually cleverer than I thought. No, I spared Scrope. He will awaken in his garderobe with a bad headache, but no more. I thought you might be chasing phantasms halfway to London by now.'

'It occurred to me that his Grace, the Earl, might be your goal and not His Majesty the King. I saw Bunce's hat that you used as bait to bring him here and I came to stop you.'

'But you didn't do very well, did you?' Will Holland sneered. 'How do you know that the other members of the society are not about to assassinate the King?'

Giles touched his eyepatch. 'Because we both know that there is no secret society. Or at least, no other secret society members here. You are on your own now, Will.'

Will Holland spun the sword in his hand. 'You intrigue me, master judge. Suppose you tell me what you know and I will tell you if you are correct. It is the least that I can do after all the time and care you have taken in teaching me all this time.'

'I know most of it, Will. Enough at least to know that you have the blood of nine men on your hands.'

Will chuckled again, a slightly manic laugh. 'My, my! What a clever judge you are. So tell me.'

'First of all, you killed Ned Bunce, the Earl's Fool, by accident. You had poisoned that pigeon, meaning to kill Dickon the falconer.'

'It is true, I admit it. I had a goodly supply of several poisons, but I was only going to use them in case I did not have a decent opportunity to execute the Earl in an appropriate manner!' He laughed, casting a glance at the Earl. 'By that, I mean with an executioner's sword.'

Giles went on. 'You had intended to kill Dickon, because you thought that he might upset your carefully made plans. These plans began when you inveigled yourself into my employ in London. I imagine that the gang of cutpurses who attacked me had been paid by you?'

'Quite correct. I had been . . . *advised* that being your clerk would be a good position, especially when it was known that you were to take up the position of Constable of Sandal Castle and Judge of the Manor of Wakefield Court.'

'And while you were here you had ample opportunities to communicate with Jasper Hirst, the poulterer. He was already an agent of the secret society run by your employer. I imagine that they had been communicating for some time with messenger pigeons.'

Holland gave an admiring laugh. 'Correct again. A most ingenious means of communication, don't you think?'

'It was,' Giles admitted. 'But when Dickon

intercepted that first message, which I now understand was about another agent who was on his way north, presumably to betray you all, you felt that you had to remove Dickon. He is a shrewd fellow and knows about birds. You couldn't take the risk of him leading me to the poulterer.'

'Well done. You have everything right so far. But that Fool stole the pigeon pie and paid for his folly with his life. I found him and slipped him into the moat.'

The Earl of Lincoln struggled against his bonds, causing Will to laugh afresh. 'Why so angry, your Grace. It was merely a Fool.'

Giles went on to try to keep Holland occupied. The situation was desperate, but he did not want to precipitate the Earl's death.

'The message was ultimately meant for you, was it not? You were being told to eliminate the agent, the priest. And you killed him first, knowing that he would be likely to seek sanctuary at All Saints Church.'

'I did. I had to prevent him reaching the Earl. He had already tried to reach the King in Nottingham and had even killed two other agents sent to stop him.'

'And since he knew you, he dropped his guard and you were able to get behind him and wring his neck. You did it on the first morning of my investigation, and then you went to Jasper Hirst's house and did the same to him. You were anxious in case I interviewed him.'

'As you were planning to do.'

'And you killed all those pigeons and broke their legs. You did it partly to make it seem as if it had been the work of a madman. Yet it also would hide any evidence of marks on their legs, where message bags had been attached.'

Will Holland nodded. 'You really have worked it out quite well. Yet were you not glad that I arrived to deal with those two men who were about to kill you?'

It was Giles's turn to laugh, albeit not a laugh of pleasure. 'You had no choice. They were agents who had been sent to kill the priest. They were mystified to learn that he had already been killed and they clearly wanted to know how much I knew. They wanted to ensure that there would be nothing leading back to your employer.'

'That is right, but I had not performed my task. The most important task of all. They were just hired killers, minions. They blundered in and would have ruined everything. I couldn't allow them to harm you, but nor could I risk them giving you any information.'

'Which is why they were killed instead of

you trying to take one alive. And they murdered Constable Crowther, so his death is also down to you.'

Holland cocked his head to one side, as if considering Giles's remark. 'Crowther's death was unfortunate, but casualties occur in war. Go on with your tale.'

'They were all members of the same society, whereas you presumably felt that you were a sole agent. They had bound themselves to their employer by the brands. That implies absolute loyalty. I imagine that they were an anti-Yorkist society.'

'Correct.'

Giles shook his head. 'But I was not thinking straight. I should not have been put off the trail by that clumsy trick of yours to poison the Earl of Northumberland's hounds.'

Will chuckled. 'The Rat, the Cat, the dog Lovell, ruled England under the hog! Actually, I thought that was a poetic touch. And poetry was appropriate for his Grace the Earl, don't you think? Anyway, I think it did put you off the scent for a while. You thought this secret society was to do with the King's closest friends. You thought that they might be traitors plotting his death.'

'It occurred to me,' Giles ceded. 'But the sheer banality of it worried me. And now that

I put it all together, you were the only person who had the opportunity to kill all of these poor people. It will be to my eternal shame that I did not make the connection until a few minutes ago. But you had fooled me with the cruel murder of the two Castle guards, Jarman and Miller, the slaughter of Sir Roger Harrington and your story of the councillor taking off with Alice. Yet a few questions remain unanswered in my mind.'

Holland shrugged. 'Ask them, Sir Giles. You have intrigued me thus far.'

Giles took a deep breath, then: 'Firstly, why are you preparing to murder his Grace, the Earl of Lincoln? Secondly, why did the priest have to be silenced? What was the secret that he carried that was so dangerous? And lastly, who are you really?'

The man that Giles had known as Will Holland laughed. 'You mean that you don't know?' He shrugged, turning his sword to and fro, but never leaving any doubt that he could instantly impart death. 'Well, it is fitting that you should both know all, especially since you are about to die. Suffice it to say that his Grace will die because of his father's sins.'

The Earl of Lincoln stiffened, staring at Will Holland with loathing in his eyes.

'His father was married to the Lady

Margaret Beaufort when they were both children, but he insisted upon a divorce when he was ten.'

'So, a woman scorned?' Giles ventured.

'More than that. His Grace there has been named King Richard's heir, whereas her son, Henry Tudor, has a real claim to the throne, better than the usurping dog, Richard Plantagenet.' He gave a snort of laughter. 'Or should I say the hog!'

Giles slowly shook his head. 'I thought that I had taught you better than that, Will. Henry Tudor's claim is tenuous. His claim is through that of John of Gaunt, the third son of King Edward the Third, whereas King Richard's line is through Lionel, the Duke of Clarence, King Edward's second son. His Grace, the Earl of Lincoln, also has a better claim than Henry Tudor by virtue of his being the grandson of Richard, Duke of York.'

Holland shrugged dismissively. 'As to that, I care little. But I do care about the way that my family were attainted. My kinsman was maligned as 'Butcher', my father was beheaded just a few months ago on a trumped-up charge of treason, and our lands were given for a while to the Stanleys. To Sir William Stanley, as it happens.'

Giles's jaw dropped despite himself. 'So! It becomes slightly clearer. You are a Clifford!

Then Butcher Clifford was the one who beheaded his Grace's grandfather on this spot and murdered his uncle, Edmund, the Earl of Rutland by the Chantry Chapel on Wakefield Bridge. I remember now how angry you were when we talked about it as we rode over the bridge on our way to the Manor Court.'

'Righteously angry!' Will Holland retorted, reaching for his mask and tearing it off to reveal his face. His eyes had the strange quality of one close to the edge of unreason.

'But your father, if it be Sir Roger Clifford that you talk of, he had no son that I know of.'

Will Holland gave a hollow laugh. 'That's right. A bastard son am I. Yet when I fulfil my part of the contract and execute his Grace, I will regain the Clifford lands. The Lady Margaret Beaufort has promised it.'

Giles nodded. 'And she is the wife of Lord Thomas Stanley. I understand your logic, if I question your naivety. Now tell me, why did the priest have to die?'

'Fie. You mean to say that you haven't worked that out? Think, Sir Giles,' he goaded. 'He was Northumberland's man and he was sent to the Duke of Buckingham to look after the Bishop of Ely, Dr Morton.'

'There is a strong link between Dr Morton and Lady Margaret Beaufort, that is well known,' Giles said. 'I imagine that Dr Morton persuaded the Duke that his allegiance should not lie with the King. He must have persuaded him to rebel.'

Will nodded. 'Close. But why should Buckingham rebel? That has been a mystery all along, has it not? And after the rebellion the Duke was summarily executed. Buckingham begged to see the King, saying that he had something to tell him, but he was ignored. Why do you think that was, clever judge?'

Giles frowned. 'It must have been because they had argued about something.'

'And what would that thing be that had caused them to fall out so badly. Until this mysterious rebellion, Buckingham had been the King's closest friend. And so think, Sir Giles, what could a priest have been used for?' He waited for Giles to respond, but when he did not, he went on with glee: 'Why, to gain access to people of importance. Remember that among other honours, the Duke of Buckingham was the Constable of England. One of his charges was the Tower of London. And there were two very important people in the Tower, were there not?'

Giles gasped as the enormity of it all sank in. 'The two princes! Jesu, I see. Dr Morton persuaded the Duke of Buckingham that if the princes were removed, then he himself would have a possible claim to the throne. He was descended from Edward the Third's youngest son, Thomas.'

Will laughed again. 'So the mists begin to clear! And now you can see what sort of a man the priest was.'

'The Earl of Northumberland told me he had been first an apothecary's assistant, then a soldier and finally a priest.'

'Aye, a killer versed in drugs and poison, given leave to enter the Tower!'

'This is the most diabolical of treacheries!' Giles said with disgust. 'And I see the hand of your employer in all this. And I now understand why he had to be silenced. I take it that assassins had already tried to silence him, hence his attempt to betray them and you to the King, and then his Grace here.'

Will Holland nodded. 'So now you know it all.' He grinned. 'She is a clever woman. And soon her son shall be King of England.'

'He will never defeat King Richard,' Giles replied, coldly.

The Earl of Lincoln struggled again with his bonds and tried to cry out through his gag.

'Oh worry not, your Grace,' Will Holland said sarcastically. 'Soon you will be freed from all this torment. Permanently freed.'

Giles raised his hands placatingly. 'Don't do this, Will. Ride away now.'

But Holland merely laughed. 'Oh, I shall be riding away for a while. But when I do ride back to the castle it will be with the news — the most deplorable news — that my former master, Sir Giles Beeston was a traitor who had trapped and beheaded the Earl of Lincoln. We fought, but I managed to despatch him.' His eyes glowed with the fire of hate. 'Which, of course, means that it would be best if I despatch you first, Sir Giles — before I execute this dog, de la Pole!'

He raised his sword above Giles in readiness to plunge the point into his heart.

There was a sudden whining noise, then a thud and Will Holland rocked forward on his feet as a small rock struck the back of his head. He staggered, his free hand instantly reaching up to his head and coming away a moment later covered in blood.

'You bastard, Will Holland!' cried Dickon, running through the trees towards Will, a catapult in one hand while he fumbled for his long hunting knife with the other.

Will Holland spun round and met the falconer before he could free his weapon. With a backward slash he cut him across the chest, causing a crimson streak to appear through the sliced leather tunic. Dickon gasped and fell to his knees clutching his chest. Then he slumped to the ground.

Giles had grasped his opportunity and rolled over on to his knees, then dived over the Earl of Lincoln to retrieve his sword. He rolled again, coming to his feet with his sword at the ready.

'Neatly done, Sir Giles,' Holland said with a grudging sneer. 'But it will be of no matter. I shall put out your good eye first, then despatch you, as I said. It will enhance my tale.'

'But you have to do it first!' Giles returned. 'I trusted you and you have shown yourself to be nothing but a craven traitor. I will not kill you, for you deserve the death of a traitor. You shall be hanged, drawn and quartered.'

With a cry of rage Will Holland came at him, thrusting, lunging and riposting. Within moments Giles felt himself giving ground. He leapt backwards, over the prostate body of Dickon, then again over the Earl of Lincoln.

Holland advanced again, gaining the upper hand.

Then the Earl kicked out with his legs, catching Holland about the ankles in a scissors.

It was enough to make him lose his footing for a moment. He dropped his guard slightly and Giles aimed a low sweeping cut. It caught

Will Holland's left hand, severing his outer two fingers, which fell to the ground and blood spouted from the stumps. He cried in agony, then immediately fought back with hatred and the enhanced strength that fury gives. Yet that fury gave Giles, battle-trained knight that he had been, an edge. In a series of moves he pierced his opponent's guard and stabbed him in the upper arm, causing him to drop his sword. Giles followed by kicking his legs from under him. Then planting his feet firmly he put his sword tip to his throat. 'Yield, traitor!'

In the corner of his eye Giles saw Dickon stir, then push himself up, wheezing with pain and the effort of it. 'Are you badly hurt, Dickon?' he called.

'A flesh wound, I think, Sir Giles.'

'Then see to his Grace, while I — '

His attention had been diverted for just a moment, but it was enough time for Will Holland to reach into his tunic, pull something out and put it in his mouth.

'Too late, one-eyed Sir Giles,' he sneered. 'A traitor's death such as you mentioned will never do for me.' He lifted his mangled hand with blood pumping from the finger stumps. 'Why look! You made me lose my ring! Tell Alice that I truly loved her, I beg you. You will find her unharmed, locked in her chamber. I had to take care of her and her father before I could bait my trap.' His face had gone ashen white and his eyes glazed over. He retched, and then gave a mirthless chuckle. 'Good poison, this. A mixture of three of the best; venom, a mineral and the deadliest plant.' He retched again and then looked up at Giles, like a drunkard trying hard to focus. 'And with me gone you may find your own head more manageable.' He giggled, and then gagged again. And then: 'In truth, in matters of poison . . . I . . . have . . . no equal.'

And to his horror Giles watched his body begin to convulse. Moments later, even before Dickon could release the Earl of Lincoln, the man whom Giles had known as Will Holland lay dead, but a few feet from the base of the memorial, where his uncle, Butcher Clifford, had so basely murdered Richard, the Duke of York.

14

The King's Messenger

The Earl of Lincoln stood beside Giles and rubbed his wrists to restore the feeling in them.

'So this was the villain responsible for all those deaths?' 'He was, your Grace. And I am ashamed that I had not discovered his crimes until now.'

Dickon was stuffing a rag under his tunic to staunch the flow of blood from his wound. 'I do not think that you can blame yourself, Sir Giles,' he said. 'He took everyone in with his apparent loyalty. I liked him well. And as for poor Mistress Alice — '

The Earl of Lincoln looked with concern at his blood-soaked tunic. 'Talk no more, good falconer. We must get you to Dr Musgrave and have that wound treated.' He reached out and laid a hand upon each of their shoulders. 'You both have my thanks in this. I was a fool to rush into his trap. You both saved my life.'

He prodded the corpse with his toe. 'So this creature was another Clifford? How they must hate our House.'

'As does the Lady Margaret Beaufort, your Grace,' Giles added. 'Shall we tell his majesty of this?'

Lincoln shook his head firmly. 'No, he must know nothing of any of this. Including what this villain said about the Tower.' He nodded his head at Giles to emphasize his words. 'We will take his body back in Dickon's cart and it will be disposed of discreetly, in unconsecrated ground.'

He took Giles a little aside. 'In particular I do not want His Majesty to know of the Lady Margaret Beaufort and her deceits. I shall deal with all this personally when the time is right. At the moment, we have nothing to fear from her husband Lord Stanley, or his brother Sir William. They have no choice but to support His Majesty. For one thing, Lord Stanley's son is at this moment held in the King's care and custody, for surety.'

He looked away, in the direction of Ned Bunce's grave. 'I will be with you in a moment,' he said as he walked off towards it. 'I must get poor Bunce's hat. It would be unseemly to leave it there.'

* * *

Much to Dickon's profound embarrassment, Giles and the Earl of Lincoln lifted the corpse of the dead Clifford and stowed it in the wagon alongside the body of the boar. Giles covered the corpse with an old horse blanket, then they made their way up the convoluted road to Sandal Castle where Giles and one of the ostlers removed the boar and arranged for it to be taken to the butchery.

The Earl once again cautioned them to stay silent about the whole affair and to transmit the same message to Dr Musgrave and his daughter.

'And while you do that,' Lincoln added, 'I shall go to the Great Hall and instruct everyone who is here in the Castle to say nothing to the returning hunting parties.'

'What of the two guards who were murdered, your Grace?' Giles asked, pointing to the body of one of the guards that still lay upon the battlement walk.

'I shall have them taken care of, and their families will be taken care of,' the Earl replied. 'Now let us be quick, before my uncle returns.'

Dickon insisted on dealing with his cart by himself in order that no one should know about the corpse that it contained. Giles agreed that he would help him to dispose of it later.

When Giles entered the physician's chamber he was relieved to find him up and about, although quite dazed.

'Thank the Lord that you were not badly injured,' Giles said. 'But without more ado, we must release your daughter.'

A much bemused physician followed with great alarm and found his daughter bound and gagged in her chamber. And just as the Earl of Lincoln had been treated, she had a sack over her head.

Once freed, Alice told them of how she had been surprised from behind and deposited thus in her chamber. Both she and her father sat and listened in stunned disbelief as Giles explained all about Will Holland's treachery and about all that had happened.

Alice had listened with tears of shock streaming down her cheeks. Now she broke down and sobbed in disbelief. 'W-Will is dead?'

Giles put a kindly hand on her shoulder. 'He was not the person that you thought him to be, Alice. He used us all. He was a devious and treacherous rogue.'

Alice suddenly stood up, wiped the tears from her eyes and dashed from her chamber, towards her private garderobe. Her father was about to follow, but Giles restrained him.

The physician stared in bewilderment for a moment, then he looked up as someone tapped on the door.

It was Dickon. He had changed his tunic, but from the way he held his chest the physician could see that he was in need of attention. 'My good Dickon,' he said. 'You look in great discomfort. Come; let me look at this wound that Sir Giles has told me about. I suspect that it may need cauterizing with a hot iron.'

Dickon managed a wan smile. 'I was hoping that you would not say that, Doctor.'

Giles waited in the physician's outer chamber, wondering whether his habitual headache would return. Indeed, from Will Holland's final words he wondered whether his clerk had been tampering with his food and drink, giving him some sort of poison that gave him headaches. It all made sense, since it would have given him reason to visit Dr Musgrave and his daughter, the lovely Alice. He could have been stealing drugs and poisons from the doctor. Perhaps there had also been some effect of the poison in slowing down his thinking.

'The villain!' he cursed, at the thought.

Some fifteen minutes later Dr Musgrave and Dickon came out, bringing with them the odour of singed flesh. Dickon's face was as white as a dove, but he looked relieved. At the sound of their conversation, Alice returned to join them.

Giles immediately noted the absence of the ring on her finger and deduced that she had thrown it down the garderobe. Accordingly, he judged it a poor time to tell her that Will Holland's last message was to say that he truly loved her. Instead, rather guiltily, he passed on the Earl's rejoinder to say nothing of the whole affair.

★　★　★

The cook, Tobias Merrion, and his staff had spent all afternoon roasting the boar on a spit in the huge fireplace in the Great Hall. King Richard had let it be known that the Council of the North would enjoy a feast and then he would address them about various important affairs that he wanted them to consider.

The Earl of Lincoln had been adamant that Giles should say nothing about the murder of Sir Roger Harrington. This troubled Giles greatly and he counselled the Earl against this course of action, but in vain.

'I shall see that his family is well compensated and in due course I will inform them that he was heroic in averting an act of treason. For now, we shall merely say that he has gone on a private errand and that he went on his own. When I tell His Majesty, he will be more than happy to give his family land

and honours. I will, of course, advise him in this matter.'

Giles nodded and said nothing. He was glad that the law was his domain rather than the world of high politics. He suspected that the Earl intended to disadvantage the Lady Margaret Beaufort in some way. In this way he would keep the Stanleys bound to the House of York, yet gain his revenge.

The Council had assembled for the feast in the Great Hall and were standing behind their chairs awaiting the arrival of the King when a shout went up from the castle gates. Then a trumpeter played, alerting the castle to the fact that a messenger approached.

King Richard entered the Great Hall and took his place at the top table on the dais beside his nephew, John de la Pole.

'Your Majesty, it seems that a messenger has just arrived,' Lincoln informed the King. 'He wears the Royal livery.'

King Richard's mouth tightened and he gestured for the messenger to be brought in.

Some minutes later, the King cursed, and then passed the message to his nephew. He sat back and drained his goblet of wine in one draught. Then he looked at his nephew for a response.

'It is dire news, Your Majesty. Tudor dares challenge you again. It is time that we crushed him for good. I say that we should move at once.'

King Richard nodded and then stood up and raised his hands to quieten the murmurings of curiosity that had spread around the Great Hall.

'My good and loyal subjects, it seems that you are all going to be given the opportunity to demonstrate your loyalty to the crown.' His lips twitched and he fiddled with his rings, both signs of his agitation.

'I have been informed by the Council in Nottingham that the upstart Henry Tudor has landed at Milford Haven and is marching northwards with an army of several thousand to claim my throne.'

The Great Hall erupted. There were cries of indignation, shouts of anger, promises of undying loyalty and of a sure victory for the King and his House.

'I know and respect all of you,' King Richard cried. 'We shall eat this fine boar as a symbol of the might of the White Boar that we shall fly before us. Tomorrow I shall ride for Nottingham. All of you shall return to your homes, raise your arms and meet me in Nottingham. Together we shall grind this pestilential House of Lancaster into the dust once and for all. Are you with me?'

To a man the Council stood and toasted the King.

Giles caught the Earl of Lincoln's eye. He noted the look of fervour in it. It was as if he accepted the horrible events that he had lived through a few hours before as a portent that victory would be theirs.

A log crackled in the fire and Giles looked over at the fireplace. Then he blinked as he beheld the smoke and steam haze about the roasting boar. For a moment he thought he saw movement in the whirling smoke.

As he watched he had the distinct impression that an ethereal Ned Bunce was looking out at him. And then the image faded. Fat dripped into the fire and made a strange crackling noise, eerily reminiscent of the dead Fool's cackle.

The whole illusion barely lasted a moment. Yet looking at his fellow diner, Dr Musgrave, he guessed that he too had seen something in the fire. Neither of them commented on it. Giles darted a look at the Earl of Lincoln, but it was clear that he had not seen the phantasm.

Giles suddenly felt ineffably sad. So much had happened, so many people had died. Will Holland had shaken his faith, made him wary of trusting anyone again. Then he thought of poor Alice Musgrave and the way that he had betrayed her love and trust.

He wondered whether the Fool, Ned Bunce, had come back to warn them all against further folly.

Glossary

ALCHEMY

An early protoscience, which had been practised in the cradle lands of civilization and spread across Europe. Alchemists had three aims. Firstly, the transmutation of base metal into silver or gold. Secondly, the preparation of a universal panacea for all ills. Thirdly, the creation of human life. These were all lofty aims, it being believed that a mythical substance called the philosopher's stone would help in their quest. In the fifteenth century a licence would be required to practice alchemy. There is evidence that an alchemist was actively practising at Sandal Castle at the time of Richard III.

APOTHECARY

The medieval equivalent of a pharmacist and doctor. They were originally members of the Grocer's and Spicer's Guild.

ASHLAR

Dressed stone blocks, often rectangular or square, used to make castles and cathedrals in medieval times.

BAILIFF
An official of a town, court or large estate.

BEVOR
An armoured metal plate worn to protect the neck.

BRANCHER
In falconry, a young raptor that is old enough to climb out of its nest on to a branch, yet too young to fly.

BURGHER
A freeman or landowner within a township.

CHANTRY CHAPEL
Chantry chapels were common in medieval England. They were special chapels within church buildings or on private land where priests could chant masses. There were four chantry chapels standing on the four main entrances to medieval Wakefield: St Mary Magdalene's on Westgate, St John the Baptist on the Northgate, St Swithens on the road to York, and St Mary the Virgin on Wakefield Bridge. Only the latter has survived to this day.

CHAPERON HAT
A type of hat that had evolved from a hood with a liripipe, into a band-like cap. It was

commonly worn at the time of Richard III, but then declined in popularity.

COGNIZANCE
The heraldic badge, emblem or device of a noble house.

COIF
A close-fitting lawn or silk cap that covered the top, back and sides of the head. It was the badge of office of the sergeant-at-law, or lawyer, in the fourteenth and fifteenth centuries.

CONNY
A rabbit (plural conies).

CONSTABLE
A person holding a particular type of office. It could refer to a high office, such as the custodian or constable of a castle, as in this story, or it could be a senior member of the town watch. In medieval times there were four watches in Wakefield.

DOCTRINE OF HUMORS
The ancient Greeks had developed the doctrine of humors or the humoral theory, which was the dominant medical theory of medieval times. It was believed that there

were four fundamental humors or body fluids (from the Latin umor or humor, meaning 'moisture' or 'fluid') which determined the state of health of an individual. These humors were blood, yellow and black bile and phlegm. Treatments aimed at removing excess of illness-producing humors by bleeding, purgation and the use of emetics.

DWALE
A poison used in medieval Europe, made from belladonna or deadly nightshade. Geoffrey Chaucer refers to it in The Pardoner's Tale' in his great work, *The Canterbury Tales*.

EWERER
The bringer of wine or heated water to the nobility.

EYAS
In falconry a nestling falcon or hawk (plural eyases).

FOOL
See JESTER.

GARDEROBE
A medieval toilet. In castles these often took the form of seat-covered holes with long

drops into cesspits, or shafts dropping into the moat. Buckets for handfuls of moss were used as cleaning agents.

HALBERD
A two-handed pole weapon, consisting of an axe topped with a spike mounted on a long shaft.

JESSES
In falconry, thin strips of leather used to tether a bird.

JESTER
An actual occupation in medieval England. A jester, or fool, could be employed by a noble house and charged with the role of entertainer. Classically, they wore multicoloured, multipatched clothes, wore a cap with three liripipes and often with a bell on the end of each. In addition they usually carried a mock sceptre or bauble. Their purpose was to amuse and entertain, with a mix of ribaldry, satire and slapstick humour.

JONGLEUR
An itinerant entertainer in medieval England. His accomplishments could include juggling, conjuring, singing, dancing, instrument playing and acrobatics.

KNIGHT BANNERET
A knight permitted to lead his own company into battle during war under his own banner. It was a higher position than a knight bachelor.

LIRIPIPE
A long peak hanging from a hat or hood. A classic head garment of the medieval era.

MANOR OF WAKEFIELD
One of the great medieval estates, with its centre at Sandal Castle. Originally owned by the de Warenne family, it later became a royal possession.

MANOR COURT ROLLS
The Wakefield Manor Court Rolls are still existent and cover the entire period of 1274–1925. They contain an immense amount of detail about people, places and events in and around Wakefield, and give a valuable insight into the working of the legal process in medieval Wakefield until the early twentieth century. The manor court house was held in the Moot Hall, situated opposite the south side of the parish Church of All Saints.

MARCHER LORDS
The Marcher Lords were powerful barons appointed by the king to guard the borders

with Wales and Scotland. The greatest Marcher Lords along the Welsh border included the earls of Chester, Gloucester, Hereford, Pembroke, and Shrewsbury. Their counterparts along the Scottish border were the earls of Northumberland and Durham.

MERLIN
A smallish type of falcon.

PANTLER
The servant in charge of the bread and the pantry.

PIKE
A long two-handed weapon, consisting of a thrusting spear mounted on a long shaft.

PILLORY
A wooden framework on a post with holes for the head and hands, in which offenders were locked, so that they could be exposed to public ridicule and humiliation.

SANCTUARY
A fugitive or suspect could claim forty days sanctuary within the 'sanctuary' of a church.

SERGEANT-AT-LAW
A now extinct legal title. A sergeant-at-law (*servientes ad legem*) was a senior barrister in

medieval times. They were often appointed as circuit judges or as judges, but were still permitted to plead in the courts. Geoffrey Chaucer has a sergeant-at-law, as one of his pilgrims in *The Canterbury Tales*.

SOKE
One of the feudal rights of the lord of a manor. In the Manor of Wakefield the lord had the right to have all corn ground in his (soke) mills, or to have bread baked in his bakehouse.

STEWARD
One who managed a castle, property or estate on behalf of a lord or king.

STOCKS
Punitive hinged, wooden framework, in which a person's feet were locked in place, and sometimes as well their hands or head. The victim was thus kept in a sitting position, a ready target for passers-by to pelt with dung or rotting vegetables.

TERCEL
A male peregrine falcon.

TITULUS REGIUS
Titulus Regius, a statute of Parliament issued

in 1483 by which the title of King of England was bestowed upon Richard, Duke of Gloucester. It was an official declaration that found Edward IV's marriage to Elizabeth Woodville to be invalid and their children illegitimate. It was repealed by the first parliament of King Henry VII, thereby legitimizing Elizabeth of York, whom he married. By their union the two warring houses were joined. He ordered that all copies of Titulus Regius be destroyed, yet one copy survived in the Croyland Chronicle, one of the primary sources of medieval English history.

UNDERCROFT
The ground floor of a medieval building, often used for storage or to keep livestock.

Historical Note

The *Fool's Folly* is a work of fiction, yet the location, some of the main characters and certain events are real.

The story was inspired by archaeological finds at Sandal Castle. Firstly, shards of alchemical apparatus, contemporary with the period of the Wars of the Roses, suggested the character of Dr Musgrave. Secondly, two medieval rings were found, one in the inner moat, possibly having arrived there via a garderobe, and another on ground outside the castle. That the rings could have belonged to lovers stimulated the author's imagination, the result being this tale.

Sandal Castle was one of Richard, Duke of York's favourite castles. John de la Pole, the Earl of Lincoln, was directly descended from the poet Geoffrey Chaucer, as well as being the grandson of the Duke of York. Upon the death of King Richard's son, Edward the Earl of Salisbury, he was named heir to the King. Among many titles and honours conferred on him, he was appointed as President of the Council of the North and President of Sandal Castle. In 1483, Richard Beeston (renamed

Sir Giles in this tale) was made Constable of the Castle and Edward Burke was appointed as the chaplain.

The Council of the North was established by King Richard in 1485 and was based at Sandal Castle in Wakefield and Sheriff Hutton Castle near York. It was continued by the Tudors and lasted until 1641.

King Richard was killed at the Battle of Bosworth Field, reputedly crying 'Treason! Treason! Treason! Treason! Treason!' Lord Thomas Stanley was at the Battle of Bosworth Field, but took no part in it. His brother, Sir William Stanley, threw in his lot with Henry Tudor at the last moment. Henry Percy, the Earl of Northumberland, shamefully failed to give his King his promised support when King Richard made his last charge. King Richard's claims of treason would therefore seem to be quite legitimate.

Legend has it that Richard's battle crown was found under a gorse bush by Sir William Stanley, and that Lord Thomas Stanley was given the honour of placing it upon Henry Tudor's head.

The fate of the Princes in the Tower has been hotly debated for many years. William Shakespeare's great play, written during Tudor times, using Tudor propaganda, paints King Richard as the most evil monarch of all time, suggesting that he was guilty of many crimes, including the murder of his brother the Duke of Clarence and of his nephews, the two young Princes in the Tower. There have been many other theories as to the fate of the Princes. The suggestion in this novel that Dr John Morton, Lady Margaret Beaufort and the Duke of Buckingham were in some way culpable is but one of several possibilities, which seems to fit the known facts.

The Battle of Bosworth Field is generally regarded as the last Battle of the Wars of the Roses. In fact, the Battle of Stoke Field in 1487 truly marks the last battle, for there John de la Pole died fighting for the House of York. It is worth considering that if he had either succeeded Richard the Third, or gained the throne himself in 1487, then the Kings of England would have had the blood of the great poet Geoffrey Chaucer in them. It is possible that had that happened history would have been spared the excesses of Henry VIII.

We do hope that you have enjoyed reading this large print book.

Did you know that all of our titles are available for purchase?

We publish a wide range of high quality large print books including:
Romances, Mysteries, Classics
General Fiction
Non Fiction and Westerns

Special interest titles available in large print are:
The Little Oxford Dictionary
Music Book
Song Book
Hymn Book
Service Book

Also available from us courtesy of Oxford University Press:
Young Readers' Dictionary
(large print edition)
Young Readers' Thesaurus
(large print edition)

For further information or a free brochure, please contact us at:
Ulverscroft Large Print Books Ltd.,
The Green, Bradgate Road, Anstey,
Leicester, LE7 7FU, England.
Tel: (00 44) 0116 236 4325
Fax: (00 44) 0116 234 0205

THE PARDONER'S CRIME

Keith Souter

1322. Sir Richard Lee, Sergeant-at-Law, is sent by King Edward II to Sandal Castle to preside over the court of the Manor of Wakefield. Sir Richard and his assistant Hubert of Loxley are forced to investigate a vicious rape and a cold-blooded murder. As the township prepares for the Wakefield mystery plays, the strangest case is brought before him. The Pardoner, Albin of Rouncivale, confesses to a crime, believed to have been committed by the outlaw Robin Hood. Sir Richard must quickly discover the truth — the stability of the realm and the crown itself may depend upon it.

THE DORSET HOUSE AFFAIR

Norman Russell

Dorset House is the home of the Claygate family, and a place where diplomats love to congregate. When young Maurice Claygate and Sophie Lenart, a notorious woman spy, are found shot dead, Inspector Arnold Box, investigating the murders, hears from Colonel Kershaw, Head of Secret Intelligence, that there are international ramifications to the case. Together the two men pursue a ruthless thief and a stolen document across France, bringing the affair to a devastating and unexpected climax in the great palace of Louis XIV, the Sun King, at Versailles.

THE DEAD HILL

John Dean

The discovery of a dead gangland figure in a quarry brings back dark memories for Detective Chief Inspector Jack Harris and the hilltop community in which he works. As the detective investigates the murder, not only is he forced to deal with the hostile villains, frightened townsfolk and colleagues who doubt his capacity to bring the killer to justice, he also has to confront part of his past that he hoped would be forgotten. And in doing so, he is forced to re-evaluate the loyalties of those closest to him.